GENIUS JONES

Lester Dent

GENIUS JONES

LESTER DENT

INTRODUCTION BY
WILL MURRAY

ALTUS PRESS
2015

EDITED AND DESIGNED BY
Matthew Moring

PUBLISHING HISTORY
"Introduction" appears here for the first time. Copyright © 2015 Will Murray. All rights reserved.
"Genius Jones" originally appeared in the November 27, December 4, 11, 18, and 25, 1937 and January 1, 1938 issues of *Argosy* magazine (Vol. 277, No. 5–Vol. 278, No. 4). Copyright © 1937, 1938 by The Frank A. Munsey Company. Copyright renewed © 1965 and assigned to Steeger Properties, LLC. All rights reserved. Restored text appears here for the first time. Copyright © 2015 the Heirs of Norma Dent. All rights reserved.
"Untitled Outline" appears here for the first time. Copyright © 2015 the Heirs of Norma Dent. All rights reserved.

THANKS TO
Joel Frieman, Chris Kalb, Will Murray, and Ray Riethmeier

ISBN
978-1-61827-182-2

Visit *altuspress.com* for more books like this.
Printed in the United States of America.

TABLE OF CONTENTS

WILL MURRAY

IN THE SUMMER of 1936, Lester Dent discovered himself separated from the Doc Savage series he had written steadily for three and a half years.

Exact details of this unusual hiatus are unknown. A year before, Street & Smith had laid plans to increase the frequency of *Doc Savage Magazine* to twice a month and hired Laurence Donovan to supplement the output of Lester Dent and his ghostwriters. Those plans were put on hold by the beginning of the year, and Donovan was reassigned to write two new S&S series, *The Skipper* and *The Whisperer.*

Having purchased two years' worth of Doc Savage manuscripts in 1935, Street & Smith did not need to buy any more for a while. Annually, Lester negotiated a new Doc contract in July, but no such agreement was signed in 1936.

Instead, after turning in *The Sea Angel,* Lester stopped writing Doc Savage altogether. Was this a sabbatical? A vacation—or a mutual but permanent parting of the ways?

We don't know, but Lester soon retreated to his hometown of La Plata, Missouri, presumably to keep down living costs. On the plus side, he was suddenly free to pursue higher literary ambitions, which in 1936 meant trying to crack two of the top pulps, *Argosy* and *Black Mask.*

Lester succeeded in both endeavors handsomely, producing the much-anthologized Oscar Sail stories for *Black Mask,* followed by a pair of novelettes for *Argosy, Hades* and *Hocus Pocus,*

which were well received. *Argosy* had
just come under the editorship of
Fiction House's Jack Byrne, who was
looking for new blood to inject freshness into the aging weekly's fortunes.
So Dent joined Robert E. Howard and
others in bringing a Fiction House
flavor to the fifty year old Munsey
magazine. Dent had written for Byrne
early in his career.

Lester Dent

An early draft of *Hocus Pocus* starred
a highly-paid stage magician who had held out for too much
money and found himself working at a gas station in La Plata,
Missouri, in order to make ends meet. This would not be the
first time that Lester Dent resorted to autobiography in writing
his fiction. This first version was rejected and Dent was forced
to completely rework the story until it was acceptable.

Lester next tried to crack Munsey's *Detective Fiction Weekly*,
but met with a resounding rejection. Giving up on *DFW*, he
turned his attention to marketing a newspaper comic strip based
on Doc Savage, and a second featuring Washington Irving's
Rip van Winkle. Neither strip sold. So he decided to focus on
composing a long serial for *Argosy*, then being edited by Chan-
dler H. Whipple.

Genius Jones was the result. Written in the summer of 1937
and printed in six parts beginning late that year and concluding
in the January 1, 1938 issue, it was the longest novel Lester ever
published, and one of the most famous. Strangely, except for
being serialized in the *La Plata Home Press* newspaper in 1939,
it has not been reprinted since the pulp era.

This rollicking tale of a young lad who was marooned in the
Arctic during World War I smacks of Tarzan of the Apes—a
character Lester read as a youth. It's an exuberant story, possessed of a wild screwball quality, and very much an example
of Lester Dent at the peak of his literary powers. He had commenced his career emulating Dashiell Hammett, and when

Hammett pioneered the screwball detective story with *The Thin Man* in 1934, Lester followed suit.

The story as published was not what Dent had originally intended to write, however. His original outline survives, and it includes a major subplot built around the idea of a so-called "static translator" which would enable people to communicate with the dead. This was a concept no less than Thomas A. Edison have been tinkering with before his death, so it was not entirely ungrounded in the scientific lore of the day.

Presumably, this version of the plot was rejected by *Argosy*, for when Dent plunged into the actual writing, the spook communicator was not part of the storyline. Lester later recycled it for a Doc Savage story, *The Pirate's Ghost*.

Moreover, in proofreading *Genius Jones*, we were shocked to discover several pages missing from the text, beginning in Chapter XII, entitled "The Caustic Samaritan," and bleeding into the following chapter. This does not appear to be deliberate, but possibly the result of a production error. This, and other excised material, have been restored, making this Altus Press release the only complete and definitive edition.

Some critics have pointed to Philip Wylie's 1932 novel, *The Savage Gentleman*, as an influence on Doc Savage. Most of this imagined influence—the concept of a father subjecting his son to a youth of special training—actually goes directly back to Street & Smith's Nick Carter, who was raised by his father to be the consummate detective, mitigating that theory almost entirely.

The Savage Gentleman was the account of a young boy named Henry Stone who is raised on an island, apart from women and entirely self-educated, ultimately becoming a splendid specimen of manhood untrammeled by civilization. This was the idea of Stone's domineering father. Wylie's novel, which might be seen as an inversion of Tarzan of the Apes, seems to be more of an influence on Genius Jones that it could possibly influence the creation of Doc Savage, a character who had been under construction all through calendar 1932. *The Savage Gentleman* was released in December, around the time Dent was writing *The Man of Bronze.*

Dent might also have been harkening back to an old *All-Story* serial he could very well have read as a boy, about an Antarctic version of Tarzan, Polaris of the Snows, from twenty years before. Charles B. Stilson was the author of the Polaris trilogy.

In any case, Lester played his Herculean new creation for its humorous potential, telling a sprawling tale of a giant man-child set loose in New York without any practical experience with modern civilization—especially women.

Cover-blurbed as a "Million Dollar Laugh Riot," *Genius Jones* kicked off with a striking Rudolph Belarski cover, and within a few months of publication Dent's agent began receiving feelers from Hollywood, which saw the screwball proceedings as potential celluloid gold. Nothing ever came of it, though.

A few years later, in 1942, DC Comics inaugurated a comic strip titled "Genius Jones." It was about a boy raised on a tropical island who had only a set of encyclopedias and other books for reading material. Thus educated, Johnny Jones is rescued and once back in the U.S., becomes a boy genius investigator called the Answer Man. Future Science Fiction great Alfred Bester originated the series, but editor Mort Weisinger, a friend of Dent's, may have purloined the idea—whether from Wylie or Dent is arguable.

Lester himself revived the idea of a character who spoke like a dictionary in subsequent Doc Savage novels, such as *The Two-Wise Owl* and *Once Over Lightly.* In a sense, all of them were variations on Doc Savage's aide, Johnny Littlejohn, who was noted for his polysyllabic vocabulary.

Genius Jones was Lester's final sale to *Argosy,* but he did begin to outline a sequel which was untitled and unfinished. In that plan, the further adventures of Genius Jones took him to Tulsa, Oklahoma, and criminal doings in its oil industry. It was a locale

Lester knew well, for it was the city from which he had launched his fiction career back in 1929. Lester never moved ahead on this outline, because by the time *Genius Jones* had reached print, he was busily writing Doc Savage once again, so his time for extracurricular writing had once again dried up. All told, the sabbatical had lasted but six short months.

Genius Jones has long deserved being reprinted, so it is with great pride that Altus Press presents this first modern edition. When you read it, you'll wish Lester had found the time to write that sequel, and many more.

CHAPTER I

WAR ON AN ICEBERG

IT SEEMS TO be a distressing fact that men will disagree about almost any subject under the sun, and fight like cats and dogs over some of them; but there is one point on which opinion is unanimous. And this proposition is that experience is a thorough teacher.

Experience is not the gentlest instructor, nor the best, nor the most welcome, since the fellow who has experience teach him something generally comes away with his ears red. But he has had a lesson nailed fast to the inside of his skull, even if it wasn't pleasant. Experience is an effective old girl.

It was on a night in April of the year 1912 when the liner *Titanic* hit an iceberg in the North Atlantic and sank, and some prominent people from England and the United States were drowned.

Then twenty-five years passed and no more liners sank from hitting icebergs, although the icebergs were still there—a safety record that was a tribute to the way experience drove a point home, the point in this instance being that it was a good idea to keep a sharp lookout for icebergs.

Captain Fritz Hannover was therefore alert for ice as his ship, the German liner *Hildenheim,* steamed across the North Atlantic toward New York, and at seventeen minutes past ten on the morning of August 20, 1937, Captain Hannover's vigilance was rewarded and he saw an iceberg. A large one.

Captain Hannover put binoculars on the berg.

"*Ach!*" he said loudly.

He handed his glasses to his officers, who stared at the iceberg, then stared at each other. "Is it imagination?" one officer wondered aloud.

"*Ach, Gott!*" said Captain Hannover. "I doubt if the same brand of imagination would come in three orders."

"Then there's a man on that iceberg!"

Captain Hannover was a bullet-headed, militaristic-looking German, aggressive, and anxious to see the day when German ships would carry all passengers who crossed the Atlantic. He saw where his line could get some newspaper publicity out of rescuing the man so strangely marooned.

Rushing to the radio room, the Captain wrote:

TO THE ASSOCIATED PRESS:
GERMAN LINER HILDENHEIM ONE OF THE FINEST SHIPS AFLOAT HAS SIGHTED MAN ON ICEBERG ADRIFT IN ATLANTIC OCEAN STOP CAPTAIN FRITZ HANNOVER TAKING PERSONAL CHARGE OF BOAT IN ROUGH SEA TO RESCUE POOR MAROONED MAN STOP DETAILS LATER

The only discrepancy in this was that the sea happened to be unusually calm.

They lowered a lifeboat, and, as it approached the iceberg, growing proximity made the berg seem huge, hard, rugged and dangerous; then a sailor discovered the equivalent of a beach on the west side, so they landed there, and Captain Hannover stepped out gingerly on the slick ice.

"Is there plenty of film in that movie camera?" he asked one of his officers.

"It's full, sir."

"*Gut.* Do not miss a single detail. The rest of you keep out of the picture. We will sell this to a newsreel company. Good advertising." He straightened his jacket self-consciously. "Take a close up, later, of the poor devil's face, showing his gratitude to me."

"Here he comes!"

HE CAME sliding down an ice hummock toward them, a shaggy apparition with what seemed to be a scarlet muffler at his throat. The descent was made by the simple expedient of sitting down and coasting, and he foot-braked to a halt some thirty feet away.

The rescue party goggled.

For now they saw that what they had taken to be a scarlet muffler was an amazing profusion of red beard. The new arrival was around six feet tall, with a nose that was straight and rather sensitive. He had a pair of solemn dark blue eyes. As he regarded them, he seemed divided between joy and uneasiness, like a young man ready to propose marriage the first time—he had worked up to it with pleasure, but the future angles had him jittery.

He had a deep, pleasant voice.

"Pleasure," he remarked, "is a state of gratification of the senses of mind. Also relish produced by expectation or enjoyment of something good, delightful or satisfying, as opposed to pain, sorrow, et cetera. Probably an instantaneous bio-chemical product. Usually of temporary duration."

Everybody stared.

The young man's upper garment was sealskin, hair-side in, equipped with a hood; and he obviously got into it by pulling it over his head, nightgown fashion. A polar bear had furnished raw material for trousers. Knee-length boots were of walrus hide.

The whirring of the movie camera urged Captain Hannover.

"Ja," he said, "we are here to take you, *mein Herr.*"

Captain Hannover looked like the pictures of Huns which formerly appeared on Liberty Loan posters.

The red-whiskered iceberg-man peered at the Captain. His grin slowly collapsed. His eyes went wide, then narrow. He was appalled, it seemed, by something about Captain Hannover's appearance.

"Hun," he said grimly. "One of a barbarous Asiatic people whose hordes came probably from the Caspian steppes about 372 A.D. Their defeat at Châlons-sur-Marne in 451 and the death of Attila in 453 terminated their sway. Hun also means a German, after allusion of Kaiser Wilhelm II, who, at the time of departure of his army for China in the year 1900, desired that his men make themselves as dreaded as the Huns of Attila."

Captain Hannover was bewildered.

"Go to the boat," he said impatiently, "so we can shoot you at close range."

The red whiskers convulsed.

"Shoot me—!"

"Ja," said the Captain. "With the—"

He never got to complete his statement. *"Hun!"* yelled the hermit.

He drove his right fist, it hit Captain Hannover's jaw. Captain Hannover arose from the ice, lit on his shoulders, his legs flew up, and he skidded toward the lifeboat, turning around and around on his back as he slid.

The tenant of the iceberg vanished around the nearest ice hummock.

A minute was required for general astonishment to subside, then the sailors sprang from the lifeboat, and one scooped up a double handful of ice water and dashed it in Captain Hannover's face and their skipper made a muttering noise, wiped his wet face uncertainly with a sleeve, sat up, blinked, and slowly lifted his right arm in a vague manner.

"Heil Hitler!" he said, solemn as an owl.

He was still dazed.

An onlooker remarked, *sotto voce,* "He'll never get that knocked out of him."

"Catch that scamp!" yelled Captain Hannover.

THE ICEBERG had appeared rugged enough from the water; but at first hand, it was an incredible proposition, there being no sharp angles, because the ice had been melting in the sun, and everything was rounded and discouragingly slick, while pools of water stood at strategic points where, as sure as a man slipped, he slid in for a bath. The would-be rescuers got soaked to the skin, shivered, swore, and in the meantime the liner whistle began an impatient tooting.

They had no sign of their quarry... until a sudden, long, ragged crash.

Captain Hannover howled and bounded behind an ice ridge, then folded down, grabbed his leg with both hands, and wet redness crawled out of his leg and over his hands, and steamed in the cold.

Meantime, a shower of ice chips fell like broken glass.

"He has a machine gun!" Captain Hannover gasped.

Fondness for shelter was immediate.

"I suggest, sir," muttered a sailor, "that the fellow may think the World War is still going on."

"If he does," Captain Hannover groaned, "it's time he was told different."

He raised his voice.

"Kamerad!" he yelled.

"No German," called the man of the iceberg, "is a *kamerad* of mine."

"If you are under the impression the World War is still on," said Captain Hannover, "it was over in November 1918."

This drew a derisive snort.

"Deceit," called the iceberg-man, "is an attempt or disposition by trick, collusion, contrivance, false representation or underhand practice to defraud another. When injury is thereby affected, an action of deceit, by law, lies for compensation."

"You don't believe us?" Captain Hannover shouted.

"No."

A sailor had brought along a boat-hook to assist himself in navigating the ice, and now he placed his cap on this and lifted it cautiously. The machine gun gobbled, the cap turned ragged and sailed away, the boat hook end splintered, and the sailor swore as the ricocheting bullets whined above his head.

"But we won't shoot you!" Captain Hannover yelled. "We have no reason to shoot you."

"Not," said the hermit of the iceberg, "if I can help it, you won't shoot me."

Captain Hannover gave low orders—he was going to leave the man on the iceberg, since he saw no reason to risk his own life, those of his men, and delay his ship, to rescue a man who didn't want to be rescued.

So they went back to their liner and passed the buck on the whole job by radioing the United States Coast Guard Ice Patrol boat the location of the berg and the information that there was a queer man on it, then sailed away, and the last they saw of the hermit, he was sitting on an ice pinnacle, contemplating their departure and manifesting the symptoms of an emotion defined as pleasure. In large bio-chemical quantities.

CHAPTER II

THE MAN JONES

THE STORY OF a lone man on an iceberg with a machine gun, a vocabulary of strange remarks, a hostile disposition, and a conviction that the World War was still in progress was a good news story, and soon the yarn was being flashed around by radio. The radio operator of Polyphemus Ward's sumptuous private yacht copied the story with other news dispatches which he regularly took down for the financier's perusal.

Polyphemus Ward was as amazing in his way as the man on the iceberg was to prove to be in his way. Polyphemus Ward had been called numerous things in his lifetime. His father came home drunk a couple of hours after Polyphemus was born in a sod shanty in Nebraska, took one look at the blessed event, and groaned. The doctor officiating was moved to remark: "I don't know which is the worst—a father as drunk as you are, or a baby as homely as that one."

To which the father said gloomily, "Yeah, but tomorrow I'll be sober."

They named the baby Polyphemus at a cowhand's suggestion, not finding out until later that the original Polyphemus was a Cyclops who, according to the *Odyssey*, imprisoned Odysseus and his companions in a cavern and devoured a pair of the company daily until his captives put out his one eye with a burning brand, after which the prisoners escaped by clinging to the Cyclops' sheep as the blind giant drove them out to pasture. Those moved to look up the name invariably remarked on how appropriately it fitted Polyphemus Ward. Polyphemus Ward devoured men's fortunes.

When Polyphemus Ward was four years old, he had his first disillusioning experience when a boy his own age—the first tike his own age he'd ever seen—stole his only prized possession, a jackknife. This single incident made Polyphemus suspect there was not an honest man in all the world, and future experiences made the conviction permanent. At frequent intervals, he was jobbed, doublecrossed, framed, and walked on, as he went about the business of getting fabulously rich.

Polyphemus Ward was twenty-one years old when he opened the Golden Glory mine, but by that time, he had learned a thing or two, and the partner who turned crooked on him went to prison, as he deserved, after which twenty million dollars net profit came out of the Golden Glory's clanking ore-cars and landed in Polyphemus Ward's bank account. Then he moved into Wall Street, which is a narrow pen with a graveyard at one end and a river at the other, where sheep are shorn artistically.

But Polyphemus J. Ward was no sheep. He was as homely as sin, had a tongue like a bullwhip, and his mind could grasp facts and figures and lay them out as though he was using bricks to pave a road for himself.

The wolves of Wall Street sprang on the sheep, and when the smoke cleared, they found themselves harnessed to the sheep's sled, pulling it and saying, "Uncle," whenever asked. As the wolves lagged, they were cooly skinned and their carcasses tossed aside.

After Polyphemus Ward became the terror of Wall Street, he began to take the shirts off international bankers. He was excellently equipped, for he trusted no one, although, oddly, he was scrupulously honest himself.

When he saw Lola Ames milking a cow on a Missouri farm near where his car broke down, Polyphemus Ward instantly realized that she was the most beautiful girl in the world, and that he was going to marry her. He did. To his everlasting disrepute, he didn't let her know he was one of the world's richest men until after they were married. But he loved her, and she loved him.

If any bitterness was needed to make the moneybags a completely sour human-pickle, two things came along to finish the job when the wife he loved passed away at the birth of their daughter, Janice, a loss that did something permanent to Polyphemus Ward.

The other was the thing about his daughter, Janice.

FUNNY PEGGER, press agent, and ex-newspaperman who had earned his sobriquet through the same process by which a fat boy is sometimes called Slim, was off duty, loafing on the bridge of the yacht when Polyphemus Ward tramped in, scowling.

"Pick up that fool on the iceberg!" Polyphemus growled.

He stamped out again.

The captain of the yacht scratched his head. "You could knock me over with a straw!" he said.

Funny Pegger grinned and said nothing.

The captain added, "Polyphemus never accommodated anybody in his life. Why this rescue? If there was a dollar on that iceberg, I could understand it."

Funny Pegger continued to grin. He was a stocky, remarkably homely, wonderfully amiable young man. He was, also, one of those rarities, a natural-born gag-man—he had a rat-trap memory, and once he heard a joke he never forgot it.

He had lately been offered five hundred dollars a week to write gags for a radio comedian, and he intended taking the job.

"I'm not entirely surprised," Funny Pegger remarked.

"No?"

The gag-man grinned. "You're not an observing man, Captain, or you wouldn't be surprised either."

"I don't get you."

"The old hickory nut has a crack in his shell, and if you look close, you might see the tender green kernel of a human being."

The captain snorted. "Impossible, Polyphemus Ward's a cockleburr all the way through."

"For six months, he's been changing."

"What happened six months ago?"

"Janice, his daughter, disappeared," Funny reminded him. "Vanished."

The yacht, a trim black giant as large as some ocean liners, sped toward the iceberg. There was a swimming pool, glass-enclosed, on board. Also, there were: Golf-practice room. Gymnasium. Billiard cabin. Card room. Badminton room. Four bars. There were so many other rooms that Polyphemus Ward had never been in some of them, and they were all air conditioned, for the boat was a floating penthouse, a castle, a château, a palace, and her designers and builders had all been able to retire after producing her.

In the yacht's launch when it went to rescue the man off the iceberg rode Funny Pegger.

On the iceberg sat the red-whiskered young man. He seemed quite calm, until a thought must have occurred to him, for he sprang up and prepared to retreat.

"Your boat has a United States flag," he shouted. "But it occurs to me that the Germans may have captured the United States. Have they, by any chance, done so?"

He seemed to have a scholarly way of stringing his words together, even when he was excited.

"They have not," said Funny Pegger. "And just to get the record straight—the World War is over."

"Terminated?"

"In 1918."

"Then," said the young man, "the Huns must have told me the truth."

Funny Pegger laughed. He walked forward, held out his hand.

The other man stared at the hand.

"What do you want?"

"Not a thing," said Funny Pegger, "except to shake your hand."

The occupant of the iceberg seemed puzzled.

"The hand," he remarked, "or the terminus of the arm, is a grasping organ sometimes called the *manus*, and consists of the phalanges, or fingers, the *metacarpus* or hand proper, and *carpus*, or wrist, and is a more specialized and prehensile organ in man than in animals, capable of pronation and supination…. Shake is an agitation with a vibratory motion, or to tremble, to shiver, quake, as to shake with fear. Combining the two, I fail to find a bearing they might have on our meeting."

Funny Pegger's mouth came open. "There," he said, "you've got me."

"Got you?"

"You wouldn't be telling me you don't know what a handshake is for?"

"Exactly. I recall reading of a custom of the sort, but unfortunately I did not attach importance to it at the time."

Funny Pegger looked blank. "Look now, could this be a line you're pulling?"

"Line?"

"A gag."

"I do not understand." The young man blinked bewilderedly. "You confuse me."

"It's unanimous," said Funny Pegger. "I'm confused by you. Do you want to be rescued, or don't you?"

"Oh, I decidedly do."

"Swell. You do so by stepping into that boat there. By the way, my name is Raymond Pegger—Funny Pegger. Have you got a name?"

"My name is Jones," said the young man.

"Anything in front or behind?"

"Just—Jones."

JUST JONES stepped across the ice to the launch. He had enough size and red whiskers to make an impressive figure.

"Any baggage?" Funny Pegger asked him.

"Baggage?"

"Machine guns, et cetera."

"I—do you think I shall need the machine gun?"

"That," said Funny Pegger, "depends. I imagine we all have moments when we'd like to use one."

"Er—I think I shall leave it, along with my skin-boat and a small supply of cured seal-meat."

The launch backed away from the floe, turned and ploughed toward the yacht. A slight breeze had sprung up, and waves smacked the bow, sending a cold spray back over the boat occupants. It was getting dark, the air was cold, and the iceberg was huge, barren and depressing.

Jones stared at the receding iceberg, an expression of regret settling on his face, with a trace of moisture in his eyes, as though he was taking leave of an old friend.

"Sort of like leaving home, eh?"

Jones looked up. "Home," he said soberly, "is the abiding place of the affections, especially domestic affections. Also the vital center or seat; the heart or core, intimately, effectively, close; and to the innermost feeling of sensibility. I hardly think that iceberg qualifies."

Funny Pegger swallowed. "Skip it," he requested. Someone had obviously been feeding the man Jones a diet of dictionaries.

The launch rounded up to the side of the yacht, davit-falls came snaking down, and the small boat was lifted and placed on its deck cradle.

Jones looked all around with the wide-eyed curiosity of a country boy in the city, or a city boy in the country.

"The doctor," said Funny Pegger, "is waiting to look you over."

Jones followed meekly to a neat white hospital cabin, presided over by a neat doctor. Jones glanced around, sniffing the anaesthetic odor which seems always present in hospital rooms.

"Carbolic," he announced. "A weak monobasic colorless or pinkish crystalline substance produced by destructive distillation of various organics, wood, coal, et cetera, and also a hydroxy derivative of benzene, used much in weak solution as an antiseptic."

"Undress," the doctor said after he had swallowed.

When Jones' sealskin upper garment came off, Funny Pegger's mouth fell open, and it remained open until Jones stood in his naked skin, after which Funny moistened his lips.

"Shades of Hercules!" he remarked.

The doctor tapped Jones, squeezed, stared, watched the little dial of the blood-pressure machine, then got out his stethoscope, stuck the ends of the forked tube in his ears and applied the business end of the thing to Jones' chest.

"Cough," he ordered.

Jones seemed impressed. He coughed self-consciously.

The doctor laid the stethoscope aside.

"Okay," he said.

Jones looked at the instrument, his serious blue eyes showed an attack of intense curiosity, and he picked up the stethoscope, stuck the ends of the tubes in his ears, calmly unbuttoned the doctor's shirt and applied the sound box to the medico's chest. He listened.

"The heart of the human being in the adult stage," he remarked, "is about five inches long and three and a half inches wide, and pumps seventy to seventy-five beats per minute, as contrasted with twenty-eight to thirty-eight beats in the case of the heart of a horse. But I've never heard one before. Ah—will you cough, please?"

The doctor started to cough, caught himself and turned red.

"What kind of horseplay is this?" he said indignantly.

Jones looked surprised.

Funny Pegger grinned. "You know, Doc, I've always wondered what you heard through them things, too. How about giving me a little listen?"

"You two get out of here!" the medico snapped.

"Sure, sure, keep your shirt on, Doc. What kind of shape is Jones in?"

"I never," said the doctor, "saw a man in better physical condition."

"Did you," asked Funny Pegger, "ever see a sweller set of muscles?"

"Never."

"Muscles," announced Jones, "consist of modified and unusually elongated cells, or fibers, which contract when stimulated. They are of two principal types, striated and nonstriated muscles, the former being mostly under the control of the will."

The doctor's jaw fell.

"I don't believe your physical build is the only extraordinary thing about you," he muttered.

CHAPTER III

THE ORIGIN OF JONES

JONES WAS SILENT as they left the hospital cabin, and wistful, as though all of a sudden, he realized that, for some reason or other, he was regarded as a queer specimen. He grew thoughtful, endeavoring to discern what put him in the freak class—what made Funny Pegger and the doctor look at him as though he was a *djinn* that had popped out of a rubbed lamp.

Funny Pegger was also silent. That was unusual. Pegger liked to talk, and ordinarily did so at an appalling rate but just now he was trying to figure Jones out and not having much luck.

Funny Pegger chewed his lower lip and mentally masticated the circumstance that Jones was apparently no normal castaway on an iceberg. There were natural things to be expected of a man found alone on a mass of ice in the Atlantic Ocean, but Jones had not conformed, had not done the expected.

For instance, Jones had not yet offered to explain how he came to be on the berg.

Funny Pegger escorted Jones to the main lounge where there was a group that included Polyphemus Ward, his executive secretary Lyman Lee, and yacht guests, among whom was the Countess Maria Montignal de Grandrieu, a onetime American heiress, now middle-aged, and more or less destitute, due to the yeoman work done upon her fortune by the Count. With the Countess was her daughter, Glacia, who needed a rich husband badly. Glacia was a strikingly beautiful and calculating piece of glass who would probably do the same thing to some man that her father had done to her mother. She sat where Jones did not at first observe her.

They all stared as if Jones were a strange insect someone had brought in on the point of a pin. Jones looked back at the occupants of the room as though they were bugs, too. He did not seem self-conscious. He walked to a deep leather chair, studied it curiously, as if he had never seen a chair before, then sat down in it as the others were doing. He bounced up and down on the soft springs, then registered pleasure.

"Comfort," he remarked, "is derived from the Old French verb *confort,* meaning a state of feeling relief, cheer, or consolation, or a contented enjoyment in physical well-being specifically, free from want or anxiety."

The cigar in Polyphemus Ward's grim mouth stuck up at a startled angle.

And about that time, Jones discovered Glacia.

JONES fell to studying Glacia. People usually studied Glacia. Seeing Glacia for the first time was like happening upon an acre of diamonds. It apparently did not occur to Jones that he cut a strange figure in sealskin jacket, bearskin pants, walrus boots, and amazing red beard. Nor did he feel inclined to make further remarks.

These people had gathered to hear his story. Jones wasn't aware of the fact, or aware of anything much except Glacia.

"Er—ahem!" Funny Pegger suggested. "Shoot."

"I haven't," said Jones amiably, "the slightest desire to shoot anybody."

Funny Pegger started to explain that they wanted to hear Jones' story, then changed his mind, for Lyman Lee was scowling at Jones, and Jones had noticed it.

Lyman Lee, of course, was irked by the inspection Jones had been giving Glacia. Lyman Lee had been monopolizing Glacia throughout the trip. Or possibly it was vice versa.

Funny Pegger did not like Lyman Lee.

If anyone else liked Lyman Lee, it would have been difficult to name him offhand. Unless it was Lyman Lee. At thirty-five, Lyman Lee held a job envied by half the financiers in the world. He was efficient at it. He was Polyphemus Ward's right hand, or, as some claimed, the velvet glove on that hand. He had the title of confidential secretary, and he knew everything to be known about Polyphemus Ward's business; he knew, some people felt, too much. For this he was paid forty thousand a year.

Lyman Lee was a large young man, too handsome, overbearing, self-centered, grasping. His dress was invariably sartorial perfection, for he usually changed suits three times a day. Lyman Lee insulted his inferiors—and these were legion—and fawned on his financial superiors. He had the eyes of a fish. He wore a monocle as if at least to hide the fishiness of one of them.

It was this monocle which intrigued Jones.

"Monocle," Jones remarked. "Probably from the Latin *Monoculus*, or single, plus *oculus*, meaning eye, thus monoculate, or pertaining to one eye. Also an affectation adopted by fops, dandies and beaux, often made of plain window glass."

That did not sink into Lyman Lee for a moment. When it did, he scowled more blackly.

Polyphemus Ward grinned and bit his cigar with relish. Funny Pegger, with difficulty, kept his face straight. The silence was so deep it almost rang.

Funny Pegger cleared his throat. "Jones," he said. "We're curious about how you happened to be on that iceberg."

Jones glanced at the assembled group, then nodded and smiled. "Of course," he said, "you would be. I was there because I got on it deliberately."

Funny Pegger swallowed. "Deliberately."

"Yes." Jones nodded. "Deliberately."

"Was there," Funny Pegger asked gently, "any reason?"

"I was lonesome."

"Lonesome?"

"Yes, very,"

"I take it," Funny Pegger ventured, "that you mean you were lonesome on the iceberg."

"Oh, no. Not on the iceberg. I wasn't bothered at all there. You see, the iceberg was slowly turning over. Presumably it was melting unevenly on one side, or something. To tell the truth, I rather appreciated the novelty."

Funny Pegger's scalp crawled. "You appreciated being on an iceberg that was turning over?"

"Pleasure," Jones stated, "can be a gratifying condition of the mind produced by the sensation of emotion, such as excitement, change, novelty, or physical activity. For example, I have discovered that if I run or leap about briskly, I seem to laugh more easily."

Lyman Lee snorted.

"This man," he announced, "is mentally unbalanced."

Jones surveyed the group. All of them, he could see, had the same impression; they agreed with Lyman Lee. Suddenly Jones felt concerned, very alone, depressed by futility. He had the sensations of a fish swimming in strange water. The thing to do, he decided, was seem relieved. He settled back, crossed his legs again, and smiled.

"Thank you," he said politely, "for bringing that up. I was intending to mention it myself for, needless to say, I have detected a strange note toward myself. I see that you regard me as unusual. My, er—conversation seems to startle you. My appearance, including my manner of dress, obviously strikes you as peculiar." He paused, "It is quite appropriate for life on an iceberg, however."

Funny Pegger grinned. "That's telling 'em Jones. Suppose you shoot your story briefly."

"I—briefly?"

"Yes."

"I was born on a ship," Jones announced. "The year of my birth was 1914. My father was Bob 'Polar' Jones, a man who made a business of taking explorers to the Arctic on his schooner."

Funny Pegger wrinkled his forehead. "Who did you say your father was?"

"Polar Jones."

Funny Pegger grabbed the back of his neck, a private device which he used to stimulate his memory. Suddenly he sprang erect. "Polar Jones!" he ejaculated. "Polar—Polar—why, of course! Polar Jones! The grand old man of the Arctic. One of the all-time mysteries is his disappearance. He vanished. Took an explorer to the Arctic and was never heard from again. Disappeared. All of them."

Funny Pegger was a newspaperman at heart, although his present job was public relations counsel to Polyphemus Ward. He was excited.

"Did you know my father?" Jones asked.

"No, no, that was before my time," Funny Pegger explained. "I've heard newspapermen talk of him. Polar Jones! He must have been a great guy. What happened to him and his schooner, anyway?"

"I'm getting to that," said Jones. "My father took me along when he sailed to the Arctic. I was very small, but my mother had died, and my father wanted me with him. That was in 1917."

"That checks," Funny Pegger nodded. "It was in 1917 that Polar Jones disappeared!"

"The explorer my father took north was Colonel Freeman—"

"Adams," Funny Pegger interrupted. "Colonel Freeman Adams. That was the explorer's name. One of the first scientists to do anything about studying cosmic rays. A bird who was ahead of his time."

"Ah—you seem to be well informed," Jones remarked.

"Any newspaperman," said Funny Pegger, "remembers a big news story. But go ahead."

"Polar Jones' ship ran aground."

"Aground?"

"In a gale. The schooner"—Jones eyed his hands grimly—"was driven so high on the glacier-covered shore of a small island that they couldn't get it off. The lifeboats were smashed. A few weeks later, the glacier moved down, shoved the schooner off in deep water, and it sank." Jones looked up at them. "Everyone was marooned on this island, which was uncharted. Food was saved, of course, and books. Colonel Adams had brought an enormous library along."

Jones lapsed into a sober silence, and the listeners looked grave, thinking of the explorers marooned in the Arctic.

"Man," Jones remarked, "a high type of animal of the genus *homo*, with sufficient structural peculiarities to justify separating him from the anthropoid apes, they having erect posture, adaption for walking instead of prehension, and greater development of the gluteus maximus and other muscles which hold the body erect. Man alone has power to articulate speech, which enabled him to develop power to reason."

Funny Pegger frowned. "I don't get your drift."

"I—drift?"

"Your meaning."

"Why," said Jones, "I was merely pointing out that man is close to the animal. Like the animal, he does not seem to be able to associate with his fellows without strife."

"I take it," said Funny Pegger, "that you mean the shipwrecked explorers began to quarrel?"

"Exactly. Quarrel." Jones eyed his fists. "The World War was going on, and there was one German in the assemblage. The cook. The other men irritated the German cook unnecessarily, I'm afraid."

"Irritated him?"

"Drove him crazy, to be exact. He finally put poison in the food."

"Poison?"

"Yes. The German cook must have been insane, because he ate of the food along with the rest, and died, too."

"You mean that everybody was poisoned?"

"Not exactly. The poison was in the beans. At my age, fortunately, I had not acquired a liking for beans, and ate none. So I escaped. Also one other man recovered, having eaten sparingly."

"Who was the other survivor?"

"Colonel Freeman Adams," Jones explained. "He was very ill from the poison, and never the same afterward, I am afraid, in his mental attitude."

Funny Pegger moistened his lips. "I'll be damned," he said.

"The rest does not amount to anything to speak of," Jones added. "I grew up on the island, and that's all."

He began inspecting Glacia again.

THEY were all seated in one of the finest yachts in the world, traveling across the Atlantic in safety and comfort, and it was doubtful if anyone present had ever experienced an adventure more precarious than dodging a taxicab. Aboard the yacht, which differed little from a fine hotel, they were surrounded with all the comforts of civilized existence. Furthermore, almost everyone present had always possessed more money than he knew what to do with, so they all of them were accustomed to smooth luxury, so much so that it was doubtful if the listeners appreciated the privation and horror covered by Jones' narrative. Except for Funny Pegger, who had been a newspaperman, and comprehended that a grisly procession of misfortune must have befallen the explorers.

"Jones," said Funny Pegger, "I want to shake the hand of a modest man!"

"I—er—what?" Jones took his eyes off Glacia. "Modest?" He was puzzled.

"I compliment you," said Funny Pegger, "on a masterly piece of understatement. You say you simply grew up on that island."

"Er—I did."

"Yes—but how? What was it like? Where did you get food? What did you think about? Where'd your education come from? Why wait twenty years? Why didn't you build a boat and leave? What—why, heck—you haven't covered half the story!"

"There were seals and walrus and things to eat," Jones said. "As for education, I recited books aloud."

"You recited books aloud?"

"Yes. At Colonel Adams' suggestion."

"But why stay on the island so long?"

"Colonel Adams did not want to leave. While I was young, he would not let me build a boat. Later, when I grew large enough to have overpowered him, I presume I did not do so because of—oh—pity. Had I tried to take him by force, I believe he would have ended his own life."

Funny Pegger squinted. "Sounds like Colonel Adams was a screwball."

"Screwball?"

"Scrambled."

"I am afraid," said Jones, "that Colonel Adams *was* mentally abnormal, if that is your meaning."

"What you're telling us is that you spent your life on that island with a madman?"

"I—yes."

"I take it," said Funny Pegger, "that after Colonel Adams passed on, you got lonesome and decided to thumb a ride on an iceberg." He whistled. "I don't see how you had the nerve."

"It was rather simple. I merely convinced myself that the compensations would be worth the dangers involved."

"Yeah. Well, I hope you won't be disappointed."

"I don't"—Jones contemplated Glacia—"think I shall be."

CHAPTER IV

THE MENAGERIE

POLYPHEMUS WARD HAD not said a word. Probably he wouldn't. Polyphemus Ward had a habit of sitting around, apparently no more interested than a snapping turtle in a shell, then suddenly exploding and spilling acid over everyone. Ordinarily, he lived in a dour sulk, but when he did cut loose, he played no favorites. He had insulted, browbeaten and put the figurative boot to international bankers, princes, dukes, lords, premiers, a few crowned heads, most of the European dictators extant, and all of his own employees that he had met. They all liked it because Polyphemus Ward had almost as many millions as Tammany has politicians.

Lyman Lee had been silent, too. He was stewing. Or at least simmering gently and threatening to come to a boil at any moment. His feathers had been ruffled by Jones' interest in Glacia and the remark about the monocle. Lyman Lee was the kind of man who got waiters fired for spilling soup on his coat. He had the kind of a mind that took a small slight, thought about it, and fanned up a considerable fire. By now Lyman Lee had worked up a violent dislike for Jones.

"This man is a liar!" Lyman Lee said unexpectedly. "There isn't the slightest doubt of it."

Jones stared at Lyman Lee with mild astonishment.

"Oaf," Jones remarked, "comes from the Icelandic word *alfr,* meaning elf, or an elf's child, usually deformed or foolish, or a simpleton, left on one's doorstep by goblins."

Funny Pegger emitted a snort of laughter before he thought. Lyman Lee sprang up, leveled an immaculate arm at the gag-man. "You're fired!" he yelled.

Funny Pegger shrugged.

"Look in your mail basket," he said. "You'll find my resignation, turned in yesterday! I'm taking a job as gag writer"—he had to add—"at five hundred dollars a week."

Lyman Lee turned shades of purple.

Polyphemus Ward spoke.

"No more of this!" he said.

Everyone jumped. A jump was the natural thing when Polyphemus Ward spoke—he had a way of sounding like an automobile accident happening. The financier's tone seemed to irritate Jones.

"I see no reason," he remarked, "for continuing this interview."

Jones arose with dignity and walked out, giving Glacia a last glance. Funny Pegger hesitated, then followed Jones.

Glacia, looking very gem-like, swept over to Lyman Lee and consoled him with a manicured hand on his impeccable sleeve.

"What a primitive person this Jones is," Glacia murmured. "Insufferable, of course, but amusing in his crude way."

Polyphemus Ward exploded a snort. "Amusing!" he grunted. "So is a barrel of firecrackers—as long as you light 'em only one at a time."

Jones and Funny Pegger headed for a vacant cabin which had been assigned to the rescued man, and Jones was silent until the gag-man grinned up at him. "I think you sold a bill of goods to the old dollar-magnet, Jones," said the humorist.

"I—what?"

"Never mind. How did they impress you?"

"To tell the truth," Jones replied, "in various ways."

"Lyman Lee, for instance?"

Jones considered. "He apparently thinks he is the last thing made by God…. By the way, who was the elderly gentleman whose voice had qualities reminding me of a bull walrus?"

"That"—Funny Pegger paused dramatically—"was Polyphemus Ward."

"Polyphemus," Jones stated, "was the Cyclops of the *Odyssey,* who kept Odysseus and his companions in a cave, devouring two daily, until Odysseus got him drunk and pierced his eye with a heated pole, after which Odysseus escaped by clinging to the bellies of the blind giant's sheep as he drove them out to graze. The Polyphemus is a type of moth, also, with a large larva, green with silver tubercles, feeding on oak, chestnut, willow, apple, cherry, et cetera."

"The only difference," Funny Pegger advised, "is that this one feeds on other men's bank accounts."

They reached the cabin assigned to Jones, one of the poorest staterooms on the yacht, hence equivalent to twenty-dollar-a-day accommodations at the Waldorf. Jones entered the room, looked around with appreciation, and went over to test the softness of the berth.

"This is wonderful," he declared. "I didn't imagine people lived so comfortably."

"Some of them don't, believe me. You camp here, Jones, and I'll see if I can scare up clothes for you."

Funny Pegger started to leave.

"Er—wait a minute," Jones requested. "I—ah—I have a question to propound."

"Propound away."

"Ummm." Jones seemed embarrassed. "In that place we just left, there was—ah—a person. It was a—woman—was it not?"

Funny Pegger staggered. "Holy mackerel! You never—saw a woman before!"

"Never," said Jones. "Er—would you call that one a girl instead of a woman?"

"That one was Glacia," said Funny Pegger. "Commonly known as a wow."

"And what is a wow?"

"A girl who doesn't occur very often, but when she does—wow!"

"Indeed?"

AFTER he left Jones' stateroom, Funny Pegger got an ache in his ribs from laughing. Funny Pegger considered himself a student of life. He believed he saw possibilities of an interesting situation. Take a young man of Jones' physique and mental equipment—Funny Pegger sensed that Jones had something extraordinary in the line of a mental machine—and add to it the fact that Jones had never seen a woman, and—well, you had something.

Funny Pegger ran into Polyphemus Ward. He started, and instantly felt nervous.

"What do you think of this Jones?" Polyphemus Ward growled.

"I like him," Funny Pegger said frankly. "And I suspect his future will be better than a circus."

"Hmmm!" Polyphemus Ward chewed his cigar. "I'm interested in him."

Funny Pegger, surprised, wondered why Polyphemus Ward would be interested. Old Polyphemus was the kind of a man who never got interested in anything merely out of curiosity.

"Any news of Janice?" Polyphemus Ward asked suddenly.

Funny Pegger had been placed in charge of the detectives who were searching for Polyphemus Ward's missing daughter.

"The radio reports said nothing today," the gag-man admitted. "Still no trace."

Polyphemus Ward would never wince at anything. However, the news made his lips tighten, as they did when he was stabbed. "Sorry you're quitting me for that gag-writing job," he said gruffly. Then he added, "But what puzzles me is why you stuck as long as you did. You only get paid—"

"A hundred a week," said Funny Pegger, "which is not bad money."

"A hundred a week doesn't sound like enough to hold you."

"Doesn't it?" Funny Pegger was very uncomfortable.

Polyphemus Ward stared at his press agent. "I was just think-ing about that," he said. Then he changed the subject. "Bring Jones to dinner tonight."

Polyphemus Ward walked away, leaving Funny Pegger feeling as though he was standing in a pan of ice water. "Now I wonder," Funny muttered, "if the old reprobate could dream what I've been up to."

Having pulled his courage out of his boots, whence it had fled, Funny Pegger moved on down the deck. He was sobered. He had started out to promote appropriate clothing for Jones, but this slipped his mind until he sighted dapper Lyman Lee taking a deck constitutional in the dusk with the crystalline Glacia. Funny Pegger got an idea. He was a practical joker at heart.

The gag-man confronted Lyman Lee, who scowled, and Glacia, who glanced at Funny indifferently. Young men with less than a million dollars didn't interest Glacia.

"Just talked to Polyphemus Ward," Funny Pegger remarked. "Can you fix Jones up with some clothes, Lyman?"

Funny Pegger didn't consider that an outright lie. He couldn't help it if Lyman Lee inferred he had been ordered by Polyphe-mus to dress their guest. "I doubt," Lyman Lee remarked coolly, "if my garments would fit that fellow."

"Sure they would."

"But—"

"Jones is going to have dinner with us," Funny Pegger ex-plained.

Glacia gasped. "That lout—dining with us?"

"Yep."

"Count me out. I'm going to go down and enjoy a headache," Glacia declared and made a face.

"Jones," said Funny Pegger doggedly, "is all right."

Lyman Lee sneered. "A faker."

"His story sounded up and up to me," Funny Pegger stated. "It was remarkable, of course. But the facts checked."

"An imposter!"

"Matter of opinion."

"Probably has some ulterior motive."

Lyman Lee apparently intended to say more on the subject of Jones, but caught himself as a man does when a sudden thought jumps into his mind. Lee's mouth, which had the shape of a woman's, pursed, and he glanced unseeingly at the ocean, where waves ran in orderly rows, crested with the last red of the sinking sun.

"All right," he said suddenly. "Send Jones to my suite, and I shall furnish him with suitable dinner clothes."

Taking the glittering Glacia's arm, Lyman Lee strolled down the deck, pointing out formations of clouds, and explaining to his companion how the clouds indicated they would have clear weather tomorrow.

Funny Pegger was dubious.

"That syrup-smeared worm," the gag-man muttered, "has something up his sleeve." He grinned suddenly. "However, my money is on Jones."

FUNNY PEGGER ambled into the radio room, borrowed a typewriter from the second-trick operator, and composed in brief, businesslike fashion a news story of the rescuing of Polar Jones' son, an item which he dispatched to the Associated Press via radio. He wrote two different and more flowery accounts, crammed with adjectives and drama, and sent these off to the two tabloid newspapers in New York which had the largest circulations.

Hardly had the stories been sent when the editors of the newspapers radioed urgent requests for more. Funny Pegger stared at the messages, then reread the stories he had sent to see what had excited the editors.

"Shades of Barnum!" he yelled.

He saw something. Something startling. Jones had newspaper "it." Jones was one of those figures that catch the public fancy. The newspapers would take to Jones like they took to Lindbergh.

"Bless me!" the gag-man gasped. "With a good manager, this Jones can coin dough."

Funny Pegger at once sent wireless messages to a dozen vaudeville agents, six major movie companies and the three largest radio chains, asking for bids on Jones' services.

He was already blissfully spending an imaginary cut of Jones' future earnings when he ambled into the corridor leading to Jones' stateroom. Instantly, he stopped. Funny Pegger's jaw fell, his eyes popped, and he felt sinkish. His hands flew up as if to push away an incredible vision.

"For the love of Godiva!" he croaked.

Jones was strolling down the corridor. Jones wore exactly what he had been born in.

"What the devil you up to?" Funny Pegger howled.

"Why," said Jones wonderingly, "I was rather warm."

"So you took all your clothes off and went for a walk!" shouted Funny Pegger.

"I—yes."

"You—were—warm!" Funny Pegger strangled.

"The reason," said Jones, "impresses me as being a sensible one."

"Walking around without clothes sensible!"

"Why not? It is warm enough."

Funny Pegger clamped hold of Jones, rushed him back down the passage, popped him into the stateroom, and slammed the door.

"Ever hear of modesty?" he demanded.

"Er—you mean it is customary not to be seen without clothes?"

"I'll say it is!"

Jones frowned. "I seem to be confused."

"What confused you?"

"The book which I read. The one with the green back."

"What," asked Funny Pegger curiously, "was the name of that book?"

"Nudist Colonies—Their Growth and Practical Sensibility."

"That," said Funny Pegger, "explains everything. Listen, my remarkable friend, don't you know anything but what you memorized from books?"

"How could I?"

"Didn't this Colonel Adams tell you anything?"

"He told me to memorize books and recite them aloud."

"All I can say," said Funny Pegger, "is wear clothes, after this."

CHAPTER V

FULL DRESS

LYMAN LEE WAS waiting in his suite when Jones came in to dress for dinner, escorted by Funny Pegger. Lyman Lee said, "I think we can manage very well without you," and shut the door in Funny Pegger's face.

Standing in the passage, frowning at the closed door, Funny Pegger rubbed the back of his neck as he did when he wanted to think hard. He was certain dirty work was contemplated. However, he couldn't think of anything very desperate that Lyman Lee could do to Jones, and there was no way he could interfere gracefully anyway, so he departed to dress himself, and to wonder.

In Lee's cabin, Jones stood smiling agreeably and not saying anything, having decided to confine his remarks to yes and no in order to avoid enflaming Lyman Lee.

Lyman Lee was a young man cured in oil. That is, his father had been a moderately wealthy small-town banker. This small-time moneybags got into difficulties with depositors' money long before there was any excuse for it and, lacking the intestinal fortitude to stand a stretch of looking out from behind bars, had stepped on the trigger of a double-barreled twelve-gauge shotgun while holding the muzzle to his chest. They scraped most of him together and buried him. And a majority of his fellow townsmen had sighed with unmistakable relief.

Lyman Lee did have one commendable trait. He was ambitious. For the rest, Lyman Lee was an amalgamation of unlovely traits. He would, for instance, go out of his way to throw a rock at a bird, just as he was now going out of his way to heave a dornick at Jones. To Lyman Lee's credit, however, let it be said that he really did believe Jones was a smart impostor, and not a young man who had grown up on a remote Arctic island, knew only what he had read in books, and was unfamiliar with customs, good, bad and senseless, of civilized people.

Lyman Lee was going to test Jones.

The two men were about of a size. Lyman Lee got out two complete sets of evening dress. Then he began putting everything but his shoes on backward.

Jones stood eyeing the process, completely puzzled. The shoes, he naturally solved at once, and he put them on. Thereafter, he watched Lyman Lee, and did exactly as Lee did—he put the trousers on so they buttoned up the back, squirmed into the shirt so that the stiff bosom was against his spine, attached the collar backward, the tie likewise, then got into the waistcoat and coat. This was accomplished with difficulty, a full dress suit being a problem in strategy, even when donned correctly.

Up to a point, Jones was silent, endeavoring to be amiable, but his enthusiasm got the best of him.

"Peacock," he remarked. "A large gallinaceous bird of genus *pavo,* native to Java, southwestern Asia and the East Indies, where they have the Javan peafowl. The fowl is chiefly notable because of the flamboyance of the male as contrasted to the plainer colors of the female."

Lyman Lee scowled, but held on to his patience.

"Does everyone wear these at night?" Jones asked curiously.

"The proper people do," said Lyman Lee shortly.

"I feel," announced Jones, "decidedly bedecked, if not quite sensible."

Lyman Lee had proved his point, or at least proved himself wrong. Jones and dress suits were strangers. Lyman was not happy about it. "You wait here a few minutes," he directed. "Then go to the dining salon. Anyone will tell you the way."

"I appreciate," Jones said earnestly, "your kindness."

Lyman Lee slipped out of the cabin, made a rush and reached an empty stateroom before anyone saw his backward arrangement of attire. Once behind a closed door, he hurriedly removed his garments and put them on the way they were intended to be worn. He smiled in thin-lipped enjoyment. It did not occur to him that what he was doing was small, mean and childish.

Jones entered the dining salon with a complete lack of embarrassment. With dress suit on backward, flowing red beard, mass of fire-colored hair, he made a spectacle that was at least astonishing.

Lyman Lee guffawed. Jones inspected the dress of the other men, then examined himself, lifting the tails of his coat, twisting to inspect them.

He grinned. "Joke," he volunteered, "comes from the Latin word *jocus,* meaning something done to provoke hilarity or humor. In ancient times, kings retained professional jokers, called buffoons, probably from the Italian *buffa,* or vanity, now meaning a droll, harlequin, clown or a merry-andrew."

Old Polyphemus Ward emitted a blast, a sound nearly a laugh, and akin to a cannon report. It was the first time in months, if anyone thought of it, that he had indicated that he might be human.

The others chuckled—with Jones, not at him—and Lyman Lee colored. His small trick had turned to bite the hand that had fed it.

The dinner was a success as far as Jones was concerned. He had the judgment to keep from ogling Glacia, to limit his remarks to necessities, and to watch the eating implements which the others used. Funny Pegger saw Jones make only one bobble, and he suspected someone else had made the mistake first.

Funny Pegger also observed that Jones was studying Glacia with enduring interest. That, to Funny Pegger, portended nothing peaceful. Jones, as a matter of fact, was restraining himself with difficulty. He had not, within span of his memory, tasted one of the dishes served, hence the thing was an exciting adventure. After a dessert of a fine old cheese that he tried with some misgivings, a sweet liqueur was served in thin glasses.

"What, if I may ask, is this?" Jones inquired.

"Benedictine," Polyphemus Ward grunted.

"Indeed," said Jones. "A liquor rather like chartreuse, and made near Fécamp, France, and originally concocted by the Benedictines, an order of monks established by St. Benedict of Nursia about the year 529 at Monte Cassino."

Polyphemus Ward gave Jones narrow-eyed interest. "Ever tasted Benedictine before?"

"Never," Jones admitted.

"And you were marooned on that Arctic island all your life?"

"Yes."

"Then where," growled Polyphemus Ward, "did you get such damned detailed information about so many things?"

"From books."

"Books?"

"He memorized books," Funny Pegger explained.

"I—er—liked definitions particularly," Jones ventured.

Polyphemus Ward gnawed his cigar. "What is—ummm—steel?"

"S-t-e-e-l?"

"Yes."

"A metal," said Jones, "named possibly after the Icelandic *stal*, the metal being an alloy essentially of iron and carbon, produced by absorption of the carbon into heated iron, also by a fusion process. Steel, for commercial purposes, is classified as soft, medium or hard, depending on carbon content of 0.25, 0.60, or up to 2.2 per cent respectively."

Polyphemus Ward blinked. "What is a—a stegosaurus?"

"A paleontological genus of large orthopod dinosaur believed prevalent in Upper Jurassic times, and notable for a dermal

armor, including a row of upright bony plates along the back,"
said Jones.

Polyphemus Ward swallowed.

"What," he asked, "is a radio crooner?"

"Crooner?"

"Exactly."

"I confess," said Jones, "to ignorance on that point. My studies
of radio theory and terminology did not touch upon any such
item as a crooner."

"I'll be chiggered!" said Polyphemus Ward, employing an
oath of which he was especially fond.

"A crooner," remarked Funny Pegger, "is a man who sings so
sweet they have to close the windows."

"Why?" asked Jones.

"To keep the flies from coming in."

After a dull silence, Funny Pegger muttered, "If anybody
wants to cackle over the egg that gag laid, they're welcome."
The party sat around in silence after that, and Jones did not feel
entirely at home, having a sensation of being out of place, and
a suspicion that his presence was dampening conversation.

What Jones did not know was that he had them awed. To
these people, Jones was a phenomenon. He knew everything.
At the same time, there was a paradox, for Jones was a vacuum
when it came to knowing simple things. He doubtless knew
that a heterocercal tail is the kind of a tail that sharks have, but
on the other hand, he had no idea what a strip-tease artist might
be. He was aware that the atomic weight of oxygen is 16.00,
but he doubtless thought a hot baby was an overheated infant.
The remarkable aspects of Jones had stunned them, one and
all.

When they did start talking, Jones became the awed one.
They were a sophisticated crowd, so their talk was based on the
popular habit of making a lightning response to anything said,
whether the reply was sensible or not, the very silliness of the
response often being amusing enough to lend fake cleverness

to the talk. It did not make sense to Jones. It wouldn't have made sense to anybody.

Cigarettes were lighted, and Jones tried one. He didn't care for his first smoke particularly.

JONES slept soundly, arose in the morning with a sense of eager well-being, an impulse to rub his hands together. Sleep seemed to have made him enthusiastic. He felt, he realized, much as Columbus must have felt when he found America.

Like Columbus, Jones decided, he was an explorer, the difference between them being that the customs of mankind was the unexplored territory in his case. What men and women did, thought, felt, was the New World for his research operations.

The late hour at which the rest of the party left their blankets surprised him. He saw hardly a soul about until past noon, which did not seem sensible, but indicated that these people did their living at night.

The first requirement for doing the things they did appeared to be to consume a succession of cocktails. Cocktails were a foundation for their dizzy repartee, he concluded, so he tried two Old Fashioneds, shortsightedly drinking them close together, so that both were down before he got a sample of the effects. The reaction gave him a fright. He resolved to have no more truck with anything that stole his mind away so unexpectedly.

The doings of the evening tended to confuse him. The staid souls played something with small pasteboards which, they advised him, was a card game named bridge, and after looking on, an operation they called kibitzing, he got the impression that bridge might be all right as a time-killer.

Sound of music drew him toward the lounge, and he ambled around on the raised orchestra dais, intrigued by the notes that came out of the instruments. One of the saxophonists grinned, handed him an instrument and he tried it, but the noise he produced was discouraging.

Couples were going through gyrations on a patch of smooth floor in the center of the room.

"What," Jones asked Funny Pegger, "are they seeking to accomplish?"

"That," the gag-man explained, "is dancing."

"What is its purpose?"

"Why, it—why—it makes you graceful, I guess."

"I see."

"What did you think it accomplished?"

"I merely noticed," Jones said, "that the most enthusiastic participants are paired male and female. I thought that might have something to do with it."

Funny Pegger grinned. "I wouldn't fool you," he said. "It does."

Jones continued his observations, and discovered he had overlooked another form of entertainment which seemed popular. Time after time, he saw two persons leaving for the darkened deck, the participants invariably being male and female. He was consumed with curiosity.

About that time, he discovered Glacia. He had rather hoped to see her. He hadn't hoped to see her with Lyman Lee.

Glacia, exquisite and white-skinned in an evening thing, was dancing with the impeccable Lyman, and abruptly, they did what the other couples had been doing—headed for the deck.

Jones sauntered after them, intent on satisfying his curiosity.

Retiring to a moonstruck niche between two lifeboats, Lyman Lee took Glacia in his arms, tilted her head back, and placed his lips on hers.

Jones stood observing with considerable interest. He was aware of sensations. He was affected. Stirred. He had a sudden desire to participate, himself.

Jones had observed the technique of cutting in on the dance

floor, noticed that it was general, and this seemed a desirable time to apply the idea.

Stepping forward, Jones took Lyman Lee by the elbow. Lee was startled, and jumped back.

"I wish," Jones explained, "to sample this diversion."

Jones placed his arms around Glacia—he found it very natural to borrow Lyman Lee's technique—and pressed his lips on Glacia's. Something kept Glacia motionless. Astonishment, probably. Glacia had been kissed plenty, but never by a young man with red whiskers.

Jones felt something go down to his toes. It came up again. Whatever it was, it was new, and he hadn't imagined there were such things. Each individual hair on his head seemed to get up on end and shake.

He was so disturbed that he released Glacia and stepped back.

"I—gracious!" he exclaimed. "Oh, my!"

"I'll be," said Glacia, "hornswoggled."

"Ah—I never did that before," Jones gasped. "I—er—feel as if something had exploded."

Glacia looked at him in an odd way.

"I have," she murmured, "a new respect for amateur standing."

"I don't believe I understand."

"It must be," said Glacia, "one of those things."

Lyman Lee found his voice and exploded. "Jones, you—you blasted freak! You red-whiskered—hitch-hiker off an iceberg! Get away from here, or I'll"—he groped for a violent enough word—"I'll knock your head off!"

Jones thought the man's excitement was out of proportion, but he wasn't anxious for physical violence on top of his other emotions. The cake didn't need any frosting.

"It—er—was explosive!" he declared.

CHAPTER VI

ONE HUNDRED THOUSAND DOLLARS

POLYPHEMUS WARD HAD fought the world. His whole life had been a great battle, and he bore the scars, one of which was his conviction that the human was so constructed that it was impossible for an honest one to reach the age of twenty-one. He trusted no one on whom he did not have a chain. The death of the wife he loved had added a permanent touch of sourness to his soul.

Then there was his daughter, Janice, who grew up with the beauty of her exquisite mother, but also with the bullheadedness of her father. Polyphemus Ward spoiled her completely. He gave her everything. Janice had always been in the storm of her father's contrariness, his explosions of temper, his browbeating tactics, so the result was not unexpected. Janice, at eighteen, was a breathlessly beautiful creature with a temper like a bobcat, a determination to have her own way in everything, and no more real human emotions than a firecracker.

Every snapping turtle can get its shell cracked, and six months ago, Polyphemus Ward awakened. A ray of light reached his understanding. He suddenly saw that Janice was something on which he had done an awful job. So he called her in, laid the law down to her, and they had a fight that lasted two hours.

Janice had something that outweighed all her other liabilities. She could reason. Her mind could take hold of a fact, nail it to the wall, examine it, then lay it out like a brick to pave her own path.

Janice told Polyphemus Ward in the heat of the quarrel that she already realized she didn't like herself. She was nothing but a spoiled little Miss Rich-Switch. Her father wanted her to reform. Check! They were in agreement on that point. She wanted to change.

The method of Janice's changing was the main dog in the fight. Polyphemus Ward said: "Bligger it to blazes—just change!" Janice said it wasn't that simple, because she had tried, and it was no dice. The conditions which had spoiled her were still all around her, and while she might struggle for a while, she would be overwhelmed again. It was like trying to wipe syrup off yourself while you stood where it was raining the stuff. Sensible thing was to get out of the rain of syrup.

So Janice got out of the rain.

She walked out. Disappeared. Polyphemus Ward hired and fired private detectives by volleys, but they failed to find the girl. With exactly five dollars in her neat little handbag, she had stepped into oblivion to solve her own human problem.

This had happened six months ago.

Polyphemus Ward at first refused to admit to himself that he was affected in a way that was changing his whole philosophy of life. Perhaps he did not know that he was. Possibly he had been infected with something without his knowledge. At any rate, the disease developed, and it was a disease of good germs, one that was slowly melting the old reprobate's shell, so that the warm meat of a human being was commencing to be visible.

Polyphemus Ward, during recent weeks, had started wondering what would become of his incredible fortune when he was gone, something he'd never considered before, his energies hitherto having gone into money-grabbing, his philosophy being that he'd get the money, enjoy what it would buy, like the power it gave him and the devil with the rest.

Now, he was feeling the urge to do the world a great good. He wouldn't have admitted that. He had never done a man a favor unless he took it back twenty times in dollars, but, without knowing or admitting it, Polyphemus Ward was getting a complex. He wanted to help his fellow man.

He was, in fact, looking around for an honest man to take over distribution of the Ward millions to deserving philanthropies.

The trouble was, he didn't think there was an honest man. The yacht steamed toward New York.

JONES was somewhat less rambunctious about promoting his education. He was cautious. He drank no more cocktails, kissed no more girls. He tied the damper down. He had discovered there were emotions inside him that could be made to burn violently. He was wary about letting air at the fire.

Polyphemus Ward found himself studying Jones, and realizing that Jones had assets, that Jones was clean metal, because he had none of the hates, eccentricities, greeds, tinsel yearnings, of other people, since he had grown to manhood without being subjected to any of these false gods of the world, and therefore had perfect ability to select the good from the worthless, true from false.

Jones, not hampered by what anyone had told him, could look at President Roosevelt and approve or disapprove of the New Deal solely on the basis of what it had done, not because someone had previously sold Jones on the idea of being Democrat or Republican. He could go to see Garbo, and if he liked her, it wouldn't be because Hollywood publicity had told him she was a great actress; if Jones thought swing music sounded like noise, he wouldn't like it just because swing music was the correct thing to go for at the moment; and if Jones thought it a sensible idea to walk down Broadway, barefooted, he might do that, too.

Jones had a scholastic education of high order—at least he had memorized whole books which contained sound philosophy of the ages. If he had been influenced, it was by this wisdom that had lived, the only wisdom that man can depend on. True,

Jones had personal peculiarities, such as his habit of launching into a monologue on some one thing when he wanted to start a conversation, but that was because he did not know how to start a conversation any other way.

One day, Polyphemus Ward ordered his yacht to decrease its speed. This was done in order to prolong the trip to New York, so the financier could study Jones. Polyphemus Ward was actually startled when Jones showed no interest in return.

Almost as many millions of dollars as Tammany had politicians did not impress Jones. Not only did Jones show no interest in Polyphemus Ward, but it was the contrary. Polyphemus Ward was an old burr who grated on everyone's nerves, and Jones did not care for his society.

Polyphemus Ward was slowly committing suicide. He was doing it with food. He ate like a harvest-hand, took little more exercise than the bronze statue of Columbus in Central Park. He liked his steaks thick, his potatoes mashed and in quantities, and he consumed enormous helpings of sweets. All he did toward working it off was knock the ashes from a dollar cigar.

Jones mentioned this.

"That steak you are eating," volunteered Jones, "will weigh at least three pounds, and will average more than one thousand calories of food value per pound. That makes over three thousand calories in the steak alone."

"Humph!" said Polyphemus Ward.

"Your daily requirement should not be much more than three thousand calories," added Jones. "In other words, that steak should be your day's food."

"Who," inquired Polyphemus Ward brusquely, "asked your opinion?"

"I merely volunteered the information," Jones explained, just as brusquely, "with scant expectation of seeing it help. To be quite plain, you remind me of a walrus I once met."

"I remind you"—the financier purpled—"of what?"

"The walrus," Jones explained, "was crawling toward a crack

into which it would fall and be killed. When I tried to turn it aside, it endeavored to bite me."

Polyphemus Ward bit his cigar in half. However, as the yacht approached New York, he grew certain that Jones was not impressed at all by the Polyphemus Ward millions.

The financier did some thinking, and as a result was seized with a remarkable idea.

A DAY and a night before the yacht was to reach New York, Polyphemus Ward spoke to Lyman Lee about various business matters which were to be taken up when they landed. Lyman Lee handled all preliminary details with utmost efficiency.

"You're too perfect!" Polyphemus Ward growled.

"I pride myself," said Lyman Lee, "on being efficient."

"The truth is"—Polyphemus Ward scowled—"you're a buzzard, Mr. Lee."

"A—a buzzard?"

"Exactly. You're a buzzard sitting around eating such morsels of my game as I give you, and when I die, you expect to gulp down most of my carcass. You expect to get to administer my money, in plainer words."

"Good Lord, P.W.—"

"Furthermore," interrupted Polyphemus Ward, "you're a potential crook, if I ever saw one. You're clever, educated, and as slick as a greased eel. But when the time comes, if it ever does, you'll turn out to be the worst kind of a crook."

"I don't—don't think so!" Lyman Lee protested, feeling guilty.

"You're a potential crook! You hear?"

"Yes—yes, P.W."

Polyphemus Ward slammed the table with his fist.

"You're a yes-man!" he yelled.

"Yuh-yes, P.W."

Lyman Lee left that conference with an inward concern greater than the expression on his perfectly made face indicated. He had heard old Polyphemus Ward hit the nail square on the head with lusty licks.

Polyphemus Ward sat and thought.

"Hell's bells!" he growled. "I can do *one* crazy thing in my life if I want to!"

Polyphemus found Jones in the lounge listening to a radio broadcast of a swing band, a comedian, and a convincing-voiced announcer who was selling pickles.

"I am puzzled again," Jones volunteered. "This radio gentleman insists that, without fail, his pickles will tone your system, correct your blood count, strengthen your muscles and give you a clear complexion. Now, while I have enjoyed the pickles of which I have partaken, I confess to some doubt about his veracity."

"In advertising," said Polyphemus Ward, "you tell 'em anything, if you can tell it so they'll believe it." He added peremptorily, "Come with me."

"But I'm interested in hearing what further properties will be attributed to the product of the cucurbitaceous vine."

The inference was that Jones didn't care for the financier's acid company.

"This happens to be important," growled Polyphemus Ward.

Jones arose reluctantly, and they went to the sun deck, which seemed deserted, and stopped in the shadow behind a large canopied chaise lounge of the outdoor variety. It was very dark.

Polyphemus Ward handed Jones a package.

"What," asked Jones, "is this item?"

"That is one hundred thousand dollars," said Polyphemus Ward bluntly, "in thousand-dollar bills."

"I—one hundred thousand dollars?"

"Exactly."

Jones attempted to return the bundle.

"Here," he said hastily, "I don't think I want this."

"But—"

"Thank you," said Jones, "but I don't want it, although I appreciate your gift."

Polyphemus Ward gurgled.

"Gift! D'you think I'm *giving* you that?"

"Naturally. It is obvious that I have not earned it."

"One hundred thousand dollars," said Polyphemus Ward, "is quite considerable of a lot of gift."

"Er—is it? A certain Oriental potentate once presented four million dollars to a stranger whom he fancied—"

"Shut up and listen to me," Polyphemus Ward growled. "Don't interrupt. I'm not used to people interrupting me. I've got too much money." He paused and scowled at Jones. "Too much money," he continued, "for any good to come of it. If I die and leave it all, lawyers will get most of it. I hate lawyers. I could will it to museums, but I hate museums, too. Stuffy places. What I want is to see my fortune do some good. Help people."

"Ah—I am surprised," Jones exclaimed.

"Why?"

"I imagine because I put too much stock in what I have been hearing about you."

"I don't give a good tinker's rooftree what you heard!" Polyphemus Ward sighed deeply. "What I'm getting at is this: I need an honest man. I think I've found one. *You.*"

"Me?"

"You're honest, aren't you?"

"Why—I suppose so. It's a good policy to follow, I believe. By the way, just what do you want with an honest man?"

"I am going to give him a million dollars," said Polyphemus Ward levelly, "to keep him honest."

"I—goodness!"

"Then I am going to hand him the job of disposing of my fortune, all but a few millions for my personal use, in a way that will benefit humanity."

Jones was confused. "But what has that got to do with this hundred thousand which, by the way, you haven't taken back."

"You give that hundred thousand away," ordered Polyphemus Ward.

"Er—what did you say?"

"Give it only to worthy people. To people, mind you, and not to organized charities. Give no more than one thousand dollars to any one person. Keep a record, and show me the record. If I think you have given it to needy persons in every case, I will give you that job of distributing my fortune to charity, and needy causes."

"Give it away?"

"Yes."

"Thousand dollars to a person?"

"No more. Less whenever best. You'll use your discretion, and the kind of discretion you use will decide if you get the million and the job."

"In other words," said Jones, "you are testing my judgment."

"That's my idea of it," agreed Polyphemus Ward. "The rest of the world would think I'm crazy."

Jones tugged his amazing red beard thoughtfully.

"This does seem a little mad," he remarked.

"As a matter of fact," replied Polyphemus Ward, "it is. It's so wacky you better keep your mouth shut about it. Nobody is to know about this. Savvy?"

"You mean that no one is to know—providing I take the job."

"Great grief, aren't you taking it?"

"It might be interesting."

Old Polyphemus Ward snorted. "It'll be interesting, if I know anything about human nature."

"I believe," said Jones, "that I should like to try this thing."

"Shake!"

The two men sealed a remarkable bargain with a hearty

handshake, after which Polyphemus Ward grunted sourly and took his departure without saying another word. Jones peered after the crusty old moneybags, shifted his gaze to the sheaf of thousand-dollar bills, and decided to stow the money in a hip pocket, after which he strolled away from the spot beside the canopied chaise lounge, where the conference had been held.

Thereafter, two eavesdroppers in the chaise lounge began to breathe freely again. In fact, they took in gulps of air like two prize fighters who had just received punches in the bread baskets.

LYMAN LEE had sat in the lounge, and heard everything. The Countess Maria Montignal de Grandrieu had sat with him, and had also heard everything. The pair of them had been sitting there gossiping about the guests when Jones and Polyphemus Ward came up and began talking.

What they had heard, and they hadn't missed any of it, had practically stunned Lyman Lee and the Countess. They sat in a stupefied silence.

"Uh—excuse me, Lyman dear," said the Countess suddenly.

Lyman Lee didn't seem to hear her.

The Countess Maria Montignal de Grandrieu flounced into her cabin a moment later. She was as agitated as a goldfish out of water, and when she tried to speak, made noises.

"Do you," Glacia asked peevishly, "have to cackle?"

The Countess got her daughter to understand what she had overheard.

"Beautiful bombshells!" said Glacia hollowly. "You mean that Jones is going to get a million dollars?"

"Yes, yes! If he gives away a hundred thousand successfully."

"Anyone," said Glacia, "practically, can be a success at giving away a hundred thousand."

The Countess sighed. "Think of all that money, Glacia dear. Just think."

"What do you think I'm doing?" Glacia demanded.

Abruptly, Glacia began to put her clothes back on—she had disrobed to retire. "But—he has those insufferable red whiskers," the Countess groaned.

"Er—he has possibilities, however," said Glacia, recollecting a kiss.

Having equipped herself with the kind of weapons that came out of a makeup case and the shop of the best Paris *modiste,* Glacia went campaigning for Jones. She found him leaning on the rail, contemplating the Pole Star. Jones gave a start of perceptible proportions when Glacia came up and took his arm fondly.

"Darling," said Glacia, "you and I must see more of each other."

Jones felt warmish.

"I—er—" he said brilliantly.

"It almost seems that you have been avoiding me," Glacia murmured.

"I—ah—thought you disliked me," Jones explained uncomfortably.

"Darling"—Glacia squeezed squeezed his hand—"I've only been trying to resist you."

IT WAS some time later when an incredulous Funny Pegger collared Jones.

"Come over here in the corner, Lodestone," he muttered.

"Lodestone?"

"Well, you've got a magnetic personality or something," explained the gag-man grimly. "You sure attract things."

"I do not believe," explained Jones, "that I understand you."

"I could be referring to Glacia."

"I—Glacia?"

"But I wasn't, although I've been what you might call a stupefied observer for the last half hour. I have another matter. A trifling bit of news for you. Do you remember that German-liner captain you shot?"

"Liner captain—ah—yes. Oh, yes. A slight misunderstanding."

"Misunderstanding or not, they're gonna put you in the clink for it."

"Clink?"

"Jail. There's a warrant sworn out for your arrest in New York. I got the tidings by radio."

"Goodness," Jones said. "Do you suppose I will have some trouble?"

"You," Funny Pegger assured him, "were made for trouble to roost on."

LYMAN LEE had been pacing his cabin for hours. He had torn off his tie and collar with savage gestures, and he was stamping in circles. Occasionally he collapsed on the berth or a chair and glared in white silence at the ceiling, while his nails bit into his palms, and his teeth punished his lower lip. He looked as if he wanted to screech.

Lyman Lee had expected to get that job of distributing Polyphemus Ward's millions. It was a goal he had worked at for years, and the shock of losing it had literally upset his mental balance.

He would have to do something…. But what? His mind hunted for methods, and because of the combination of circumstances, his mind had become something of a mad dog among minds.

It was nearly three o'clock in the morning when Lyman Lee dressed in dark clothing, took his butcher knife, and went toward Jones' cabin.

CHAPTER VII

TARGET JONES

THREE O'CLOCK OF the morning preceding the arrival of Polyphemus Ward's yacht in New York harbor, preparations to receive a strange fellow named Jones were already under way. Final editions of morning papers had been put to bed, and night editors were writing notes to leave for editors on the day trick, notes suggesting it might be a good idea to have reporters and cameramen meet Jones.

There was something that appealed to the public in the idea of a young man being rescued off an iceberg in mid-Atlantic. The story had caught on. It was a story not just about a poor devil, a nobody, marooned on an iceberg, but the son of Polar Jones, who had been famous in his day, and whose death had been a long-standing mystery since the schooner on which he had taken Colonel Adams to the Arctic in 1917 had disappeared with all aboard.

So the story of Jones, son of Polar Jones, picked off an iceberg, had taken hold, was building circulation, and was therefore going to get plenty of attention from the press, particularly since it was rumored Jones himself was a pretty odd specimen.

The story had good color, too. Polyphemus Ward, Jones' rescuer, was one of the richest men alive; and in his time had socked more photographers and broken more cameras than any other industrial Merlin. That didn't make the press any less gleeful about smearing his glower on the front pages now that it had the chance.

And Poly-
phemus Ward's
big yacht was
good camera
fodder. The craft
was the most
luxurious thing
afloat, widely
known, and
daily stories
about the float-
ing château were
sure to sell a lot
of papers to the
gentry on the
left, who could
wave them
under the noses
of friends and
shout: "Look at
Polyphemus
Ward's yacht!
Down with the
rich!"

ABOARD
Ward's yacht,
the center of all
the commotion slept poorly. Usually he placed himself on the
berth—he'd never ceased to marvel at the comfort of mat-
tresses—and it required only one deep sigh to put him to sleep.
This morning he was pitching, tossing, turning, grinning, groan-
ing, frowning, smiling, and gazing vapidly at nothing. Jones was
experiencing some of civilized man's troubles. He had, in fact,
both the big ones. He had money trouble, and he had woman
trouble.

A slight noise caused Jones to open one eye. It was inkish in his stateroom. Then a patch of shadow caught his eye. It was near the door.

Some one was after Polyphemus Ward's hundred thousand dollars, Jones realized. He had never encountered a thief. About the only thing he knew was the definition of the word thief in the big dictionary he'd read on the island.

"I say," he remarked, "that money is in my custody." Jones strung his words together carefully at all times.

The big shadow flew toward Jones. A hand reached out to grab him and out of it stuck a sliver of steel—a knife blade. And so Jones was having his first fight with a man.

It was a grim desperate encounter without Queensbury courtesy, or rules.

Jones spun, met the rush with his feet. He exerted force. The assailant, caught in the middle, flew back. But the knife came down and shaved skin off Jones' leg.

Jones came out of the berth. Having spent his life where nights were six months long, he had probably moved around more in the dark than several generations of average citizens.

He grabbed the knife-wrist, lunged with it against the wall. The blade entered the wood and broke at the hilt. Jones got a wallop on the back. It started him coughing. A foot crunched his bare toes; the foe grabbed Jones' remarkable red beard and Jones howled.

Jones picked up his opponent bodily, threw him at the other wall. Bulkhead panels cracked. A picture jumped off the wall.

That decided the fight.

The other man staggered up, dazed, scared, took a run and leap, got through the door, and sped away. Jones, jumping after him, tripped over a chair, fell and saw a whole constellation. Arising, Jones stumbled down the passage. But the other had taken a lead, and was not to be found.

Jones was returning to his cabin when Funny Pegger turned the lights on in the corridor.

Funny Pegger's stateroom was located close to the one inhabited by Jones, and he had heard the uproar. Pegger stared at Jones accusingly. "You have been," said Funny Pegger, "taking another walk without any clothes."

"I should hesitate," Jones said breathlessly, "to dismiss my recent exertions as a mere walk."

FUNNY PEGGER followed Jones into the stateroom and stared at the knife blade sticking in the wall. He popped his eyes at Jones' damaged leg.

"For the love of little lambs! What happened?"

"I awakened," explained Jones, "to find I had a visitor. I accosted him, and without more ado, he sprang upon me."

"You mean he tried to kill you?"

"I rather got that impression," Jones admitted.

"Great blazes! Let's get a hunt started. What did he look like? Who was he?

"I am afraid," Jones explained, "that there is no use searching. I could not describe him because, unfortunately, it was too dark to see him very well."

Funny Pegger threw up his hands. "What was he after?"

"Why the—" Jones stopped. He remembered that nobody was to know about the hundred thousand dollars because old Polyphemus Ward was afraid they would think he had gone crazy.

"Well," said Funny Pegger, "what was he after?"

"I—cannot say," Jones said uncomfortably.

"Your lying," said Funny Pegger, "will improve with practice." He looked around the stateroom, lifting strewn blankets, scrutinizing the knife blade and examining the hilt which was still wrapped with a flannel cloth.

Jones' assailant had been cautious.

"No fingerprints," he remarked. "In fact, no clues at all. Look here, Jones, did you have much of a fight?"

"There was some difficulty before it was settled."

"What you needed," said Funny Pegger, "was a western settler."

"A western settler?"

"The contents of a six-shooter," said Funny Pegger, the inveterate gag-man.

The two men set about straightening up the stateroom. Jones put the blankets back in place, at the same time making sure the hundred thousand dollars was concealed.

"You've got Atlas stopped," he remarked.

"Atlas," said Jones, puzzled, "was the Titan son of Iapetus and Clymene; he warred against Zeus, and as a punishment was forced to support the heavens on his head and hands. I fail to detect any similarity."

"No?" Funny Pegger grinned. "I might point out you seem to be supporting some trouble on your hands."

"You refer to the recent raid?"

"I also refer to the fact that I would like to know what your raider wanted."

"I do not choose to explain," Jones said.

"I'm your friend."

"I know that," Jones said sincerely. "But I still do not choose to explain."

Funny Pegger shook his head slowly as he stared at Jones. "Okay," he said. "You can think of more ways of sticking your neck out."

"I—sticking my neck out?"

"Laying yourself open."

Jones was bewildered.

"There was a library on my father's schooner when it was shipwrecked in 1917, and by studying the books diligently I hoped to fit myself to cope with the outer world, if I ever succeeded in reaching it. Oh—I did not imagine the English language would change in twenty years so extensively that I could not understand it at times."

"I am referring," said Funny Pegger, "to Glacia."

"Er—to be sure." Jones colored warmly. "The wow."

Funny Pegger shivered dramatically. "You said it."

"You hinted," said Jones with enthusiasm, "that she had qualities, and I am beginning to agree. On that point, our minds seem to run in the same path."

"All great minds run in the same path."

"Er—possibly."

"But so do little pigs."

Jones frowned. "I seem to detect a satirical note."

"I like women," said Funny Pegger, "but I like toast and coffee, too—and I don't like them cold."

"Cold?"

"Glacia," said Funny Pegger, "is a piece of calculating ice. She's out to grab off a rich guy. She's got no more money than a grasshopper has pants. Her mother, the countess, was a sap heiress who married a foreign title, and he blew all her shekels for her. Glacia is out for heavy sugar, and make no mistake about that."

Funny sighed. "What floors me is the play she started making for you last night. Until then you were as popular with her as Mussolini is with Ethiopians. All of a sudden she began to purr and show you her teeth. It gets me."

"I did seem to detect a change," Jones confessed.

"You've never seen a woman before." Funny Pegger contemplated Jones. "God made the earth, and rested. God made man, and rested. Then God made woman, and neither man nor earth has had a minute of rest since. All I can say, Jones, is that you'll learn. You'll learn."

"I am beginning to think," said Jones, "that I shall be enthusiastic about this learning."

Funny Pegger groaned, "Time wasted," he muttered. "Let's get some sleep. Big day ahead tomorrow. We reach New York."

He stepped to the door. "That is, if you can get any sleep after what's happened. How's your iron?"

"Iron?" Jones didn't understand. "Iron is a malleable, ductile, readily oxidized silver white metallic element with an atomic weight of 55.84, and rarely found native except in meteorites. It's melting point is 1530 Centigrade, its specific gravity varies between 7.86 and 8.14, while its weight is 491.508 pounds per cubic foot. The content of iron in the human body is—"

"Ample, in your case, I hope." Funny Pegger grinned. "Let it ride. I'm hitting the hay. By the way, how did your visitor get in? How'd he unlock the door?"

"The door," Jones explained, "wasn't locked."

"Why not?"

"I didn't know how."

Funny Pegger swallowed.

"You slay me, Jones! You know the specific gravity of iron and the names of the papa and mama of Atlas, but you don't know how to lock a door." Funny Pegger shook his head. "Here, I'll show you. You use a key. That's it on the dresser."

"I wondered," remarked Jones, "what that bit of metal was for."

CHAPTER VIII

KETTLES ON TO BOIL

THE IRON IN Jones fell down on the job. He lay on the berth intending to sleep, but the unusual turmoil inside him kept him wide awake. He was realizing that his fellow man in New York was going to regard him as a strange kind of a bug.

To be sure, the attitude was mutual, as Jones already considered his fellow man, judging by those he had so far met, a rather unique style of goods, but this might be a case of the raindrop calling the ocean wet, since it was a minority opinion. If anyone was an unusual article, it was conceivably himself, but he had the good sense not to feel inferior about it, on the theory that no man need feel inferior when he has done his best, because, although some men get farther than others, some men do not have as many obstacles to overcome as others.

His fellow man baffled Jones. He couldn't quite make him out, and wondered if he should be uneasy—the people he had met struck him as being eccentric, which meant that either they or Jones belonged to the category Funny Pegger described as screwballs.

Polyphemus Ward particularly baffled him. Being a self-made man, Ward should also be a wise man, the two things usually going hand in hand, or so the books said. But Ward had handed Jones, a comparative stranger, a hundred one-thousand dollar bills to give away.

It made Jones wonder who was screwball.

Jones felt under the mattress. The sheaf of thousand-dollar

greenbacks was still there. "I am to give that," Jones reminded himself aloud, "to needy persons, no more than a thousand to a person." He shrugged. "Oh, well, it should be easy."

It was indicative of his lack of experience with money—the things it would buy, and the mad capers men cut to get it—that his mind did not dwell in more than a passing way on the prospects of receiving a million outright, "to keep you honest," as old Polyphemus Ward said.

Jones did rather like the idea of playing angel to the needy. He couldn't think of anything more desirable. He went to sleep and dreamed rosily about a pleasant future.

But Lyman Lee did not sleep.

He sat in his cabin, wearing cream silk pajamas and a matching cream silk dressing gown and stuck cigarettes in a long holder and smoked them up rapidly. On a table were a pencil and sheets of paper which he had covered with stars, crosses, funny faces and other doodlings. A miserable scowl was on Lyman Lee's good-looking face, a blacker funk behind it.

He had the nerves of an oyster, so he had not been scared at any time, except for a bad moment or two after he had entered Jones' cabin with the knife, and discovered Jones could get around like a circus acrobat. It had been too dark for Jones to recognize him, so he was not worrying about that.

He knew, now, that he should not personally have tried to take care of Jones and the hundred thousand dollars, and he was irked at himself for being impulsive. He usually farmed out his dirty work, but there was no one on the yacht whom he could trust with the job, so he had tried himself.

He had tried and failed.

Lyman Lee had not changed his mind. He still felt robbed. He had worked with efficiency for years for old Polyphemus Ward; he knew as much concerning the Ward business as Polyphemus Ward, and he couldn't see the sense of the Ward millions being administered to charity by Jones.

Lyman Lee had expected the job. He had dedicated his life

to getting it, having spent in his imagination the million that Polyphemus Ward was going to give the administrator of the wealth to keep him honest, purchasing, in his thoughts, a Rolls Royce, a penthouse, a flashy yacht, maybe a racing stable—everything he'd ever wanted.

Now they were gone.

Suddenly, Lyman Lee took a fresh sheet of paper and wrote:

PAUL SHEVINSKY
72 RITZ LANE
NEW YORK CITY

He chewed at the inside of his lower lip while he consulted a small code-book and composed a radiogram.

Paul Shevinsky was the man to take Jones over. Paul was Lyman Lee's lawyer, but only the two of them knew that. Paul had a number of clients no one else knew about, a few of them in penitentiaries, but not as many as would have been if it hadn't been for Paul Shevinsky. When he heard about Jones, Shevinsky would be sick, too, because he had looked forward to administering the Ward millions with fully as much expectation as Lyman Lee.

A kind of partnership existed between the two of them dimly resembling a collaboration of two pirates, an arrangement which persisted because Lee respected the shyster lawyer's connections with the most talented gentry of crookdom, and because Shevinsky had a wholesome awe for anyone with the reptilian sort of brain that Lyman Lee possessed.

The message Lyman Lee put into code read:

THE JONES OF THE ICEBERG HAS BEEN GIVEN ONE HUNDRED THOUSAND-DOLLAR BILLS TO GIVE TO NEEDY PERSONS. IF HE DOES A GOOD JOB POLYPHEMUS WARD INTENDS TO HAVE HIM ADMINISTER WARD FORTUNE TO CHARITY. SUGGEST YOU THINK OF SOMETHING.

He took this to the radio room and had it transmitted. Within an hour, there was an answer, which he decoded.

HAVE THOUGHT OF THIS: SOMEBODY HAS GONE CRAZY.

Lyman Lee scowled and replied:

IT IS ON THE LEVEL.

To which, in short order, came a response:

HOW ABOUT PROVING JONES INSANE AND HAVING HIM COMMITTED STOP JUDGING FROM NEWSPAPER STORIES, CAN DO.

Lyman Lee contemplated the desk top for a time, then coded instructions.

GO AHEAD AND PROVE JONES NUTS. SOME-THING MIGHT ALSO BE DONE ABOUT THE GERMAN LINER CAPTAIN WHOM JONES SHOT IN LEG.

Having sent that, Lyman Lee took a large drink of whisky and went to bed. He felt better.

JONES greeted the dawn with vim, vigor and pleasant delusions about the future, since this was the day of days when they would reach New York, when he would see his first skyscraper, look at his first automobile, perhaps partake of his first ice cream soda.

Jones dressed in his borrowed clothes, combed his long red hair, carefully, untangled his impressive red beard, made two rounds of the deck, relishing the salty tang of the morning air, and entered the dining room to dispose of bacon and eggs. Next, he went in search of Polyphemus Ward. He wanted to clarify a detail or two that had been bothering him. It was a clear morning, not a cloud, with the temperature pleasantly cool for August, and blue vastness of the sea flung away to the horizon was made mysterious by smoke from an occasional steamer. The yacht was near enough New York to encounter sea traffic.

Polyphemus Ward sat at a table on the sun deck and scowled at a bromo. The financial tycoon wore old sneakers, flannel trousers, furry tweed coat, and a towel tucked in around his hippo neck. Jones was reminded of a picture of a rhinoceros he had seen in a book, labeled: "Male of the species."

"Good morning," Jones ventured.

"What do you want?" asked the moneybags.

"I—er—how are you this morning?"

"What do you care?" growled the financial power. "You're not a doctor."

If this is one of the world's richest and most astute men, Jones reflected, I wonder what the others will be like.

"A crab," Jones remarked aloud, "is a crustacean belonging to the order of Decapoda, or to suborder Brachyura, and also to the group Anomura which are known as hermit crabs, or purse crabs. They can walk in any direction without turning."

"Are you," Polyphemus Ward inquired acidly, "referring to me?"

"Well, the remark occurred to me."

"Take your remarks," Polyphemus. Ward requested, "a long way away from me. You've got your job. I don't want to see anything more of you until you've done it. Or failed to do it. I don't want to be bothered. Understand?"

"There is a matter I wished to discuss," Jones replied thoughtfully. "You see, I have slept on your proposition and—"

"Look here now, Jones. You can't back out!"

"On the contrary," said Jones, "I am more enthusiastic. The prospect of using a hundred thousand dollars to help the needy intrigues me. But a point or two needs to be clarified."

"What point or two?"

"First, is there a time limit?"

"Thirty days."

"Excellent. A month should be ample. Thank you for being so generous."

"What's the other point?"

"Ah—I lack funds for personal operations."

"Broke, eh?"

"I am without financial assets."

"And you want to know if charity begins at home?"

"To tell the truth," said Jones, "that hadn't occurred to me. But it's a thought."

"No." Polyphemus Ward slammed the table. "Every cent of the hundred thousand goes to needy people."

"But if I become needy myself? I might, you know."

"Your own hard luck."

"It seems to me that you are endeavoring to make this as difficult as possible."

"Yes. That's the idea. It's all a test of your judgment. You take receipts for every cent of this money. And I'll have detectives investigate and see whether you picked needy people."

"I understand that perfectly," Jones replied. "Also, I am to tell no one about this."

"You bet you're not."

"Ummm."

"If you can't say anything but, 'Ummm,' you can get out of here!"

JONES strolled away and shortly found himself collared by Funny Pegger. Funny chuckled. "I noticed you locking horns with the bull of the woods."

"You refer to Polyphemus Ward?"

"How'd you get along with him? He give you the geological survey?"

"I—the what?"

"The stony stare."

"He spoke rather tersely," Jones confessed.

"The old reprobate is as tight with words as he is with money."

"I don't believe I understand."

"Skip it." Funny Pegger grasped Jones' arm. "You and I have some talking to do," and moved to two deck chairs.

"I've been consulting booking agents by radio," Funny explained. "Fixing it up for you."

"But I do not wish to buy any books. And I certainly have none to sell."

"No, no. These guys book you for theater and radio jobs. Jones, you're going to land on the velvet."

"Velvet?"

"In the dough."

"Dough," said Jones, puzzled, "derives from the Icelandic *deig*, or possibly the Sanskrit *dih*, meaning to smear, and means a mass of moist flour not yet baked. Er—I fail to perceive the connection."

"All right, all right, I'll put it the classic way. Mr. Jones, I have communicated with the representatives of a radio hookup, a vaudeville organization, and a tabloid newspaper, all of whom agree to pay you substantial sums for your services."

"Pay me for what?"

"Oh, you can tell them how you speared seals for a living on the island."

"My problem," said Jones, "is not to make money, but get rid of it."

"What? What's that?"

Jones said hurriedly, "I mean—thank you very much. I—er—appreciate your efforts in my behalf, which I shall have to decline."

"Decline?"

"Yes. Thank you."

Funny Pegger groaned. "You can't do this! You can't let me down."

Jones considered the point. "I do not see how I am letting you down, as you put it."

"You don't, eh? You're taking money out of my pocket, that's what you're doing. You're gypping your manager out of his cut."

"Manager?"

"I was coming to that," Funny Pegger explained. "You need a manager. Look around. Who do you see? Me. Who's the best manager you could get? Me. Who's the best friend you've got?"

"You, I believe," Jones said sincerely.

"Check."

"Nevertheless," Jones declared firmly, "I'll have to insist on postponing decision on this matter."

Jones was uncomfortable. He liked Funny and ordinarily would have been pleased to work with him. But that was hardly advisable now. For, although Jones was sure it would be simple to dispose of a hundred thousand dollars, to be safe, he'd thought of devoting the first few days exclusively to the matter. A week at the most.

"By the way," announced Funny Pegger, "there's another little thing."

"I—thing?"

"The German liner captain you shot in the leg."

"Yes, I remember," said Jones. "As I explained, that was an error. I thought the World War was still in progress."

"It was an error all right. The German captain has sworn out a warrant for your arrest when you hit New York."

"I believe you previously mentioned that complication."

"The complication," said Funny Pegger, "has had pups."

"Pups?"

"Not only are you to be arrested, but they're gonna put you in the booby-hatch."

"Gracious! You mean an institution for the insane?"

"That's it. I understand some lawyer named Paul Shevinsky popped up this morning and volunteered to do the job."

"Paul—Paul Shevinsky."

"You see you have friends ashore."

"I do not know anyone named Paul Shevinsky."

"That," said Funny Pegger, "makes it one of those things."

"How did you learn this?"

"The radio. A wonderful invention." Funny Pegger added grimly. "And don't underestimate this Shevinsky. He's big-time stuff, and his middle name is shyster. I asked some of my newspaper pals about him. Shevinsky should have been barred from law practice long ago. But he's slick. You're practically occupying a straitjacket right now."

"But I'm not insane!" Jones gasped.

"You'd better practice saying it," advised Funny Pegger. "With a good deal of conviction. I hope the judge believes you."

JONES walked gloomily to the upper deck to be alone and ponder. He imagined jails were unpleasant places. Likewise, he had no desire to visit, in the capacity of inmate, any institution for the irrational. Not even to oblige an unknown lawyer named Paul Shevinsky.

Paul Shevinsky—why on earth should a perfect stranger volunteer to prove he was mentally sub par? It wasn't logical. Jones had been carefully building his knowledge of men, and he had found a queer brick; he had found a number of odd pieces of masonry so far, but Paul Shevinsky was far the oddest.

Jones brooded.

Glacia appeared on the upper deck, glancing about as though in search of something. Apparently it was Jones, for she came toward him, looking crisp, bright and altogether beautiful.

"Bad boy!" she said gaily. "You've been avoiding me."

"Er—not at all."

"You darling, I've been looking everywhere for you."

"You have?"

"Everywhere, simply everywhere! I even imagined you might have fallen overboard. My heart almost stopped."

"Oh, did it?" Jones said, experiencing a glow.

"Absolutely," said Glacia fondly. "Just think! I wouldn't have seen you again, ever. Not ever." She turned her wide eyes up to him. "I don't think I could have stood it."

"Not actually!" gulped Jones.

"I am sure," said Glacia dramatically, "that I couldn't. Life would have been empty. Just a shell!"

"Indeed!"

"Life would have been a mockery!"

"Er—"

"And not worth the candle!"

"I—ah—see," said Jones.

He didn't. Not exactly. Yesterday he had been as popular as an ant in Glacia's consommé, but last night she had taken a great interest in him. The shift was a little too fast for Jones. However, he was warmed by it.

"Poor boy." Glacia slipped her arm in his. "I've heard about your trouble."

"Er—you mean the matter of the captain's leg?"

"Yes. The other, too. That horrible lawyer." Glacia patted his hand comfortingly. "But don't you worry. I'm going to help you."

Glacia being comforting would melt the heart of a sheik with a large harem, and what it did to Jones, whose experience with the female of the species was limited, was something indescribable.

"I—ah—" was the best he could do.

"You sweet, mistreated boy," Glacia purred.

There is, in every critical situation, a point where action, not words, is called for. Such an occasion was here. It was powerful. It was compelling. By some natural impulse, Jones found his arms around Glacia, and discovered that his lips were against hers. The following ten seconds were so momentous that, as soon as he could organize, he released Glacia and stepped back.

"Goodness!" he exclaimed. For some moments, bells continued to ring and things went up and down.

"Darling," said Glacia, "darling, it was all right for you to do that."

"I—the explosion again!" gasped Jones.

There was silence. Glacia appeared to be waiting for something.

"Aren't you," she asked, "going to continue?"

"Continue?"

"And ask me if we are engaged, silly."

"Are we?" Jones asked wildly.

"What a cute way of asking me." Glacia said warmly. "Of course we are."

Jones was bewildered.

"Engaged," he gulped, "to be married?"

"You darling! Of course!"

Jones opened his mouth to get out that she had wrongly interpreted his words, but Glacia kissed him, and that fixed that.

There was a small animal of caution trying to warn Jones, but the kiss drove it scurrying away.

"You'll come to live at our apartment," Glacia informed Jones. Now that she had staked out her gold mine, Glacia certainly had no intentions of letting it, so to speak, run around loose.

"But—would that be proper?"

"Mother will chaperon us," Glacia explained.

"I—I'd rather not. I have some business to transact," he added desperately.

Glacia's smile sweetened. "I'm going to help you, darling."

Jones colored uncomfortably, recollecting he had promised old Polyphemus Ward not to tell anybody about the hundred thousand.

CHAPTER IX

INNOCENCE AT LARGE

JONES WATCHED GLACIA'S triumphant departure, and felt inclined to listen for the thunder that follows lightning. He was engaged. *Whang!* Just like that.

He did not believe he felt quite as he should. He had just acquired a mate, or at least been given a breathtaking shove in that direction, and he imagined such an event should be an occasion of joy and dancing on the decks. He felt sinkish.

He felt trapped.

He began to experience a doubt that was a sort of spike-tailed devil. Soon there was to be a herd of them.

Jones had just sampled another privilege of the human male—he'd been treated to the whole repertory by a scheming woman who was also beautiful, but like many men who get taken, he did not have a true perspective. He could not conceive that a woman had roped him. He thought it had just happened. There was innate chivalry in Jones, which was unfortunate, because there seems to be something about chivalry that convinces a man that female hearts are universally pure. This, unfortunately, works out rather badly sometimes.

The yacht hardly rolled, the sea was so calm, and there was a steady sighing sound as the bow cut water and threw it aside, leaving a long wedge of wake stretching out behind, widening until it blended with the horizon. Directly ahead appeared the shabby-looking vessel which was the Ambrose Lightship, the sea-signboard that marks the entrance to New York's harbor.

The yacht ploughed on, picked up a lane of buoys marking Ambrose Channel. Coney Island was on the right and Sandy Hook on the left, and directly ahead was the Statue of Liberty, carrying the torch.

Funny Pegger appeared beside Jones. Jones pointed at Liberty. "That, I presume," said Jones, "is the Statue of Liberty."

Funny Pegger nodded.

"Er—what are those big buildings in the background?"

"Those," explained Funny Pegger, "are known in the vernacular as skyscrapers."

Jones experienced a sensation of shrinking, of becoming unimportant. Although he was not aware of it, he was looking at one of the most impressive sights in the world.

Captains of incoming liners frequently remark on a strange silence which grips their passengers as they are confronted with the skyscrapers on the lower end of Manhattan Island.

"You wait here until I come for you," directed Funny Pegger. "As your manager, I've arranged a bang-up welcome for you."

Jones entered into the formality of quarantine-inspection with genuine pleasure. Their little tugs, black as water beetles, came out to push with their noses against the hull of the yacht, turning her around and easing her into a long green-shedded wharf near the foot of Wall Street. Husky sailors flung heaving lines, long light lines with a lump of lead enclosed in a Turks head knot on the end. The heaving lines were used to drag out the hawsers with loops spliced in the ends to drop over pilings. Men sweated the lines tight, put out fenders and rub-boards, set up gangplanks, and four businesslike gentlemen in trim uniforms marched up the gangplank. The latter were the U.S. Customs agents.

Automobile horns bleated on Front Street, nearby. Tugs tooted. Steamer whistles moaned. Newsboys shouted, stevedores hollered, people on the dock squealed at friends on the yacht. People ran, yelled. A seaplane came from the seadrome near the foot of Wall Street, scudded out on the harbor, lifted off the water, motor bawling. A swarm of men collected at the shore end of the gangplank. The men carried cameras, microphones, notebooks.

"Bring on Jones!" shouted the newspaper and newsreel men.

"Soon as the customs go through our pockets," yelled Funny Pegger, "I'll lead him to slaughter."

Jones passed a hand across his forehead. There was perspiration. Slaughter struck him as the appropriate word. He became aware of a strange feeling that was growing, and he suddenly wished he could leave all this confusion like the seaplane had left the water. He didn't like this excitement; it confused him. He had lived, in the past, a life of absolute aloneness; everything that he had done, he had accomplished alone.

In the face of the tumult around him, his instinctive reaction was that he wanted to solve his problems as an individual. His job was not to become a celebrity—it was to give away one hundred thousand-dollars in bills. He didn't want Funny Pegger to manage him. He didn't want to marry anybody yet, including Glacia. What he did want, he realized all of a sudden, was to work alone, as he was accustomed to.

One of the springlines which held the yacht to the dock terminated at a big cleat near where Jones stood close to the stern, and Jones' eye followed this down to the dock while the seed of an idea germinated, grew and flowered in his mind, all in the space of a few seconds.

Jones obeyed an overpowering impulse. He slid down the rope to the dock.

ONE of the newspapermen, seeing Jones, pointed and emitted a shout. Funny Pegger craned his neck. "Jones! Hey, what the blazes?" Jones commenced running.

"Come back here!" Funny Pegger howled. "Hey!... He's running away! *Jones!* I'm your manager! Stop him! Stop Jones!"

Stop Jones? Not if he could help it! He put back his head and stepped out. The newspapermen angled to cut him off, but they didn't make it.

Out into Front Street, Jones dashed. He took a turn to the right, a turn to the left. He got out and traveled in the middle of the street, where there was plenty of room. Rather sooner than he expected, the sounds of pursuit were lost.

He could communicate with Funny Pegger later, after he had disposed of the hundred thousand.

Jones proceeded up the middle of New York streets with enthusiasm, vigor at high level, his eye bright, and began looking around for a needy man. Came a rattling noise behind him, and a screech. A loud toot followed. Jones turned curiously and found himself confronted by a large mechanical device, equipped with wheels, two headlights, and a sloping glass window, from behind which an irate stranger leaned.

"Whatta d'you think this is?" the motorist inquired.

Jones contemplated the mechanical device.

"Automobile," he hazarded. "A self-propelled vehicle suitable for use on street or roadway, usually propelled by internal combustion engines consuming inflammable or volatile fluids, such as naphtha, gasoline, petrol or even alcohol."

The motorist blinked. "Ya wanna get run over?"

Jones was astonished. "No," he said. "Certainly not."

"Then whatcha walkin' in middle of the street for?"

Jones considered. "Am I to understand there is something incorrect about my behavior as a pedestrian?"

"For the luvva mud!" sputtered the motorist. "What is this, anyhow?" But he evidently had business more pressing than arguing with a red-bearded psychotic, because he clashed gears, tooted his horn, and drove around Jones, who stood in the middle of the street and considered the departing vehicle in some puzzlement.

It had seemed to him that there was more elbow room in the street, and therefore that was the sensible place to walk. It wasn't apparently. He was willing to learn. He transferred his course to the sidewalk and proceeded on his search for a needy man.

Jones noticed that people were turning to look at him. Occasionally they bumped into each other in their absorption. And they said such things as: "Did you see *that?*" Or: "Santa Claus has his whiskers sunburned." Another favorite crack seemed to be: "His girl must have given him a necktie for Christmas." Jones commenced to feel uncomfortable. The only visible difference between himself and the other men was that they didn't have long red hair and a remarkably fiery beard. But even so....

However, interest was not one-sided, for Jones was making elaborate observations of the passersby. He felt let down. Some of the people he saw looked worried, even unhealthy, and they all seemed to be in an unnecessary hurry. Jones wondered if making a living was as hard as all that.

A mound of reddish earth stood near the sidewalk. On this sat a man attired in ragged, extremely grimy khaki pants and a shirt which was in danger of falling apart. The man's face was remarkably dirty.

As Jones saw the individual, he was suddenly reminded that his immediate mission was not to observe humanity, but to distribute money. Here was a man who looked needy.

"Er—good morning," Jones began.

The man glanced up, not unpleasantly. "H'yah," he said.

"I beg your pardon," Jones said, "It is my intention to ask you—ah—rather an embarrassing question."

"About money?"

"Why, how did you know?" asked Jones, puzzled.

"A touch, ah?" The man considered, then reached into a grimy pocket, fished out a fifty-cent piece, which he extended. "Here you are, pal."

"Are you," asked Jones, "giving me that?"

"Sure."

"Gracious!" Jones swallowed. "There is, I am afraid, a misunderstanding. My intention was not to solicit alms, but to distribute them."

"You mean," said the other, "that you were gonna give me dough."

"Dough?"

"Were you gonna pass me a shekel?"

"The shekel," Jones replied, "was the ancient money unit of Babylonia and Phoenicia, as well as the Hebrews, the Hebrew shekel being of gold with a weight of 252 ⅔ grains, and valued at ten dollars and eighty-eight cents. It was not used prior to the year 139 B.C., and I do not believe it is used as an American medium of exchange."

"What," asked the man, "are you driving at?"

"I was defining the shekel."

"What," asked the man in a louder voice, *"are you driving at?"*

Jones was confused.

"I had the impression," he explained, "that you were a needy man."

"Needy?" the other looked indignant. "Buddy, I'm a sandhog. I get twenty bucks a day for digging in this tunnel down under me. I wouldn't change places with Henry Ford, J.P. Morgan, or Polyphemus Ward."

"I perceive that I have made an error," Jones announced. "Ah—good morning, and thank you."

With which, Jones took as dignified a departure as he could manage. Apparently you couldn't tell a needy person by looking at him.

HE PROGRESSED a few blocks and a voice accosted him. "Spare a dime for a cup-a-cauffee, mister?"

Jones examined a short, seedy man who needed a shave, a bath, and a trip to a dry-cleaners'.

"Are you soliciting alms?" Jones inquired.

"No. I'm just askin' for a dime, mister."

"You are a needy individual?"

"Mister, I ain't eat since yesterday," mumbled the other.

"Excellent!" Jones was elated. "Just a moment, please," he

said. He produced his sheaf of bills, shucked one off the top and presented it to the needy man.

The man seized the bill avidly, and started to depart.

"Wait, if you please," Jones said in haste. "It is essential that I secure your name and address and a few facts about yourself. Merely routine data for a record."

The man stopped. He happened to glance a second time at the bill. His eyes popped.

"A grand!" he exploded.

The man turned the piece of currency over to scrutinize the other side. "Jeepers creepers!" He peered at Jones suspiciously.

"Is this the McCoy?" he gulped.

"I didn't," Jones replied, "know that individual pieces of currency had names. I am sure I do not know whether that one is named McCoy."

The man flung the bill at Jones.

"I ain't gettin' roped in on no gag!" he snarled. He took a nervous and rapid departure.

CHAPTER X

ALL ABOUT MONEY

WITH AN AIR of dignity, which was entirely synthetic, Jones retrieved the thousand-dollar note. He was confused, and further than that, depressed, for it seemed that he had started out confidently to climb a mountain that was slicker than he had anticipated.

Lifting his eyes, he saw a clock, which told him he had been ashore more than hour, and involuntarily, he did some mental arithmetic—he'd allotted a week to disposing of the money, which meant six working days. He would, therefore, have to give away sixteen thousand, six hundred sixty-six dollars and some odd cents as a daily quota, or if he worked an eight-hour day, he had to give away slightly in excess of two thousand dollars an hour.

These statistics made him suspect a hundred thousand might be a lot of money.

The size of the bill must have frightened away his last prospect. The thing, then, was reduce the bills to smaller denominations.

He set out walking rapidly, with a definite objective—a bank. He covered a few blocks, and found one.

It was a cold-looking structure with shiny brass doors. Jones entered and at once noticed that two men in gray uniforms were giving him attention. He did not know they were bank guards, nor was he aware that a bomb exploded in Wall Street in 1920, killed thirty persons, injured two hundred, did two millions damage, and that ever since this event Wall Street has been jittery about men with whiskers.

Jones moved to a grille, where a well-dressed young man surveyed him coolly.

"Ah—I wish some money changed."

The teller frowned. However, New York is a city of strange people and the financial district has its share, so the bank cashier decided to think nothing of it.

Jones produced one hundred thousand dollars. He laid the roll on the black marble slab in front of the window. "It is my wish," he stated, "to have these reduced to smaller denominations."

The well-dressed young man on the other side of the bars was accustomed to handling money, and a hundred thousand dollars would not have startled him, ordinarily. However, Jones was very whiskered, and the bills looked new enough to be counterfeits, and the bank had a motto: Be cautious.

The teller was cautious.

"If you don't mind," said the teller, "I shall call an officer."

Jones was shocked. "Officer?"

"Yes."

"I would prefer," said Jones firmly, "that you do not do that."

Jones had heard Funny Pegger refer to policemen as officers. And he remembered, with an unpleasant feeling, that the police wished to arrest him for shooting the German liner captain in the leg.

The bank teller frowned. "You do not wish me to call an officer?"

"No."

"It will only take a moment."

"No," Jones said stubbornly.

"Nevertheless," said the teller, "I shall have to call one of our officers." With which, he pressed a button.

Jones knew what happened when you pressed buttons. The

servants on the yachts had been summoned in that fashion. Without more ado, he reached for the hundred thousand.

Jones' excitement convinced the banker something was amiss. He decided he was dealing with a crook trying to pass counterfeits. He snatched the money for evidence.

It was no time for ceremony. Jones grabbed the cage, piled over the top, seized the money. The teller showed fight. Jones gave that man a shove which turned him end over end. Then Jones bounded out of the cage.

An alarm bell rang. Men shouted. Jones dashed for the door, reached it, raced down the street. Looking back, he saw the bank guards pursuing him, guns in their hands; but they were well-trained and did not shoot because of the danger to pedestrians.

Jones put back his head and stepped out. Every time he came to a street intersection, he turned.

Having distanced his pursuers, he trotted into an alley, sat down on an ashcan and panted for breath.

FASHIONING the thousand-dollar bills into a compact roll, he stowed them in a pocket. He was actually relieved to get them out of sight. They represented a bull he held by the tail.

"Gracious!" he remarked gloomily.

Jones had been accustomed to dealing with factors which were predictable, things which did about what was expected of them, like a seal or walrus, for instance, that could be depended on to flee when scared, and fight when cornered.

Man was a different article. The shabbiest looking one had money, one who needed money wouldn't take any as a gift, and the bank that was in business to change money wouldn't do so.

Jones needed advice. A mentor was his immediate requirement. Someone he could consult.

Funny Pegger occurred to him naturally. Jones decided to find Funny Pegger.

As he walked along, Jones noticed a pole which bore red and

white stripes, and peering through the window of the place of business it marked, got an inspiration. He entered the barber shop, seated himself in a white chair and leaned back.

"I wish," he advised, "to dispense with a considerable portion of my hirsute adornment."

The barber pondered.

"Shave and haircut, you mean?"

"Exactly. I desire to look like other men."

The barber surveyed his customer. "With that build, you'll never make the grade."

"I fail to see why not," Jones responded.

"You wouldn't be, now, one of them bearded wrestlers, like Man-mountain Dean?"

"Please," said Jones, "start operations."

The barber picked up his clippers and a comb. About to take first cut, he drew back and grinned in admiration.

"Mister," he said, "we couldn't, now, make a deal."

"Deal?"

"I never saw whiskers like them. Now, no offense, you understand. But I'd like to have such whiskers to put in my window. Kind of a display. I might, maybe, shave you for nothing if you'd give me the whiskers."

"Er—would you make a telephone call or two for me, also?"

"Why, sure."

"I am very anxious," Jones explained, "to find a man named Funny Pegger. He told me he had a wide acquaintance among newspapermen, so I presume you might locate him by calling some reporters."

"Then, it's a deal."

"It is," said Jones, "a transaction."

The scissors snipped.

JONES surveyed the results. He saw a firm face with a long jaw, flat cheeks, well-shaped lips, high forehead over serious blue eyes. There was a lean impression generally. Jones was more satisfied than he had expected to be. His face had changed considerably since his last look at it.

"What beats me," said the barber, "is why you let a good-looking phizz like that get covered up with hair."

"You," asked Jones, "approve of it?"

"Approve? Pal, I wish we could trade."

"Er—indeed?"

"You've got Robert Taylor stopped. And Gable—phooey!"

"Who," Jones inquired, "are those gentlemen?"

The barber grinned. "Don't kid me. Now that you've had an unveiling, I can see you'll have your pick of the girls."

"You think so?" Jones asked thoughtfully.

"You'll have to club 'em away with a stick."

"I should dislike," Jones said, "to do that."

"Well, that's up to you."

Jones digested these remarks as he left the barber shop. On the streets, he noticed attractive girls in numbers, but resolutely kept them out of his mind, the experience with Glacia having lent him at least some caution. Glacia who had happened to him rather fast, had half convinced him that women were lightning that struck you before you could dodge.

The barber came back from the telephone and said, "Your friend, Funny Pegger, now lives in Greenwich Village."

"Another town, you mean?"

"No, no," the barber said, and explained that Greenwich Village was just a section in the heart of New York which didn't look much different from the rest of the city.

"How do I go to get there?"

The barber gave directions.

CHAPTER XI

MERELY MURDER

CAPTAIN FRITZ HANNOVER was enjoying the bullet-wound in his leg. He had a private room in the hospital, food he liked, a pitcher of beer whenever he wanted it, a relay of pleasant-faced nurses, and it was not necessary to be on an ocean liner bridge or answer silly questions put him by passengers who wanted to be seen talking to the Captain.

Too, getting shot in the leg by Jones had turned out to be a better break from a publicity standpoint, than if he had managed to rescue Jones from the iceberg without a hitch.

Captain Hannover's picture was on front pages of newspapers; better still, so was the picture of his ship, and the free advertising pleased his owners. His salary was going on; there was the money from his accident insurance policy; also there had come a cablegram from an official high in the conclaves of the German Government.

The cablegram congratulated Captain Hannover on his bravery and his escape, told him he was a brave man, a true follower of *der Fuehrer;* then bluntly ordered a grand gesture of forgiving the iceberg-man, Jones, for the shooting. Jones was to be forgiven because the world must know that the New Germany was the soul of heroic gesture.

When the nurse said there was a visitor, Captain Hannover presumed it was another newspaperman and asked that he be sent right in.

But the captain looked at the visitor without too much plea-sure.

"Ach!" he muttered. "Back again, *ja?"*

The newcomer was large and thirty years or so of age; his body was as loose as a sack. He had a large nose, cow lips, one chin when he held his head up, and three when he happened to glance at his feet.

"I am Paul Shevinsky," he told the hovering nurse. "Captain Hannover's lawyer. May we be alone?"

The nurse left.

Paul Shevinsky lit a cigarette, squinted one eye at the smoke, then brought papers out of his inside coat pocket. He had the lazy-bodied air of a catfish, the size of his nose and lips gave his face a poisonous swollen look; around him was the scent of gardenia.

"Here are some papers for you to sign," he said.

"Of what nature?" asked Captain Hannover.

"A deposition stating that you believe the man you found on the iceberg to be insane."

"I am sorry," said Captain Hannover. "I have changed my mind."

Paul Shevinsky took the cigarette from his lips and moved a fleck of tobacco around with the tip of his tongue. He dropped the cigarette into a beer pitcher that was almost empty. He folded his papers in his hands once, neatly.

"What has got into you?" he asked.

"I have," said Captain Hannover, "changed my mind."

"You won't sign this?"

"And," said Captain Hannover, "I am going to withdraw the complaint against the iceberg-man—Jones—for shooting me."

Paul Shevinsky got out another cigarette. The tips of the two forefingers on his right hand were dark brown with nicotine.

"Am I to take it," he demanded, "that you're not going to press any kind of a charge against Jones?"

"That is right."

"Why?"

"That is a personal matter."

"If you've been bought off," said Paul Shevinsky, "I can raise the ante."

"You get out of here!" Captain Hannover said.

"Now listen—"

Captain Hannover picked up the beer pitcher.

In a low ugly voice, "You get out of here!" he said. He made a motion with the pitcher.

Paul Shevinsky got out.

PAUL SHEVINSKY walked to the nearest drugstore, entered a telephone booth and dialed a number.

"Lyman," he said.

"Yes, Paul," said Lyman Lee.

"The captain has decided not to press charges against Jones."

"What?"

"We're blown up."

"You—but why? Why did he back out?"

Shevinsky raised his beefy shoulders and looked hurt.

Lyman Lee swore bitterly. "Let me think."

Lee was silent so long that Paul Shevinsky had to deposit another nickel in the telephone.

"Paul—"

"Yes."

"Suppose something happened to Captain Hannover?"

"What could happen to him?"

"He might die from that wound in the leg," suggested Lyman Lee.

"Not a chance!" snorted Paul Shevinsky. "It's only a flesh wound—oh! Oh—I see. Yes, I do see."

"It would be kind of tough on Jones, wouldn't it?" Lyman Lee asked.

Paul Shevinsky's forehead got wet, although it was cool in the telephone booth. He blotted it with a handkerchief, and wiped his lips.

"Yes," he said. His voice was different. "It'll be tough on Jones."

Twenty minutes later, Paul Shevinsky was in conference with a longish middle-aged man who had a very pale face. "That's the set-up, Hover," Paul said.

Hover contemplated his colorless hands. His eyes had become prominent. He swallowed. "I don't like it any too well," he muttered. "What will it pay?"

"A grand."

"Double it."

"I won't double anything," Paul Shevinsky said.

Hover got up and walked around. The room was large, and by the window there was a wooden table, and on the table two microscopes, one large and one small, also a collection of jars containing germ cultures. Through the window was visible the other buildings and campus of the college in which Hover was a professor.

"All right," Hover said.

Paul Shevinsky grinned, shook hands with Hover, and left....

Hover entered the hospital and said to Captain Hannover, "I am Doctor Augustus Albert, and I am employed by the insurance company in which you have your accident policy."

"*Ja,*" said Captain Hannover. "Insurance is pretty nice, *nein?*"

Hover nodded. "Everyone should have insurance." He opened a small dark bag. "It is necessary for me to examine your wound."

"*Ja.*"

During the course of the examination, Hover emptied the contents of a glass phial on the bullet-wound in the German-liner skipper's leg, and was not observed.

"You're going to get well in a hurry, Captain," he said in a queer voice.

"*Nein.* I like it here." Captain Hannover chuckled.

Hover got his hat and bag and left.

Later Captain Hannover began to complain of fever....

After he had died, they examined his corpse. Said the doctor: "He died from an infective germ that spread at great speed from the bullet wound."

Said the District Attorney: "The man who inflicted the wound is therefore guilty of murder."

Said the police rule-book: "Code signal *thirty-one*—arrest for murder."

Said the police radio: "Signal thirty-one. Signal thirty one. A man known as Jones, six feet two, one-ninety, red hair and possibly red beard. Has the habit of reciting unusual facts. The man Jones may make himself conspicuous because he has almost no knowledge of civilized customs."

JONES strode along New York streets. His destination was Funny Pegger's apartment in the Greenwich Village section. Jones had become pleasantly aware of a marked change in the general attitude toward himself, for the men no longer noticed him in particular, and the women noticed him in a different way. It appeared that his status had been altered by the simple magic of the scissors. His self-consciousness was gone. He felt warmed. Yes, he was one of them, and no longer looked or felt like what Lyman Lee had once called him—a hitch-hiker off an iceberg.

Having reached Greenwich Village, he next located a street called MacDougal Alley, wherein Funny Pegger was supposed to live.

Then he saw the girl.

He was suddenly presented with the sensation of having the earth and everything else substantial whisked from under him.

She came around the corner, went past and gave no evidence of noticing him.

This girl distinctly had qualities. She was a long girl, a well-shaped girl, with a firm little chin, warm rose-colored lips, a slightly snub but delectable nose, large devastating blue eyes, and a wealth of coppery red hair. However, Jones had been seeing girls with similar assets in varying degrees, and they hadn't made him feel as though he had been given a little push behind the knees.

The quality this girl had was something besides looks. A look at her was like a glance at an electric spark. She radiated energy. The way she carried her chin showed vitality and intense joy in living. The girl was a diminutive, auburn-haired dynamo in a streamlined mounting.

A series of collisions between his feet and the sidewalk revived Jones and he realized that he was following the titian-haired girl.

She turned into a recessed doorway and rang a door-bell, then as she waited, she chanced to turn. Her blue eyes—instantaneously it seemed—began to disapprove of Jones, who stood not much more than an arm-length away. Unfortunately, no one had told Jones it was unorthodox to survey a strange red-headed girl with frank approval.

"As a rule," the young lady remarked coolly, "the easier they are on the eye, the harder they are on the pocketbook."

"—indeed?" said Jones.

He continued to scrutinize her, noting such details as a little dimple to the left of a nice mouth.

"I presume," she remarked with more edge, "that you are an astronomer?"

"Astronomer?"

"A man in search of heavenly bodies."

"The planet Venus," stated Jones, "moves in an orbit between Mercury and the earth, at a mean distance of 67,000,000 miles from the sun. Venus was also an ancient Italian goddess of bloom and beauty."

The titian-haired young woman considered this remark for a moment.

"Scat!" she said.

"Eh?"

"You weren't," the girl inquired, "thinking of lingering?"

"To tell the truth, I was not contemplating departure."

"What were you contemplating?"

"I was considering indulging in—er—osculation."

"You were?"

"Yes indeed. I have found it highly exhilarating on the two previous occasions in which I participated."

The red-headed girl's toe began to tap the floor.

"Osculation," she said, "is a large word for kiss."

"Exactly."

"Try it—"

"Why, thank you!"

"—and see how high you bounce!"

THE DOOR, the bell of which the auburn young woman had punched, opened. A short round young man with a humorous mouth appeared.

It was Funny Pegger.

Jones was astounded for a moment, then realized that it wasn't such a great coincidence because Funny Pegger lived on this street.

Funny Pegger looked at the girl.

"The Indians are coming!" he gasped. "Vix, what brings—?"

Vix grabbed Funny Pegger's arm and pointed at Jones. "Sock him!"

Funny Pegger surveyed Jones. There was no recognition in his eyes. It dawned on Jones that Funny Pegger didn't know him without his red whiskers.

"Sock this clown," the girl commanded Funny Pegger, "a good one."

"Why?" Funny inquired.

"He annoys me."

Funny Pegger snorted. "They all annoy you, if I remember rightly."

The red-headed young woman's ire widened quickly to include Funny Pegger.

"Are you going to swat him one?"

"I doubt it."

"Why not?"

"I never," said Funny Pegger, "hit anybody I don't think I can't lick."

The young woman stamped a foot, indignation mounting.

"It seems," she told Jones, "that you will have to hit *him*." She pointed at Funny Pegger.

Jones was confused. "Er—why should I?"

"Because I would approve heartily."

Jones brightened involuntarily. "You really wish me to—er—sock him?"

"Absolutely!"

Jones was conscious of an intense desire to do anything this young woman wanted. His fist lifted—lifted rather absent-mindedly, since he had no real intention of striking his friend.

Funny Pegger was not asleep. When Jones' fist came up, he lunged in, struck. Jones gasped. Out of self-defense, he seized Funny Pegger. The two young men rolled head over heels out of the entry onto the sidewalk.

A moment later, a large red-faced policeman was holding them by their respective collars.

"Sure, and what's goin' on here?" inquired the policeman.

"Officer," snapped the red-headed girl, "these men were annoying me."

"Sure, and then me duty is to throw their pants in the can."

Funny Pegger yelled, "Vix! Hey, Vix, you can't do this!"

"Maybe I can't," Vix said sweetly, "but the officer can."

He did.

The indignity of being hustled toward jail, literally by the scruff of his neck, brought a remark from Jones.

"Vixen," he stated, "is the name of the female of the fox species, and also designates a shrewish, ill-tempered woman with no patience."

Funny Pegger peered at Jones. He said, "Love a duck!" He had recognized Jones—no one but Jones made quotations.

A bit later, the gag-man got an opportunity to whisper to Jones. "Your name," he breathed, "is Holmes."

"Er—I understand. A pseudonym is called for," whispered Jones.

They reached jail, were booked, and Jones remembered to give the name of John Holmes.

"You can come back in the morning and appear against these two in court," the desk sergeant told Vix.

"Swell!" Vix said. "Can I watch you hang them too?"

Jones and Funny Pegger were taken to another room and relieved of belts, shoe laces, and their pockets were emptied.

"Great Moses!" said the cop, ogling one hundred thousand-dollar bills which he had taken out of Jones' pocket.

"I do hope," volunteered Jones, "that you will not lose that."

"We've got a nice strong safe." The cop eyed Jones. "A little later, we may let you tell us what mint you own."

Funny Pegger had been ogling the money in pop-eyed silence.

"Wait a minute!" the gag-man blurted. "Jones! You can bail us out!"

"I—which?"

"Give these gentlemen in blue uniforms part of that money," explained Funny Pegger patiently.

Jones perceived instantly that this was out of the question, it being most emphatically part of his bargain with Polyphemus Ward that he should not use any of the hundred thousand for himself.

"Impossible," he said firmly.

"But—"

"No," said Jones. "We go to jail first."

"You bet you will," a cop said.

Funny Pegger and Jones soon found themselves consigned to adjacent jail cells. It was only a question of time until they made the discovery that, by keeping their voices low, they could conduct a private conversation.

"Who did you rob?" Funny Pegger demanded grimly.

"Rob?"

"You got that hundred thousand somewhere, didn't you?"

"But I did not rob anyone."

"You earned the dough I suppose."

"Well—no."

"Let's have your story. It had better be good."

JONES, in the middle of an uncomfortable silence, wished he had not promised old Polyphemus Ward not to tell anyone about their bargain.

Funny Pegger said, "Go ahead. I'm practically drowning in suspense."

"I—er—can not impart information concerning the hundred thousand," Jones muttered.

"You *what?*"

"Silence," said Jones, "is the entire absence of sound, and is supposed to be complete only in a region of vacuum, such as interplanetary space."

When there was no answer from the other cell, Jones grew embarrassed.

"Ah—Mr. Pegger," he ventured.

"Go away! You've no idea how you aggravate me!"

"I confess to a mistake in judgment in separating myself so abruptly from your company," Jones said gloomily. "I am referring of course, to my flight from the yacht. At the time it seemed the thing to do."

"Running out on your manager was just the thing, eh?"

"I—er—felt urged to depend on myself," Jones said.

After that, conversation rather hung up on a snag, because, to each remark Jones made, Funny Pegger bluntly demanded to know where the money had come from. Almost an hour passed, and the gag-man persuaded the jailer to furnish him with the late editions of the afternoon papers.

"I want," Funny Pegger explained sourly, "to read the latest about a man named Jones."

The instant he looked at the front page, Funny Pegger grew rigid. With great haste, he read the rest of the way through the story that startled him.

"Jones!" he hissed. "Can you take a little shock?"

"I shall do my best to cope with my problems," Jones said.

"Your problems," muttered Funny Pegger, "are going to take some coping. You remember that German-liner captain you shot in the leg?"

"I—what about him?"

"You're only charged with murder now."

"Murder?"

"Yes. M-u-r-d-e-r. The thing they invented electric chairs for."

"But I—I don't understand!" Jones gasped.

"The German-liner captain died."

"Died?"

"As a result of the hole your bullet made in his leg, this paper says. So now you are charged with killing him. That's in the paper, here, too."

"But it—it was a superficial wound!" Jones exclaimed.

"That puzzles me, too," Funny Pegger muttered. "And it happened rather damn suddenly, if you ask me."

Jones groaned.

Funny Pegger also groaned.

"You need all the cooperation you can get," he explained.

CHAPTER XII

FIT TO PRINT

JONES, DUE TO the strange course of circumstances, had only a limited acquaintance with the customs of mankind, but this nubbin was enough to make him begin to suspect that he would never learn anything whatever about the human race. He knew as much about mankind as a wild camel in the desert of Rub' al Khali would be expected to.

Excellent prospects of spending his first night in New York in one of its jails did not embarrass Jones particularly. He had too many other troubles, and being in the bastille rated among the lesser ones; it was only a lamb in the flock. If stone blocks and steel bars offered sanctuary from his other troubles, he would have actually welcomed them. Being in jail didn't perturb him because there was no point in being bothered about a mouse with so many rats around.

Jones was also somewhat disgusted with himself over the way he had underestimated everything. To give away a hundred thousand dollars had seemed simple. That so many difficulties, none anticipated, could appear, made him feel futile. The increasing complications were undermining his confidence in himself.

The jail cell was five feet wide, seven long, and Jones' head came within half an inch of the ceiling when he stood. There was a bed—a hard board-shelf twenty-four inches wide and six feet six inches long. It certainly wasn't there for comfort. Even Jones didn't think it could actually be slept on. Jones tapped disconsolately on the east wall of his cell to get the attention of Funny Pegger, who was next door.

"The word clue," Jones stated, "means a bunch of worms, but it also denotes a thread, or yarn, which one may grasp and follow out of a labyrinth."

"I lean toward the first part," Funny Pegger remarked. "It kind of describes my opinion of a guy who won't use part of a hundred thousand dollars to bail himself and his manager out of the clink."

Jones wished he hadn't promised to tell no one about the hundred thousand. He couldn't explain to Funny Pegger that he was not to use any of the money for himself.

"I am puzzled by something, Mr. Pegger—"

"I am puzzled by that hundred thousand dollars the cops found on you," interrupted the gag-man. "Where'd you get it?"

"Er—what I started to say," Jones continued, "was that it seems rather odd that the German liner-captain should have died suddenly from a superficial bullet wound in the leg. At the time I shot him, while under the mistaken impression the World War was still going on, I purposefully inflicted a very minor injury."

"You sure of that?"

"Quite sure. I merely perforated the calf of his leg."

"That," said Funny Pegger, "is something to think about."

Jones cleared his throat. "I have been thinking. A rather grim suspicion has occurred to me. Would you care to hear it?"

"Jones, I find almost anything you do or think is interesting. Proceed."

"Do you suppose someone poisoned the German captain in some fashion, so that the man's death would involve me in serious difficulties?"

Funny Pegger considered this in startled silence. "Ain't that kind of far-fetched conceiving?"

"Perhaps. It is merely deduction on my part."

"Were there," Funny Pegger asked suddenly, "any detective novels on the island where you dug out your remarkable education?"

"Why, yes. A volume concerning a chap named Sherlock Holmes."

"That explains this brainstorm of yours."

"The only trouble," said Jones gloomily, "is that I can not conceive of a motive for anyone desiring to place me in difficulties."

"You're stumped?"

"What?"

"You're puzzled?"

"Oh, yes."

"Which brings us back," Funny Pegger said, "to that hundred thousand dollars and where you got it."

JONES longed to put into Pegger's friendly ear the story of the hundred thousand. He wanted the gag-man's advice about how to get people to take thousand-dollar bills as a gift. But old Polyphemus Ward had directed that the thing be kept a secret.

"I'm sorry," Jones mumbled. "I am not at liberty to impart information concerning the money."

"I can see," snorted Funny Pegger, "that you trust me!"

"But I do!"

"Oh, sure! But maybe you're right. They say you can trust a newspaperman with anything but your money or your woman. In that case—" He broke off, gave a startled grunt. "Speaking of the devil!" he muttered.

Jones pressed an eye to the bars and saw a tall, carelessly dressed young man approaching in the company of the jail guard.

"Psst!" hissed Funny Pegger. "Jones—duck! There comes a reporter I know. Get back in the dark! If anybody discovers you're Jones, the man off the iceberg, you'll turn into a permanent fixture here! Remember, you're wanted for shooting the German captain."

Jones withdrew to the murky rear of his cell.

The newspaper reporter hailed Funny Pegger with a loud laugh.

"Hello, jailbird!" he said. He peered through the bars. "Where's your stripes?"

"Heh, heh," said Funny Pegger nastily.

"How'd you get in here, boy?"

"If I recall, it was with the assistance of a cop," Funny Pegger explained. "How'd you know I was in?"

"Oh, word went around, as words will do. Had a fight over a woman didn't you?"

"Uh-huh."

"Where's the fellow you mixed it with?"

"Search me," Funny Pegger said calmly.

"Holmes was his name, wasn't it?"

"So I heard."

The reporter fortunately did not pursue that point, and eventually departed, gloating at every step.

The masterpiece of satiric journalism he turned out was cut to newsworthy proportions by a businesslike copy-desk man, was assigned a relatively inconspicuous position on page fourteen, and ultimately came to the attention of Lyman Lee, who was having fried snails and champagne in a small, smart restaurant east of Madison Avenue. This is known as the power of the press.

Lyman Lee looked up and summoned a waiter, who plugged in a telephone at the table. Shortly, Paul Shevinsky was on the wire.

"Paul, have you read in the late papers about that Pegger fellow being in jail?"

"Just saw it," said Paul Shevinsky. His voice had a meaty

sound which seemed to convey over the telephone a picture of his well-stuffed face.

"Did you also see that the man Pegger had a fight with was carrying one hundred thousand-dollar bills?"

"I—heaven love us! Then the other man is *Jones!*"

"Obviously."

"But how come the cops don't know it?"

"Jones probably shaved off his whiskers. The police wouldn't know about the hundred thousand."

"We'd better tip them off." Paul Shevinsky chuckled queerly. "The German ship captain died from the leg wound Jones gave him, you know."

Lyman Lee frowned. "I wouldn't talk too much about that."

"Maybe you're right."

"I wouldn't say anything to the police just yet, either."

"No? I don't follow you there, Lyman."

"The hundred thousand."

"Oh."

"A hundred thousand," said Lyman Lee, "is a fairish sum."

"It is, at that."

"Jones," continued Lyman Lee, "is supposed to give it away to needy people."

"Yes, I know."

"I thought you might know some needy people."

Paul Shevinsky was silent for a time, and coughed once before he spoke. "Ever hear of the man called 'Forgetful' Osborn?"

"I haven't," Lyman Lee said, "had the pleasure."

"It's not always a pleasure," Paul Shevinsky chuckled, "to know Forgetful."

"I don't follow you."

"Forgetful Osborn is one of the slickest con-men in the racket," Paul Shevinsky explained.

"So—?"

"Forgetful is the fellow to sic on that hundred thousand. He'll think up something in the line of needy persons."

"Now," said Lyman Lee, "we progress."

"I'll contact Forgetful, then call you back later," Paul Shevinsky said.

"I'll be at my apartment," Lyman Lee told him.

The waiter took the telephone away, and Lyman Lee inserted the miniature fork in a snail with the air of an expert at extracting tender morsels from hard shells. By now, he knew enough about Jones to realize that unusual young man had, for all of his strange mannerisms, a hard shell.

CHAPTER XIII

THE CAUSTIC SAMARITAN

JONES AND FUNNY PEGGER had had a long period of silence, during which Jones was trying to make mental progress in the direction he considered most important—the matter of the German captain's suspiciously sudden death. His thoughts kept jumping the track and racing to the red-haired young lady, Vix, who was an interesting subject. Jones was having trouble keeping Vix out of his mind. He tapped on the cell wall to get Funny Pegger's attention.

"Mr. Pegger!"

"What," asked Funny Pegger, "is on your mind?"

"To tell the truth, a member of the opposite sex."

"Any particular member?"

"Yes," said Jones. "I refer to the young lady who is responsible for our present circumstances."

"Oh, you mean Vix," said Funny Pegger. "The sparkler who had us clapped in here."

"Er—would she happen to be your fiancée?"

"Vix? That wildcat! Not a chance. She has the idea that nothing in trousers is worth wasting time on."

"Indeed? Then I take it that she is fancy free?"

"You take it correctly," Funny Pegger advised him. "But if you want advice, I'd say lay off Vix."

"Why?"

"You're inexperienced with women."

"But," said Jones, "I shall have to learn."

"They usually tried to get some practice before they climbed in the ring with Jack Dempsey."

"I don't believe I understand."

"Start with kittens," suggested the gag-man, "and work up to the tigresses gradually."

"Oh." Instead of being cautioned by the warning, Jones found that he was aroused by it. "I find it difficult to see why she had us consigned to jail, when as a matter of fact she started the trouble herself."

Funny Pegger snorted. "That's an example of what I mean. Women are trouble. They don't like the color of your eyes, so they give you the works."

"You think that she was unfavorably impressed by such a small detail?"

"She was impressed by something. I wouldn't know. By the way, what started her off?"

"Nothing at all, I merely mentioned my intention to kiss her."

A strangled explosion came from the next cell, "Is that all? Are you sure?"

"Oh, yes."

"Thank your stars you're not hanging from the nearest lamp-post!"

Jones considered this.

"The kiss," he announced, "comes from the Icelandic word *koss,* and means to press with the lips, which are compressed on contact, then separated, and is a salute of greeting or reverence. A kiss is also a sweet-meat composed of sugar and beaten egg whites, and baked, also a bit of confectionery, or a sugar-plum."

"Which leads up to what?"

"I don't know," Jones confessed.

Keys rattled in a lock, iron doors clanged, and the jailer approached, accompanied by the auburn-haired young woman whom they had been discussing.

"I'm bailing you two out," Vix declared. "I'm sorry I lost my temper."

JONES stepped out of the cell, filled with gratitude so profound that it crowded out of him all memory of her feminine contrariness that was responsible for their arrest. He hunted for words to express his feelings, but saw Funny Pegger scowling at him, which he correctly interpreted to mean that silence was the policy.

"If you've got a rabbit foot, rub it," whispered Funny Pegger, "and maybe the cops won't recognize you."

They recovered their belongings, and Jones placed the sheaf of one hundred thousand-dollar bills in a pocket rather self-consciously, aware that Vix was staring at him.

They marched out of the police station. The three of them entered a waiting taxicab, gave the driver Funny Pegger's address; and the cab rolled through gathering dusk, between elderly red-brick buildings, past fruit stores whose proprietors were putting away wares for the night, past groups of children engaged in throwing balls back and forth across the street. Vix broke the silence first, after they had been riding for some time.

"Was that a hundred thousand dollars?" she asked, "or am I having that old trouble again?"

"Er—your eyes were all right," Jones admitted.

Vix looked at Funny Pegger. "I can't understand you having a friend who isn't broke."

"He was broke when I collected him as a friend," grinned the gag-man. "Where he got that hundred grand is beyond me. But I'm not surprised. Not at Jones. Nothing Jones does will surprise me. Ever."

The red-haired girl, Vix, gave a convulsive start. She stared at Funny Pegger, but she pointed at Jones.

"Jones?" she asked.

"Yes," admitted Funny Pegger.

"Off the iceberg?"

"Right."

The girl made her hands into fists and appeared inclined to poke Funny Pegger. Then she pounded her forehead dramatically.

"Sometimes," she said, "I do the cutest things. All I've done now is get an accused murderer out of jail. It must be a kind of gift."

Her tone distressed Jones, who did not want her getting the impression that he had homicidal tendencies. He wondered if she was, and glanced sidewise at her, but could tell nothing from her face. His inspection accomplished nothing but a great tumult within him—parts of his interior seemed to jump around and other parts go into a cramp. Vix was more than a pretty, red-headed girl. She had dynamic energy; she was a girl who had to be doing something all the time. She bubbled, as it were, over. There was sparkle to her eyes, to her smile, to the quick, graceful movements of her hands and body. She was distinctly what Pegger had called a wow. And Jones decided he liked it.

THEY reached Funny Pegger's rooming house, left the cab, and entered. "Thanks, Vix, for getting us out," said Funny Pegger drily. "Of course, you got us in, too." His grin was wry. "I only hope I can return the favor sometime."

The young woman compressed her lips. "If you think I'm leaving now, you have another guess coming. You got me into this. Now you can explain what it is."

"I got you into it? *I* did?"

"Of course."

Pegger snorted. "It seems I remember you telling a cop we were annoying you?"

"Weren't you?"

"Not half as much as you were annoying us."

"Exactly!" said Jones. "I did nothing but say I wanted to kiss you."

"Jones," Funny Pegger said, "you'd better keep your finger out of it. There's sharks in the water."

Jones looked injured.

"Mystery," he said, "was originally a religious rite to which only privileged worshippers were admitted, hence came to mean the wholly unknown, an enigma, beyond human comprehension—leading poets refer to woman as the mysterious sex."

Vix pointed at him.

"Just what kind of thing," she inquired, "is this Jones?"

Funny Pegger sighed, grasped the young woman's elbow, and spoke to Jones. "I'll take her in the next room and explain. Can't do it here. She's allergic to you, or something."

"Allergic?"

"Letting her see you is like showing a hay-fever victim a goldenrod patch."

Their departure to the next room left Jones alone to contemplate something distressing that had just occurred to him. He liked Funny Pegger. Liked him a lot. The last thing he desired was to cause the gag-man any trouble. But trouble might be exactly what he would bring Funny Pegger. Jones was charged with a major crime—murder probably qualified as major. Funny Pegger was harboring him. Anyone who knowingly aided a criminal became an accessory, and liable to severe penalty, or so Jones recollected having read in a law book which had been on his Arctic island.

It all narrowed down to this: If he permitted Funny Pegger to help him, he would be getting the friendly gag-man into difficulties. The proper solution for that was for Jones to leave. That would solve the dilemma nicely. Still… for two large reasons, Jones didn't wish to leave. First, he needed the tubby gag-man's aid. Secondly, the auburn-haired Vix was beginning to fascinate him—he distinctly wanted to see more of her.

It took almost five minutes of wrestling with the problem to see that the important thing was not to get Funny Pegger in trouble. He must leave.

He walked to the door, opened it silently and stepped out into a street now dark except for illumination from the corner street-lamp.

Automobiles had ceased to be a novelty to Jones, so he paid no attention to the one that drew up beside him until the beam of a strong flashlight sprang out in his face. He looked around and saw a limousine which seemed a block long.

"Hello, Jones," a voice called cordially from the wheeled castle.

JONES had heard the voice before. He threw a glance up and down the street, picking his course if he had to run for it.

"You are Jones, aren't you?" asked the voice, rather anxiously. "This is Lyman Lee, your old friend."

Jones thought it incongruous of Lyman Lee to designate himself as a friend. On the Ward yacht, the fellow had been obnoxious.

Jones went over to the shiny car. "I—hello," he ventured.

"I hardly knew you without the whiskers," Lyman Lee said. "What a change they made. I'll bet there isn't a policeman in town who would recognize you."

Jones winced. "Er—let us hope you are correct."

Lyman Lee laughed pleasantly. "Get in the car, Jones."

"Get in? Why?" This was a reasonable question.

"Because I want to help you," Lyman Lee explained heartily. "You see, I know more than the police do. One of the things I knew was that you and Funny Pegger were very good friends, and I had a hunch you'd go to Pegger. So I came to warn you."

"Warn me?"

"Yes. You should not associate with Funny Pegger. It's the worst thing you could do."

"It is my belief," said Jones sincerely, "that Funny Pegger is an estimable person."

"Of course. They don't come any finer. But you can see that the police may find you with Funny Pegger, and Funny will be in trouble."

"Er—that seems logical."

"You bet it is. But I can help you, Jones."

Distinctly against his better judgment, Jones entered the car, which Lyman Lee occupied alone, and the machine went into motion. The huge car swept along with the impressive effect of a dark cloud, with a radio speaker mounted in the top making quite pleasant music after Lyman Lee turned it on. City streets at night, the strolling, neatly-dressed people, the sidewalk cafés which were a feature of this section, made an interesting novelty to Jones. He wished he had sufficient peace of mind to enjoy it.

Jones studied Lyman Lee. There was certainly nothing wrong with the latter's profile, at least. It occurred to Jones that he had not seen another man as lovely at this one.

Jones tried to push away doubts. On the yacht, he had disliked Lyman Lee; his impression had been that the feeling was mutual, and furthermore, he'd suspected Lyman Lee had base qualities, but he might be mistaken, although instincts kept insisting to the contrary.

"Character," remarked Jones thoughtfully, "is a sign, sometimes cabalistic, placed on an object or individual, and significant as a mark of some ulterior fact."

"What?"

"I was just wondering if one should disregard signs."

"I see," said Lyman Lee. Obviously he didn't. The large car rolled into a more pretentious part of town. Lyman Lee stopped before an only mildly imposing structure of reddish stone. "I'm going to rent you a room here," he explained. "This is a quiet place. You won't be bothered."

"Why, thank you."

"By the way, how are you fixed for money?"

"Er—I am without personal funds."

"Here's twenty," said Lyman Lee generously.

"But—"

"That's all right."

"I—thank you."

"I'll look you up later," said Lyman Lee.

Jones watched the swanky car leave, and assured himself he must be mistaken about Lyman Lee.

THE ROOM was large, airy, and Jones' first act in examining it was to scrutinize himself in the full-length mirror in the closet door. He no longer looked like a freak off an iceberg. In the glass, he saw a tall, well-built young man with red hair who appeared, if anything, a year or so older than twenty-three.

The room was equipped with essentials: bed, dresser, clothes closet, chair, telephone, a bathroom, items to which he had become accustomed on the Polyphemus Ward yacht. The bed was not as soft as the one on the yacht, he found when he bounced on it. His exploring progressed to the telephone book, which fortunately had a clear explanation of its purpose printed in the front. That seemed to exhaust possibilities for exploration in the room.

He counted the sheaf of thousand-dollar bills. One hundred of them were still there. Giving away that money was going to be much tougher than anticipated, he was beginning to realize. He put the roll back in a pocket, feeling futile again.

Furthermore, he was hungry. He had not eaten since breakfast on the yacht, and the excitement of approaching New York had caused him to slight that meal. The logical cure for being hungry was to find an establishment dispensing food, so he yanked his hat down to hide his red hair, and left the rooming house, taking however, a careful bearing so as to be able to find the place again. He walked toward a more brightly lighted part of town.

Numbers of people wore evening attire. Brilliant electric signs advertised products of which Jones had never heard. A large glass window marked "Cafeteria" interested him after he saw people eating inside, and observation showed him how they got their food, so he entered, pulled a green ticket out of the contraption by the door and got tray, knife, fork, spoon, paper napkin. He collected enough food to make the other customers stare in astonishment, paid for it with part of Lyman Lee's twenty, and ate. Then he leaned back, imitated a nearby diner in manipulating a toothpick, and felt he was beginning to do rather well.

There is enough animal in man that foods seems to equip him with a feeling of spurious well-being. Jones was feeling less like a lamb on strange wolf range.

After leaving the cafeteria, Jones decided to stroll around and make another effort to find a needy man. He felt all primed to make another attempt to give away a thousand-dollar bill. Almost immediately, he saw a likely-looking prospect. What Jones didn't know was that his prospect was one of the tribe of petty criminals that seems to flourish under the nose of New York's allegedly brilliant police department. This fellow was a car-watcher. Actually, he was a petty racketeer, shabby, dirty, vicious, and an outstanding example of what the psychologists call antisocial. He was accosting a motorist and hinting that the motorist might find his tires slashed and paint job scraped with a knife point unless he contributed fifty cents to the watcher—who, of course, would keep such vandals away.

Jones thought the poor man was soliciting alms.

"I say," Jones remarked, by way of introduction.

The small-time crook scowled at the largish young man who had accosted him. "Yeah?" he muttered.

"Are you," Jones inquired, "a needy person?"

"Brother," said the other, as a matter of policy, "I ain't had nothin' to eat for two days. And me poor family is starvin'. I ain't," he added quickly, "been able to get on relief."

Jones felt it advisable to try a smaller amount, since a thousand dollars seemed to do strange things to needy people.

"Would one hundred dollars be of assistance to you?" he asked.

The thug batted his eyes, wiped his nose on the back of his hand.

"I ain't doin' nothin' shady enough to pay that big," he growled suspiciously. "Uh—not until I—uh—know you better."

"Honesty," said Jones irrelevantly, "comes from an old Roman word *honestus,* which at various times has meant a plant known as the satin-pod, also a virgin's bower, as well as freedom from fraud or guile, the conventional meaning."

"Huh?" said the other.

"Honesty," added Jones, "is the best policy."

"Oh! Well—sure."

Jones extracted a thousand-dollar bill from a pocket, presented it to the man, and commanded: "Have this changed into currency of lesser denomination, if you please. Bring the money back to me, and you will receive your hundred dollars, in return for which I will expect you to give me some data concerning yourself for my records."

The man seized the banknote, probably with the same avid gesture he had used to snatch a few purses in his time.

"I'll be right back, buddy," he said unconvincingly.

He walked away with feigned unconcern until he could not restrain himself, then ran. He rounded a corner, got under a bright light, and peered at the bill. He really saw the denomination for the first time.

"Jeeps!"

He stared at the banknote, eyes protruding slightly. His mouth opened, shut. Suddenly, he put back his head, tore full speed into a dark side street. He stopped. He perspired.

"Jeeps!"

He changed stance from one foot to the other. He took off his hat, put it back on, chewed his lower lip.

Abruptly, he dashed out of the alley, and to the ticket window of a movie. He shoved the banknote at the blonde.

"Ich—ich—is that thing McCoy?" he croaked.

The theater cashier happened to be expert as well as blonde, and she knew, after a few moments of examining the piece of currency, that it was genuine.

"I think it's okay," she said. She shoved it back. "But we don't change anything bigger than a ten."

The small-bore crook snatched the bill, raced down the street. He came to another foolish stop. When he wiped sweat off, his hand shook until his knuckles knocked against his skull.

"Love a duck," he gasped, "I've gone nuts."

His eyes rolled; he mopped his lips with his tongue. He went into a species of trance, and walked stiffly back to Jones, carrying the bill as if it was something venomous held by the nape of the neck. He gave the banknote to Jones.

"Here!" he said.

Jones didn't want the bill. He had ninety-nine others just like it which he had to give away.

But the man dropped the note at Jones' feet, turned and dashed down the street.

Jones slowly bent over, picked up the bill and sorrowly replaced it with the others. It seemed that no one wanted to be given even a hundred dollars.

CHAPTER XIV

THE POOR IN SPIRIT

JONES SPRAWLED ON the bed in his room and tried to figure his fellow man. He was baffled by *homo sapiens*. They did not behave according to logic, the men being as erratic as the women, if not more so.

An electric clock on the dresser made a tiny whirring, audible only as there were lulls in the mumbling of the city at night. It was dark in the room, and quiet, and a little stifling as well, it seemed to Jones; almost undesirable when he compared it to the clean air of the Arctic, which he was accustomed to breathing. He began to wish he was back on the lonely island. The place had advantages he hadn't appreciated. There'd been no such things as old Polyphemus Ward, no hundred thousand dollar bills—in a flash, Jones was wide awake. His face was grim.

He seized the telephone directory, found Polyphemus Ward's telephone number, and got connected, doing it the way it said in the front of the book. A voice informed him that Polyphemus Ward could not be disturbed.

"Get the old rep—er—gentleman on this telephonic device," Jones commanded emphatically. "Tell him this is Jones, the—ah—possessor of one hundred thousand dollars."

That was effective.

"Young man," roared Polyphemus Ward's crusty voice, "I told you I wanted to hear nothing out of you until you had succeeded or failed in your job."

"I wish to make a report," Jones said.

"Report? Report what? Have you lost my hundred thousand?"

"The report," said Jones stiffly, "concerns the state of my feelings."

"What?"

"If you were in this neighborhood," stated Jones grimly, "I should be inclined to give you an—er—sock on the jaw, even if you are an old man."

"By Harry, the door is open! You—you—whippersnapper! Old man, am I?"

"A bullying, cantankerous, squalling old reprobate of a moneybag," Jones said additionally. "I do not number you among my friends."

"You don't, eh?"

"You," said Jones, "did a worse trick to me than anybody."

"Worse trick!" Polyphemus Ward yelled. "Giving you a chance to get a million dollars and a job—that's a worse trick, eh?"

"I am sure of it."

"What," snarled the financier, "are some of the tricks the others did to you?"

"Thus far, I have become engaged to a girl I am not sure I want, been accused of murder, been in jail and out, attacked by a thief, pursued by bank guards with guns, sought by police, inveigled into fisticuffs with my best friend by a girl, and the same girl has cast aspersions on my intelligence."

"Look out for that girl," Polyphemus Ward advised.

"I shall continue to endeavor to solve my own problems to the best of my ability," Jones replied.

"What about my hundred thousand dollars?"

"I still have it."

"All?"

"Every cent," said Jones disgustedly, "Which again reminds me that I consider you a cranky, browbeating, insulting old grab-dollars who doesn't care how much grief he makes for other people."

Jones hung up. He felt much better. He made a mental note to berate old Polyphemus Ward again the next time he got to feeling low.

AS FOR Polyphemus Ward, he threw the telephone across the room, kicked a chair, hurled his cigar at the fireplace and sat down. He was in his chair three or four minutes and began to grin.

A man hadn't dared insult him in a dozen years. He found the novelty refreshing and further proof that Jones was not overawed by the fact that Polyphemus Ward had as many millions as Tammany has politicians. The financier considered himself a judge of character, and he had rated Jones well from the beginning, but there had been a time, after he had given Jones the hundred thousand, when Polyphemus Ward had wondered if one of the world's richest men had gone crazy. Doubts, big ones, had assailed him. He hoped Wall Street wouldn't hear about it. They'd be sure his mind had slipped.

The telephone talk had renewed his confidence in Jones.

"Givens," he growled at his butler, "I think I've picked a winner."

"Yes, sir," Givens said.

Polyphemus Ward scowled. "Givens, you're another yes-man. Don't you know that no one ever got a million dollars by saying yes."

"No, sir," said Givens hopefully.

SHAKESPEARE said sleep was the hand that soothes dull care away, and Jones found this to be correct, awakening in the morning with healthy energy plus desire to be up and at it. He whistled as he dressed, instinctively sang as he swung to the door, bounced out into the corridor—and collided with a man.

"Excuse me," Jones said.

"Oh, to be sure," said the other half of the collision vaguely. "Oh, yes—I beg your pardon. I didn't intend to bump into you."

"No, no. I did the bumping."

"Er? Why yes, yes, I'm very clumsy."

The man seemed completely absent-minded, and was a smallish, roundish sort of a benevolent-looking sheep. Apparently he had dressed without thinking, for his tie was awry. He wore large horn-rimmed spectacles in front of large soft eyes which reminded Jones of an infant seal.

"Yes, yes, to be sure. Ah—where shall we have breakfast? Mr.— Mr.—?" The nice little man peered at Jones, then looked confused. "Ah, bless me! I'm sorry. I—goodness I—I thought you were a gentleman who was to meet me for breakfast. Won't you excuse me?"

The little man went away nervously, leaving Jones feeling sorry for him because he was obviously such a confused, helpless lamb.

JONES himself headed for the cafeteria where he had eaten the night before, entered, pulled a ticket out of the contraption that rang a bell, and began loading his tray, only to discover he was standing next to the absent-minded little man from the rooming house.

The little man looked blankly at Jones.

"Ah—haven't we met before?"

"About five minutes ago."

"Why—yes. Oh, I remember." The little man chuckled jerkily at his own confusion. "It seems we are having breakfast together after all, doesn't it?"

"Yes, indeed," Jones agreed politely.

They filled their trays, moved to a table and sat down together. Jones was impressed by the extent of his companion's forgetfulness. The benevolent fellow seemed completely distraught—he fiddled with knife and fork, stared into space, then began putting salt in his coffee.

"I believe," Jones suggested, "that sugar, rather than salt is the proper combination with coffee."

"Why—oh, goodness! To be sure!" The other twittered nervously. "You see, I—I'm afraid I'm not completely myself this morning. I'm really at a loss to know what to do. You see, a man was to meet me, and he hasn't appeared. Oh, gracious! He hasn't come, and I just know that means he has decided not to give financial support to my poor orphans. I don't know what we shall do, I really don't. But—oh, please excuse me. I didn't intend to bore you."

Jones was thoughtful.

"Orphan," he remarked, "is a child deprived of parentage, and commonly refers to such individuals when in need of care, I believe."

"Yes. Yes, exactly."

"You," Jones inquired, "have some orphans?"

"Oh, a large number. Poor things. I do not know what they shall do, now that we have no money. But—I must be boring you. Please don't pay any attention to me. I'm just distraught."

THE SUBJECT of orphans was not boring Jones. When he got back to his rooming house, he sat on the bed and thought. The more he thought, the more interested he got. He took the idea of orphans whole-heartedly to bosom, sprang up, went out into the hallway and knocked on the door of the benevolent little man.

"May I come in?" Jones asked. "I wish to discuss the matter of orphans to greater extent."

"Yes, yes—of course. It's very kind of you to sympathize with me. I've noticed that so many people are bored by the troubles of other people. Do come in."

Jones entered a quietly furnished room in which there were some books. "Let us," he suggested, "get down to the basic facts."

"Why—I—of course."

"What is your connection with the orphans?" Jones inquired.

"They are my hobby. Some people collect stamps as a hobby. For my part, I collect orphans. My name is Goodman—Clarence Goodman, and once I had a fairish amount of money. A few years ago, I purchased a large house, and began taking in poor homeless children. The depression came, and soon I had lost my own money, after which I managed to raise small sums from people I knew. But lately, I have been unable to find more benefactors. My last prospect, a rich man, did not show up this morning, as you are aware."

"You gave all your own money to such a good purpose?" Jones inquired admiringly.

"Oh, I was quite glad to do so."

"You were?"

"Charity is wonderful."

"It has been my experience that charity is a hard thing to manage," Jones remarked.

The little man frowned. "Why, I do not believe I understand."

"It's a long story," Jones said, "we'll put it aside for the moment."

The benevolent little man sighed in a broken-hearted way.

"If it were a matter of pennies, it would be simpler," he murmured disconsolately. "But it isn't. To tell the truth, I have exactly one hundred orphans, and it requires about a thousand dollars a year each to maintain them."

Jones smiled.

"A few thousand dollars would take care of our immediate needs," the other said. "Perhaps kind providence would provide our later needs."

"Hmmm," said Jones.

"Are you interested in charity, may I ask?"

Jones nodded happily.

"To tell the truth," he explained, "I have decided that I must go in for charity on the bulk scale."

"Bulk scale?"

"Finding one needy person is too slow. I am already twenty thousand dollars behind schedule."

"Twenty thousand—I do not understand."

"I do not understand, either." Jones shook his head slowly. "People baffle me. One would think it a simple matter to give away—but I won't bore you with my troubles. I see you have your own."

"I do have, indeed."

"At least," Jones said, "I can fix yours."

"Fix mine?"

"I can provide cash to operate your orphan institution for six months."

"You mean—you—fifty thousand dollars?"

"Exactly. That will put me nearly two days ahead of schedule."

"But—but—" The little man seemed about to faint.

"And later, if things go well," Jones added, "I shall be in a position to aid orphans further."

"Oh—oh—I—" The little man swayed. "I feel—oh, so happy!"

Jones suddenly remembered all men are not honest.

"Of course," he stated, "I should like to see this institution and the orphans."

"You can—at once!" exclaimed the benevolent little man.

CHAPTER XV

IT HARDLY EVER RAINS

THEY DROVE NORTHWARD out of the city in a little old rattletrap of a car that was somehow nice and homey like its owner. The benevolent little man seemed to be so happy that he was in danger of driving them into other motorists. He actually shook with joy.

Jones himself was experiencing a pleasant warmth. He was discovering the existence of a fine unconscious quality in the human being that enables him to draw delight from doing good for others, one capacity that makes man different from animal and indicates there may be such a thing as a soul.

The orphanage was a long, two-story, rambling old structure in much need of repair. Jones stepped out of the car and looked at it. It gave him a heart-clutch. There were children running and playing, and the little tikes weren't too well dressed. One little girl, seated on the sagging front steps, was bent over and sobbing gently, and Jones' benevolent companion stooped over the child and patted her head.

"What is wrong, honey?" he inquired gently.

The little girl sniffled. "Hungry," she said miserably.

Jones noted that his companion seemed about to shed tears as they moved on.

"We're actually out of food," the little man explained.

Jones was moved, and as he continued his inspection, he became convinced he would never find a more deserving receptacle for fifty thousand dollars.

"Er—there hardly seems to be a hundred children here, however," he suggested.

"No, no, some of the little darlings are out on a hike in the country this morning," the little man replied. "Ah—sometimes the good people of the countryside give them something to eat."

"Goodness! You mean they beg for food?"

"They—they can't—starve," the little man said, and his voice broke.

Jones became determined. "I will give fifty thousand dollars at once," he announced. "We shall draw up a legal document stating that each of these one hundred needy children is receiving five hundred dollars."

"The money will be in my custody—"

"Of course."

The little man smiled tearfully. "There is a notary public nearby who will witness the document, stamp it and make it legal."

The notary public was a long lean gentleman, notable chiefly for a drooping moustache and a chew of tobacco.

"You're just like an angel," the little man told Jones repeatedly.

BACK in New York, in his rooming house, Jones could not restrain his enthusiasm. He bounced delightfully on the bed, feeling as an angel probably must feel after some conspicuous benevolence. Charity, as the little man had said, was wonderful. Half the hundred thousand disposed of at one lick! The job wasn't going to be so tough. Jones even felt inclined to think of old Polyphemus Ward as a friend.

He desired to share his exaltation with someone, and thought, naturally of Funny Pegger. Why not? He could communicate with Funny Pegger via telephone, and at least tell Pegger he was making his own way gloriously.

Funny Pegger was listed in the telephone book. Shortly Jones had him on the wire.

"I—er—thought you might be wondering about me," Jones explained.

"I was!" yelled Funny Pegger.

"You were?"

"Yes. I was at the zoo this morning."

"Er—I do not see why you should be angry with me. You're—ah—barking."

"Am I?"

"However," added Jones hopefully, "isn't there a saying that a barking dog never bites?"

"How can he," asked Funny Pegger, "when he's biting?"

"I—ummm—just wanted to tell you I am progressing very well."

"Where are you now?"

"In a rooming house, in a room numbered eleven. And I believe the house is number seven on a thoroughfare designated as Cheare Street."

"The combination should bring you luck."

"Yes. I'm very grateful to Mr. Lee for bringing me here."

"Grateful—to who?"

"Lyman Lee."

"To *who?* Whom?"

"I told you—"

"Never mind. I must have heard you. I—oh, my—can you reach your bed from where you're sitting?"

"Why, yes."

"Can you take hold of the bedstead?"

"Oh, yes."

"Do that," said Funny Pegger, "and don't let go until I get there."

JONES contemplated the telephone, squinting one eye doubtfully, reflecting that Funny Pegger had sounded like a man seized with pains. But there was not a great deal of time to puzzle about the phenomenon, because a taxicab slid to a halt in the street in a remarkably few minutes, and Funny Pegger dashed in, accompanied by Vix, in person. Jones stared.

"Won't you come in and take your things off?" he asked politely.

"What kind of a girl," Vix inquired, "do you think I am?"

"Er—"

Funny Pegger said, "Don't mind her, Jones. I forgot to nail her down before I left." He frowned darkly at Vix. "You take a back seat. Keep your nose out of this."

Funny moved nearer to peer at Jones strangely.

Jones became uncomfortable. "Er—is something wrong?" he wanted to know.

"That's what I wonder."

"I don't understand."

"Nobody else does, either." Funny Pegger shook his head in a dazed way. "Boy, this gets me. You say Lyman Lee parked you here? Never mind—that's what you did say. And it ain't the natural ways of nature, at all. Lyman Lee—well, it just couldn't happen."

Vix nodded her head so vehemently that her bright hair flew.

"Lyman Lee never does anything for anybody except himself. He's for number one, always. He even tried to marry—"

"Ahem!" said Funny Pegger.

Vix bit her lip. "Well, he did. He tried to marry Polyphemus Ward's daughter for her money! Can you imagine anything worse than marrying a woman for money?"

"Yes," said Funny Pegger. "Marrying one for beads, like the Indians used to do."

The red-headed girl stamped a foot.

"Some day you're going to choke on one of those mummies you call gags," she said.

"Most cats can see in the dark," retorted the gag-man. "But some can talk."

The girl subsided.

"Now that I've disposed of her," Funny Pegger said, "maybe I can satisfy deep curiosity about you, Jones. First crack out of the box, tell me why you skipped out on us."

"Why—ah—I merely thought it advisable," Jones said uncomfortably.

"Come on, come on, why?"

"Well," explained Jones modestly, "it was my desire to keep you out of my difficulties, since you were kind enough to befriend me."

Funny Pegger eyed Vix. "I told you."

"Which makes twice in my life I lose," Vix sniffed. "The other time was when Schmeling smacked Louis. Go ahead. I'm busy catching my breath."

Jones wished she wouldn't act as if he was something which needed pursuing with a fly-swatter.

Funny Pegger scrutinized Jones.

"I've got it!" he yelled suddenly. "You're pleased about something!"

"Why—I—" Jones swallowed.

"Come on. What is it?"

"I have just given away fifty thousand dollars," Jones confessed, and grinned.

"You—to—" Funny Pegger staggered.

"Bear up, my lad," Vix advised. "Remember! Jones has a perfectly level head. You told me so."

"Levity," said Jones in an injured tone, "is a tendency opposite that of gravity, and designates a lack of earnestness in deportment or character."

"Fifty grand!" Funny Pegger croaked.

"Exactly."

"Gave it away!"

"Very successfully," Jones smiled.

"You—who took you?"

"What?" Jones frowned.

THEN he explained about the orphans. Funny Pegger said, "Let me hold onto something," and went over to take hold of the bedstead. He listened, then stared at the auburn-haired girl. "Your car is outside?" he croaked.

Vix dashed for the door. "I'm ahead of you."

Jones found himself bustled outside and shoved into a car which he suspected must be nearly as old as himself.

"Where were these orphans, Genius?"

"Genius?" Jones was puzzled.

"Genius," said the girl, "is you!"

"Genius. That's her idea of a name for you," Funny Pegger explained.

Jones thought it a dubious compliment.

"The orphans are in a northerly direction," he said.

The rambling orphan home looked more dilapidated than ever as Vix brought her car up before the place and made the elderly machine stop by switching off the motor while still in gear.

Jones stared around for orphans. Something slipped inside him.

Suddenly, Jones sprang out of the car, ran to the ancient house, wrenched the front door open and leaped inside. No one in sight. He ran through that room into another. He saw cots in neat rows. None were occupied. The next three rooms were all empty.

Vix and Funny Pegger came and stood beside Jones, but did not say anything, and he did not look at them. The only audible thing was Jones' breathing.

A long rumbling thump came from the rear of the house and Jones, racing to the sound, found himself looking at a middle-aged fellow, a stranger, who was dragging chairs to one wall and stacking them there, and who at once stopped working and stared at Jones.

"Funny thing," the stranger remarked as if to himself. "Them birds rented this place for a month, but only used it today."

He scratched his jaw.

"They got a lot of child actors up here, and was rehearsin' 'em all morning, or something," he added.

He shook his head.

"Then they all pulled their freight in a dickens of a hurry," he continued.

The man took out a tobacco plug and bit it.

"Anyhow, they paid me in advance, so let somebody else worry," he finished.

Jones walked out and got in the car, and Vix and Funny Pegger got in with him, and Vix started the engine, then Funny Pegger pulled in a deep breath.

"*Genius* Jones!" he said. "Of all the—"

Vix reached out and slapped him.

"Ouch!" yelled the gag-man. "What—"

"Only a dog," Vix said grimly, "bites a rabbit after it is caught."

SHE JERKED the gears in mesh, turned the wreck by backing into the driveway, then drove toward New York, and all three of them were silent, but Jones managed, somehow, to remain more speechless than the other two. Automobiles that tooted horns behind them seemed to jeer.

They entered Jones' rooming house, and Jones went to the door of the room used by the benevolent little man, and it was locked, but the lock splintered out with very little noise when he threw a shoulder against the door.

He stalked in, gazed gravely at the room's emptiness, then tramped to his own room, sank on the bed, and with a curious kind of interest, contemplated his hands.

He blocked the hands into fists. They became formidable. They were capable fists. Jones stood up.

"My trouble," he said emphatically, "has been imitation."

There was new firmness in Jones' voice.

"Until now," he stated, "Jones has been under the impression that he did not understand people. Jones wished to learn about people, so he has been imitating them."

Vix looked interested.

"A notable thing about sheep," Jones said, "is that they follow a leader. One sheep takes the initiative, and the others imitate. I have been a sheep. But a sheep who tried to follow many leaders." He hit the bed with a fist. "I have been a sheep!"

"Check!" Vix agreed.

"I have changed."

Vix nodded grimly. "It's about time."

"Instead of imitating people," Jones declared sharply, "I am going to do things to people!"

"Try, don't you mean?" Vix inquired.

"I mean what I said. Do things!" He repeated this as if he fancied the sound.

"What things, for instance?" Vix inquired.

"A variety." Jones put out his jaw. "I have thought of several."

"Great! Now you look just like Mussolini," Vix told him.

"You wouldn't," Funny Pegger asked Jones, "be thinking of looking for Lyman Lee."

"That," said Jones, "is my first project."

If Jones had anything additional to say, loud banging on the street door kept it back. Vix, bright hair flying, ran out into the hallway. She flashed back inside the next instant, slammed the door, turned the key.

"Lyman Lee is out there now!"

"Excellent!" Jones declared.

"It's not excellent at all," Vix headed Jones off. "Lyman has a flock of cops with him and they're hunting you."

CHAPTER XVI

THE CONQUERING HERO

SOUND OF POLICEMEN striding down the boarding-house hall was as the noise of the Indians coming. As awesome an uproar as he'd ever heard. The newborn Jones—the new man—shook. The new Jones, that determined d'Artagnan who was going to do things to people, quailed. Almost, he fled back into the nest of misfortune where he'd watched. But Jones gave the newborn artificial respiration with words.

"Ram," he announced, "is the male of the sheep species, hence the most courageous. Also an engine of war for butting or battering. Er—the word denotes qualities of strength. I," he said impressively, "have become a ram."

He sprang erect. "The window!" he commanded. "Open it and see if retreat is feasible."

Vix got the window open and looked. "Coast clear," she said.

"Out!" Jones said.

"But "

"Out!" Jones thundered. "Action is imperative."

The red-headed girl looked as if she wanted to discuss it. The whack of a policeman's fist on the door changed her mind. She went out of the window. Jones sprang out after her—a tall young man, wide at the shoulders, with brick-colored hair and a shaky but earnestly summoned expression of ferocity.

The window opened into backyards with clotheslines, ugly wood-fences, old boxes, tin cans, dog-kennels—everything that might be expected in the backyards of a block of New York

City rooming houses. They fled across this hodgepodge, climb-
ing fences, upsetting ashcans, and landed with almost a complete lack of ceremony in a yard where a long man with a
freckled hide was sunbathing in the nude, and he sprang up,
clothed only in a newspaper he had been reading, and swore in
Finnish as they ran on into a back door, through a house, where
a large blonde woman began to yell bloody murder, and on out
through a front door. The fugitives ran a block, and Jones called
a stop.

"Mr. Pegger," Jones puffed, "you will detour and get Miss
Vix's car."

"But—"

"Transportation is a necessity. Obtain the car, please."

FUNNY PEGGER squinted in an amazed way at Jones, then
dashed off. A few moments later, he returned with the old car,
and they drove away from there.

"Where to?" Funny Pegger asked Jones, who was breathing
deeply.

"Er—Miss Vix, do you reside in an establishment of your
own?" Jones inquired.

"I have an apartment, if that's what you mean. And just to
keep the record straight—I pay the rent myself!"

"Good," said Jones. "We shall—ah—ask you to shelter us."

"You—what?"

"I—shelter us."

"Shelter you? Listen, if you think I take in stray hitch-hikers
off icebergs and fat gag men, you're mistaken! Guess again."

"I—ah—think that is unreasonable."

"The fat part is unreasonable," said Funny Pegger. "I'm just
plump."

"Mr. Pegger, do you know the location of her dwelling place?"

"Yeah."

"Then pilot us to it," Jones ordered.

"You do, fat man, and I'll never speak to you again," Vix raged.

Funny Pegger sighed. "I'll just drive around until we decide which dog gets the bone."

"You—er, won't?" Jones inquired.

"Right," Vix snapped, "—er, won't."

"You can see," said the gag-man, "that it's a case of being bitten by the polar bear or clawed by the tiger."

Jones considered this. He wanted to waver, but he felt that it was a crucial moment, a deciding point at which he either went on being Jones, man of action, individualist, or he slunk back to the fold with the other sheep.

"Miss Vix—" Jones ventured. "I—"

"*No!*"

"You are involved in this too deeply to withdraw. You got me, an accused murderer, out of jail yesterday, and you were consorting with me a few minutes ago when the police came."

"Consorting, indeed!" Vix flamed. "Sounds indecent. And another thing—you got me into this!"

"On the contrary," said Jones, "you sought me out—I suspect, for the pleasure of further irritating me. I am sorry, but you must—er—take your medicine."

Vix nipped her shapely lower lip, tapped a toe angrily.

"Well," said Funny Pegger, "where do I drive to?"

"To my apartment!" Vix said, and stamped the floor.

Enjoying a warm glow of victory, Jones arrived at Vix's little apartment, looked around and approved. The place did not have the sumptuousness of Polyphemus Ward's yacht, nor was it as ordinary as the boarding house, but rather in between. There were little frills, feminine, pleasant, and rooms included one for living, one for sleeping, a kitchen, a bath. Jones ambled into the bedroom and gave the bed an experimental punch. Beds were his first interest, soft beds of civilization being in such contrast to hard pallet of Arctic moss that Jones had never ceased to be intrigued.

"This one seems above average," he remarked.

"You," Vix informed him, "sleep on the kitchen floor."

"I—kitchen floor?"

"You can put your feet in the refrigerator and feel at home."

"I shall decide that point later."

Funny Pegger smoked a cigarette and seemed thoughtful. "Want some advice, Jones?"

Jones brightened. "I would welcome it."

"Give yourself up to the police. Take the fifty thousand you've got left and fight the murder rap. With that kind of dough to spend, you might beat it."

Jones' hopes dropped. "I—er, can't."

"Why not?"

Jones wondered if this wasn't at least the thousandth time he had regretted promising Polyphemus Ward not to tell anybody about their deal with the hundred thousand dollars.

"I—well—just can't," Jones mumbled disconsolately.

HE WENT into the living room, selected a comfortable chair, collapsed, folded his hands, and his attitude became one of deep concentration. He found that he had to overdo this concentration to keep from getting an utterly defeated feeling. With the police hot on his trail, how could he give away fifty thousand dollars? And what about the fifty thousand he had lost?

Vix and Funny Pegger contemplated Jones. They were impressed. To Vix, this was a surprise, since from the first, she had noticed that whenever she was around Jones, she wanted to throw things at him. It was a sort of nervous reaction. An instinct. But of late she had discovered that Jones gave her a feeling akin to awe and she resented it. She wanted to bite him with words.

"Genius Jones," she remarked, "is becoming a Titanic personality who needs no advice. He makes us feel rather small, like a little grub."

"Little grub," said Funny Pegger, "is an idea. I'm hungry."

"All I have is some apples," Vix snapped. "I can't cook, and if you think I intend to learn at this late date, you should have an alienist look at your head."

She went into the kitchen, rummaged, and came back with two apples, one of which she handed to Funny Pegger, who inspected it and found a wormhole which looked as though it was inhabited.

"Here, you take this one," Funny said. "I'm a vegetarian."

Jones continued to sit and think, occasionally clamping his fingers on the arm of the chair, as though he had encountered a stretch of rough mental road.

"I'm gonna get a newspaper," Funny Pegger said, "and see how famous we're getting."

He got his hat and departed. Jones remained in the chair, his chin cupped in a palm, and was more or less that way when Funny Pegger returned with a handful of newspapers.

"Look at these," he said.

ACCUSED SLAYER ESCAPES
At Least Two Others Implicated; Girl Aids Flight

"That's us," Pegger announced gloomily. He glared at the newspapers, pushing out his lips as Mussolini must have done when he read about the Spanish chasing his soldiers into a harbor. Suddenly, he hurled the journal to the floor and jumped on it. "They identified me!" he groaned.

"My pals!" he yelled. "I worked with these newspaper clunks! What do you think they called me in these stories?"

"What?" Vix inquired.

"A second-rate gag-man with an ever-ready fund of second-hand jokes! My pals! They'd eat their own brother!"

"Are you just finding it out?" Vix said. "By the way, what did they call me?"

"Quick," yelled the man Jones. "Speed is essential."

"An unknown red-headed beauty."

"Beautiful, eh?"

"Don't mean a thing. A newspaper man can't write red-headed without putting beauty after it."

Jones suddenly came out of his trance and jumped to his feet. "I am ready," he said, "to proceed."

"Toward the electric chair, perhaps?" Vix inquired.

Jones managed to head off a wince before it had visible proportions.

Jones ran fingers through his red hair. "First," he announced, "I shall summarize briefly the obstacles which I must demolish."

"Demolish is a good word, too," Vix said.

Jones resolutely ignored her, and held up one capable looking forefinger. "First," he said, "there is the remaining fifty thousand dollars which I must give to needy persons."

Funny Pegger came bolt upright. "Jones! You madman! You idiot! Are you still—"

"Second," Jones interrupted, holding up another finger, "I must make fifty thousand dollars to replace what I lost, or recover the money from whoever got it." He consulted the clock. "I have twenty-eight days and nine hours in which to do that."

"Hell and damnation!" Funny Pegger shouted. "Jones, why the devil you trying to give away a hundred thousand dollars?"

Up went Jones' third finger. "I must defeat unknown persons who are plotting against me," he said.

Vix tossed her bright hair.

"Now that you've got it in a nutshell," she said, "crack it!"

"Nothing around here needs cracking," Funny Pegger muttered. "It's cracked enough as it stands now."

Jones looked uncomfortable. "I do not think you are justified in insinuating there may be a flaw in my mentality."

Funny Pegger stamped the floor. He waved his arms. "Justified? I'm not justified? My remarkable friend, when anybody goes around trying to give away one hundred thousand dollars, something is screwy. But *screwy!*"

"It is perfectly sensible," Jones insisted.

"Tell us!" Pegger pleaded. "Make us understand."

"I'm sorry, but I cannot explain," Jones said with flat finality.

"Why not?"

"I made a promise."

Funny Pegger fell heavily in a chair and fanned himself with both hands. "This is gonna give me heart trouble." He pointed a ringer at Jones. "Ain't I your manager? Don't you want to take me into your confidence?"

"You're fired," Jones said.

"I'm what?"

Jones help up a fourth finger. "Fourth," he said, "I am now getting rid of my manager."

Funny Pegger stared at the four fingers. "You've counted up to four fingers in the trap, Jones. What about the others?"

Jones scrutinized his hands. "They are competent hands—I hope."

"What about Glacia?"

"Er—Glacia? Oh, yes. Glacia."

"Don't Glacia rate a finger, too?"

"I—finger?"

"If I recollect, she was throwing her hooks into you."

"Hooks?"

Funny Pegger grew grave. "Say, just how far did that get?"

"Ah—I—well—" Jones found himself embarrassed.

Vix was now staring at Jones.

"Just who is this Glacia person?" the red-headed young woman demanded with some frost.

Jones decided he would rather, much rather, not explain about Glacia. He said so, as firmly as he could.

"But I prefer," Vix insisted, "to discuss her."

"Ah—we shall drop Glacia," Jones said desperately.

"That," Vix said violently, "is what you'd better do."

Jones stared at her.

FUNNY PEGGER peered at Vix, then grasped the back of his neck with one hand, a Pegger habit when the brain was probing, after which he began to grin. He wiped the smirk off when he saw Vix eyeing him. He shifted subjects.

"So I'm fired, eh?" he remarked to Jones.

"I did not hire you in the first place," Jones reminded him. "You merely informed me you were my manager. But answering your question—yes, you are fired."

"As an ex-employee, may I ask why this change in you, Jones?"

"Change?"

"Where did the sheep-like Jones go?"

"But I told you. This is my new attitude," Jones explained. "Hitherto, I have been convinced that, due to my unusual upbringing, I lacked experience to cope with the world boldly. I am changing my philosophy. Henceforth, I go get them."

"Sounds all right in theory," Funny Pegger said dubiously. "Who do you get first?"

"Whom," Vix said. "Whom do you go get?"

"I think I shall—ah—sort of try my new claws out on Polyphemus Ward," Jones replied.

Vix said: "Oh, oh, *oh!*"

Funny Pegger shuddered. "Do you want carved angels, or just a plain tombstone?"

"I beg your pardon?"

"Never mind. You might as well be eaten by the lion as by the jackals."

Jones swallowed. "The new Jones," he said bravely, "is not readily frightened."

"The Genius Jones!" Vix suggested.

"Exactly." Jones considered. "Genius Jones—you know, that rather fascinates me. I have never needed any name other than Jones, but here in New York, I notice approximately seven columns of Jones in the telephone book, which is confusing. However, none are named Genius."

Genius Jones strode to the telephone and seated himself. He had called Polyphemus Ward once before, and he had a memory developed by memorizing whole books, so he recollected the Ward number. He called and got someone on the wire who objected to putting him through to one of the world's most important financiers.

"This is a matter of a million dollars," Jones said.

He'd discovered money was the magic word which got you through to Polyphemus Ward instantly.

"Mr. Ward.... This is Jones—"

"I've told you time and again," Polyphemus Ward yelled, "that I want to be shut of you until you give away that hundred thousand!"

Jones looked a trifle desperate. "Be quiet, please," he said. "This telephone seems to lose efficiency when you scream. Also, you sound, er—silly."

Jones held the receiver away from his ear until it stopped smoking.

CHAPTER XVII

A GIRL IN THE ARMS

"MR. WARD," JONES said firmly, "you can render me a measure of service." Jones made an effort to sound both friendly and firm—the new man stooping pleasantly to an inferior.

"What? What? Measure of what?"

"You can do something for me."

"Young man, who do you think you're talking to? What the devil do you think I am?"

"I haven't time to take that up in detail," Jones said. "The point is this: You are going to perform a service for me."

"I most certainly am not! Except stomp on your sassy face when I catch you. By Satan, I know what I'll do. I'll hire detectives to help the police find you!"

Jones cleared his throat. "They might be no more efficient at that than they were at finding your missing daughter, Janice." Shocked sound came over the wire, followed by silence.

"How—how did you know about that?" Polyphemus Ward asked.

"Everyone knows you had a daughter who left you six months ago because she couldn't stand your devilishness."

"That's a lie!" yelled Polyphemus Ward. "Who said so?"

Jones ignored the question. "About your doing the thing I want done—er, you are going to do it? I will"—Jones glanced at Vix and Funny Pegger—"not mention the reason specifically, because others are present. It is your wish, I believe, that the matter be kept secret."

Polyphemus Ward gulped. "You mean that hundred-thousand-dollar test and—and—you idiot! You stupid, unwashed refugee from an iceberg! Shut up! Someone might hear us!"

"The newspapers would be glad to hear about it."

"You—you—"

"So would Wall Street. They would think you had gone mad. The stock of the companies you own would probably drop half. I wonder what that would cost you?"

"You—you—"

Polyphemus Ward got words coming, kept them coming in a barrage, such words as Jones had never heard, because there are no dictionaries of profanity. The volcano finally blew itself dry.

Jones frowned. "Here," he said, "is what you are going to do for me."

"What? In a pig's eye, I will!" The man of money swore some more. "I'm done! The deal is off! Give me back that hundred thousand, or I'll see you in the penitentiary! The whole thing is off. You hear? Off!"

"You made a bargain," Jones insisted. "It was no idea of mine. And now you are going through with it, willing or not."

"I'm cursed if I will! Uh—what do you want done?"

"I wish you to bail Funny Pegger and a girl named Vix out of jail," Jones said.

Behind Jones, Funny Pegger sprang to his feet and yelped: "Jail? Jail? What's this?"

Jones waved Pegger back and said into the telephone, "You will bail Mr. Pegger and er—Miss Vix out of confinement, providing they are in need of such aid."

"I won't! Let them rot in there!" roared Polyphemus Ward. "Who is this Vix?"

"That is all," Jones said. "Er—I do not think of anything further. Goodbye."

"Goodbye, dammit! And don't call me again! Uh—are you all right? Need anything else? Not, by gad, that you'll get it!"

"No," Jones said, "but thank you."

JONES hung up, and the next instant, Funny Pegger grabbed him and shook him. "Jail! What was that talk about jail?" Funny Pegger shouted. "We're not in jail."

"You might be, you know," Jones explained.

"Jail? Me?" Pegger bounced up and down in his agitation. "Not me! What do you think I ran away from your rooming house for? Why have I been parked in here instead of out seeing about that job that I was gonna get writing for the radio? Already I've been in the can once on your account. That's my limit. What do you think I am?"

Jones got out his handkerchief and mopped his forehead.

"I—er—made that telephone call for the purpose of ascertaining if I could bluff a man," he announced. "But I also had an objective." He looked embarrassed. "You two have befriended me, and as a result find yourselves in complications with the law. I was endeavoring to devise some expedient whereby you might be aided."

"So you made old Polyphemus Ward promise to bail us out if we got in, eh?"

"I—yes. I knew about bail. You kindly explained bail to me when you and I were—ah—in jail ourselves."

"Murder," said the gag-man, "is different."

"Ah—different?"

"Bail don't do you no good."

"Oh, my," Jones muttered forlornly. "I did not know that."

"Vix and I are blamed close to being accessories after the fact. I don't know whether bail will do *us* any good, either."

Jones inspected the pattern of the rug. "I am sorry," he muttered. "I thought I was helping you." He gazed at Funny Pegger and Vix. "I do appreciate your kindness, you know," he said.

Funny Pegger looked queer and got up and came over and gave Jones' shoulder a punch.

"Sure, guy, I know," he said sincerely. "That was a smart move you just made. On the level, it was." The gag-man shook his head slowly. "But it gets me. Old Polyphemus Ward is a pill nobody ever swallowed. Plenty have tried. He's hard. Old Polyphemus wasn't born—he was quarried."

Jones nodded. "Yes. Yes, I have secured such an impression. However, he listens to reason."

"Reason? What reason? The talk you gave him sounded like blackmail to me."

Jones mopped his brow again. "I cannot discuss that matter."

"You've got some dirt on Polyphemus Ward?"

"Dirt?" Jones put on a look of determination. "Polyphemus Ward is in the notion of cooperating with me, but I do not wish to make any more elaborate explanation."

Funny Pegger windmilled his arms.

"You're gonna drive me bugs!" he yelled. "Don't you realize I'm your manager?"

"You have been discharged," Jones said patiently.

Funny Pegger put his head back.

"Ye-o-o-w-w!" he yelled wildly. Then he went over and fell into a chair.

JONES eyed his two companions, and wiped his forehead. The eccentric behavior of Pegger confused him, and he wished Vix would not persist in regarding him as she would prospective quarry for a fly swatter. She rattled him. He had problems to cope with, and the erratic actions of his companions made it hard for his mind to cope with them properly. He began to pace circles around the apartment living room, head bowed to invite thought, jaw thrust out, hands swinging at his sides.

"Napoleon," suggested Vix, "usually tucked his left hand in the front of his coat. And don't stop now to tell me who Napoleon was. I know."

Jones frowned at the red-headed young woman who was fast getting to be his personal briar. Suddenly, he had an idea.

"Do you," he inquired, "apply artificial coloring to your hair?"

"Do I—" Vix surveyed him as if in search of a place to bite. "Them's fighting words, mister!"

"I merely wish," Jones said stiffly, "to inquire if you can purchase a chemical compound which will darken my hair. It is my intention to don a disguise."

"Scat," Vix said, "before I explode! Is my hair dyed! You iceberg hitch-hiker!"

Jones became vexed. "Gab," he announced, "comes from the Old French *gaber,* and at one time meant to project the teeth, but now designates prattle, chatter, unmeaningful talk, a strong possession of the female sex."

Vix parted her lips, plainly having a great deal to say, but instead of saying it, she squealed, for Jones had picked her up bodily. Vix's pert face became a racetrack for emotions, all of them fully life-sized, as Jones carried her toward the door.

Jones deposited Vix outside.

"Aren't we," Vix asked caustically, "going to fight for my honor?"

"I—honor?"

"My error. Just a mistake in identity. I thought it might be flesh and blood. Pardon, please. It's just a walking collection of definitions."

Jones was bewildered. "Er—purchase the hair dye," he commanded. "And acquire some food. After which you may come back in."

And he closed the door and locked her out.

Jones had acted solely with the idea of getting something done without a lengthy argument which he felt he couldn't win, anyway. He had taken Vix in his arms for business reasons—but instead of walking away from the door, he stood there and peered at the panel, not seeing the door, exactly, for his visionary capacity seemed in temporary suspension. He was experiencing sensations. He felt warmish. The way his pulse had commenced acting was best described as boom, boom! He felt dizzy. Boom, boom! Inside him. Boom! Boom! Boom! Boom!

"Goodness gracious!" Jones gasped.

CHAPTER XVIII

FOR LOVE OR MONEY

INTERNAL COMMOTIONS WERE things with which
Jones had very little experience. Up to the moment of quitting
his iceberg, the problems of his daily life had been almost wholly
external. Food. Shelter. Defense from unfriendly animals. But
things had changed almost overnight. Having exposed his outer
shell to the complications of civilized existence, he had found
that things could go on in the inner ego that were fully as
violent, intricate, and astonishing. He had kissed Glacia and
his heart had got into an elevator and swooped dizzily around
his insides. He held a red-haired girl in his arms and even more
sensational things had happened. A munitions factory had just
blown up in his stomach. Star shells ascended, screaming, to
his brain.

With a dazed expression, he held up his hand and erected
another finger.

"What's that for?" Funny Pegger asked.

"Er—Vix."

"Vix?"

"I—it just occurred to me that she had become a factor."

The gag-man shook his head and made a clucking noise.
"How many fingers between Vix and Glacia?"

"I—none."

"Not enough," said Funny Pegger gloomily. "Not nearly
enough!"

Jones wished he had never promised Polyphemus Ward not

to tell anybody about that unhappy hundred thousand dollars. It would have been a relief to spill the whole thing into Pegger's lap. The gag-man had a breezy way of talking about problems, a manner which made them seem less acute.

Vix came back carrying a bottle of hair dye and an armload of groceries, but she was obviously resentful about her shopping trip, and she frosted Jones with a look, and said nothing, and began preparations for dinner. Vix had said she could not cook, but that was an understatement, because the meal she turned out was tasty. Civilized foods were by now not as much a mystery to Jones as they had been when he was first taken off the iceberg, and he managed to get through this dinner with only one uncomfortable experience, that one coming when he sprinkled a large quantity of the violently strong sauce known as tabasco on a pork chop, and as a result had to dangle his tongue in a glass of water while his eyes watered uncomfortably.

Unexpectedly Vix threw her napkin down. "I'm through! I won't get mixed up in this when I don't even know what it is!"

That led to a battle in which Vix put up a gallant fight for her rights—and lost. Finally she abandoned the field. "Look," she said. "I'm just a babe in the woods. I admit it. I quit. I'm going to sleep, heaven willing. And there's something behind that door that comes down and hits you in the head. I think it's a bed. You two take that—and I hope it crushes you both." Then, head held high, she retreated to the bedroom and locked the door, and for good measure, made a noisy business of stacking chairs against the door.

"**SHE SEEMS** piqued with us," Jones said thoughtfully. "It is a pity."

"She seems something," Funny Pegger admitted. "But I don't think you called the turn."

"Turn?"

"Skip it. That's my secret." Funny Pegger considered, then chuckled. "No, I don't think you called the turn. You wouldn't. You lack experience."

"Lack experience?"

"With the deadly half of the species."

Jones found himself reminded of something. "Hmmm. I suppose I am inexperienced. Ah—by the way, what is Vix's profession?"

"Vix? She's a warbler on a commercial spot."

"A what?"

Funny Pegger explained: "Vix is a singer on a commercial radio program which goes on the air once a week, and she makes two hundred dollars a week. *Sabe?*"

"Oh, I see. But won't this keep her from her employment?"

"Hardly. She's on the air a total of about five minutes each week."

Jones was astounded. "Do you mean that it is possible to earn a comfortable livelihood by working only five minutes each week. Why, that is only twenty minutes per month, or a total of four hours of work in a year. Imagine! Working four hours and making nine thousand six hundred dollars!"

"You're confounded, eh?"

"Somewhat."

"So are a lot of people. It's just one of those things."

Jones fell silent and closed his eyes, but instead of sleeping, he found himself mentally gathering the remarkable aspects of mankind and lumping them together. They made a pile that he could not understand. Four hours a year.... Doubtless men with shovels dug eight hours a day, six days a week, throughout the same year, for less financial return.

"Brains," said Funny Pegger unexpectedly, "is the answer."

"Eh?"

"I got a hunch what you're thinking. The world pays off on brains."

Jones hoped so. He intended to tackle his difficulties with brains. He had noticed, in comparing himself with other men, that he had more than an average share of brawn, but the amount of brains was more ethereal, the quantity he possessed more difficult to measure. His thoughts, prodding around, began to stir up the resting animals that were his troubles, so that he saw them in a milling pack, and distinguished their teeth. He was awed.

"I believe," Jones remarked in the darkness, "that earning money is more difficult than giving it away to people."

"Such has been my experience," Funny Pegger chuckled.

"Then," said Jones, "I shall first make fifty thousand dollars."

"That sounds very sensible."

"Thank you."

"—except that you said something about making it in twenty-eight days and some odd hours."

"Yes. I must make it, and also give it away in that interval, as well as give away the fifty thousand I already have. I was to give away a total of one hundred thousand dollars, you know, within thirty days after reaching New York."

"My God, I know!" Funny Pegger said wildly. "Don't bring *that* up again!"

Jones took a turn about the room, hands jammed in his trouser pockets. "How," he inquired, "does one go about making fifty thousand dollars in twenty-eight days?"

"You're asking me?" Funny Pegger demanded.

"Yes."

"You're sure asking the right guy."

"I'm glad of that," Jones said, relieved.

"I've only spent a little over twenty-eight *years* trying to make fifty thousand."

"*Years?*"

"At present date," Funny Pegger said, "I've got four dollars and eighty-six cents."

"I had hoped," Jones complained, disappointed, "that you would be more fitted to advise me."

Later Funny Pegger demonstrated a snore which could have emanated only from a man deeply asleep.

WHEN Jones awoke, it was broad daylight, and he lay wondering if he hadn't a subconscious mind, or something, that went ahead while he was asleep and did sensible thinking, or else sleep was cool rain that washed away mental fogs and left everything clear-cut, for he found that the dawn had brought him a clear idea of the sensible way to proceed. He would pick his troubles off one at a time, the first, and possibly the most troublesome, being the missing fifty thousand dollars. He would concentrate on that. Hopping out of bed, he strode into the bathroom and nearly scalded himself before he discovered how to manipulate the hot and cold faucets of the shower. The morning was sultry, foggy, with the sky leaking rain that ran off the roofs in strings and squirmed along the gutters, and the bleat of automobiles sounded like barking seals. It was a morose, drizzling world which Jones contemplated through the window, but he believed he could cope with it.

He knocked on the bedroom door.

"Go away!" Vix ordered sleepily. "I'm in the habit of getting up around noon."

"In five minutes," Jones said, endeavoring to sound convincing, "I shall expect you to be preparing our morning meal."

"In five minutes, I'll be asleep again, please God."

The pert voice through the door was not at all obedient, not meek, and Jones got the feeling that it was a symbol of the difficulty he might have in picking his troubles off one at a time. He was perturbed. Rather than engage in a crucial struggle this early in the morning, he decided to get his own breakfast. The mechanics of the gas stove baffled him, but he went ahead and turned several gimmicks, applied a match, and there was a loud cough and an uprush of flame which nearly relieved him of eyebrows.

He called Funny Pegger. "This device has me puzzled." Jones pointed at the stove.

The gag-man shook his head wonderingly. "You can't light a gas stove," he remarked, "but you expect to make fifty thousand dollars in—um—it's twenty-seven days and some odd hours now, isn't it?"

Jones stood by and watched Funny Pegger crack eggs, mix them and concoct an omelette.

"Egg," Jones remarked, "the oval or spheroid reproductive body produced by birds, reptiles and some animals. The *membrana putaminis,* or skin is usually associated with a hard calcareous shell in the case of birds, while the skin of most animal eggs is more or less resilient."

"Meaning eggs can all be cracked?" Funny Pegger inquired.

"Why, yes. Cracked. Yes, indeed."

"And eggs can be scrambled, too. Let's hope you don't scramble yours."

JONES sat before the window and contemplated the weather. It had ceased raining and the sun shone, but there came a few whoops of thunder and a splatter of lightning, and it began pouring again—something like the progress of a man's life, Jones reflected.

Vix put in an appearance, yawning elaborately, wearing a low-cut hostess gown which revealed the nice shape of her arms, disclosed the exquisite lines of her back, and rather assisted imagination otherwise.

"It's new," she said. "Like it?"

Funny Pegger wanted to know where the rest of it was.

"Goodness!" said Jones, who was definitely thrilled.

Vix swept into the kitchen to prepare her breakfast, and Jones loosened his collar and contemplated the kitchen door, wishing to consult Vix, and at the same time, not relishing the task. He felt the need of a quotation to bolster determination.

"The diamond," he stated, "is the most unyielding substance known, with a hardness measurement of 10, and specific gravity of 3.52."

"Where do diamonds come from?" Funny Pegger inquired.

"Why, from blue clays in South Africa, and elsewhere."

"Wrong. They come from suckers."

"Suckers?"

"Skip it. I keep thinking of the fifty thousand dollars in your jeans, and their brothers that got away." The gag-man sighed and stared morosely at the floor.

Having gripped his courage firmly, Jones entered the kitchen.

He said: "Miss Vix. I understand you earn nine thousand six hundred dollars with four hours' work."

"What?"

"Er—you work five minutes per week. I understand."

Vix brushed a tendril of copper-colored hair back from impudent blue eyes.

"Is this a proposal?" she inquired.

"I—proposal?"

"If it is," Vix said, "I hope you're good at dodging things."

Jones hesitated, confused, because there was that boom-boom inside again. To keep to his point and prevent the inner man from getting excited and dashing into the jungles, he made his mind drop everything for a moment and dwell on the iceberg, a procedure he'd discovered had a cool, stabilizing effect.

"I desire," Jones said earnestly, "to make money."

"Who doesn't?"

"I wish to make fifty thousand dollars," Jones continued doggedly, "and the sooner the better, because after making it, I must turn around and give it away."

"When you talk like that," Vix said, "people scream and fall over. Haven't you noticed?"

With a small sound, two pieces of toast popped out of the automatic toaster, and simultaneously, two upright wrinkles of impatience appeared on Jones' forehead.

"Ah—how do people make money quickly?" he asked solemnly.

Vix cupped her chin with a palm in an attitude of concentration. "Stock market," she said with equal solemnity.

"Eh?"

"The stock market."

"By that," Jones ventured, "I presume you mean the purchase and resale of industrial securities at a profit?"

"That's the grass which lures the lambs."

"Er—where does one find this stock market?"

"Wall Street."

Jones brightened. "Wall Street," he announced, "is not straight, has a river at one end, and at the other end a church which was built by the pirate, Captain Kidd."

"I've heard that one," Vix said.

"Who hasn't?" Funny asked.

"Can you," Jones suggested, "mention further means of making money quickly?"

"A crap game."

"And what is a crap game?"

"A pastime of chance," Vix explained, "otherwise known as galloping dominoes or African golf, wherein you lays your money and you watches 'em roll, uttering such remarks as: 'Stay away, snake eyes!' 'Baby needs shoes!' or 'Eightur from Decatur!'"

"It sounds rather silly."

"Then there's the nags."

"The—what?"

"Ponies. Oat burners. They run races, and you bet on the horse that wins. With luck."

Jones drew himself a drink of water from the faucet, at the same time looking thoughtful. "In these methods you have just mentioned," he remarked doubtfully, "an element of chance seems to exist."

"An element?" Funny snorted.

"Nobody makes money in a hurry unless they gamble," Vix said.

"They don't?"

"Not," Vix said, "that I've noticed."

CHAPTER XIX

A HERO MUST TO BATTLE GO

JONES MADE HIS way out of the kitchen, selected a chair in the living room, and sat down. He accepted what he had just been told at face value, although none of the three money-making methods seemed sound in a general economic way, since they entailed, unless he was mistaken, the taking of re-muneration without return of useful service—getting some-thing for nothing, which was against the laws of nature as he understood them. He had noticed that every living creature had to work to survive; the Arctic fox had to chase the snowshoe rabbit for food, the rabbit had to hunt grass, and the grass had to send out roots; it seemed a profound natural law that each must pay with effort for what was received, and it followed that it might be unsound for men to go contrary to that law. Jones did not, unfortunately, let his mind walk far enough up that road. Nor did it occur to him that Vix had been kidding. He still lacked the experience with people to tell with accuracy when they were being facetious and when they were in earnest.

He wished to earn fifty thousand quickly, he had asked Vix about means, and her suggestions—stock market, craps or ponies—seemed logical, so Jones intended to try one or all, preferably without delay.

"We shall disguise Jones," he announced abruptly.

Disguising Jones required an hour. Funny Pegger and Vix dyed his red hair a somber black, and his eyebrows the same hue; his suit was dark gray and there were probably hundreds of suits exactly like it in New York City, so they did not do anything about that.

"Do you think I shall manage?" he asked anxiously.

"They probably won't recognize you," Vix said. "But I wouldn't bet on anything else."

Funny Pegger took the cigar he was smoking from his mouth and contemplated it distastefully.

"What would you be planning to do?" he asked. "Or would that be a secret, too?"

"I've been thinking," Jones replied.

"Thinking," said Funny Pegger, "has killed a lot of people."

"I—"

"But *not* thinking has killed more."

Jones finished squinting at himself in the mirror, then went to the window and observed that it had stopped raining. The air was cooler. The sun shone invitingly, and he was reminded that he was dallying away time.

"I am," he stated, "going forth to make fifty thousand dollars." He was, to be precise, going to invest some of Ward's remaining fifty thousand in Genius Jones, Unincorporated. It was, he felt, a likely proposition.

Funny Pegger grinned. "Take a plenty o' powder and ball for that thar musket, Daniel Boone, 'cause it's a long, long trail you're a startin' on."

Jones frowned disapprovingly at the gag-man's levity. "I am," he said, "in earnest."

"They say you have to be. You gotta plan?"

"I intend to utilize the stock market, the ponies, or the craps."

Funny Pegger let fall his cigar. "The *what?*"

"The craps. I have been told they make one money."

"You—who—who—?"

Vix, coming out of the kitchen, stared at the gag-man. "Owl," she remarked, "is a large-eyed bird which roosts in trees, and eats mice and says *who-who!*"

Funny Pegger peered at Jones, "Who gave you such ideas?" He whirled on Vix. "He's off again!" he shouted.

"He's some fun, eh?" Vix inquired.

The gag-man groaned. "He wants to make fifty thousand dollars."

"But he's got one," Vix said.

"I know. He's going to use it to play the stock market, bet on the horses, or shoot craps."

"Well, I'm not going to worry—what? *What?* He's going to do what?" Vix took a stiff step forward and stared at Jones.

THE CIGAR Funny Pegger had dropped was burning the rug, a curl of yellow smoke rising slowly. Jones, disturbed by the way his companions stared at him, changed from one foot to the other. "Er—good morning," he said nervously. "I shall leave now."

Vix made vague swimming motions with both hands. "Fifty thousand—stock market—horses—craps—" Suddenly she shouted at Funny Pegger, "Don't you let him out of this apartment!"

"I won't. Don't worry."

Jones took two steps in retreat. "I must confess," he stated, "that I find you are both entirely incomprehensible to me."

"Jones!" Funny Pegger begged. "Don't you leave here with that money."

"But why should you be so concerned?"

"This is the first time I ever had a friend with fifty thousand dollars."

Jones was vaguely resenting the situation, resenting rather his inability to adjust himself to the erratic behavior of the gag-man and the red-headed girl. It bothered him, for he found himself liking both of them remarkably well. He could see that they were not in sympathy with his desire to make fifty thousand dollars at once, and he believed he saw their viewpoint, or rather their lack of the correct one—they didn't know just how necessary it was for him to make the money, and it was certain they couldn't comprehend why he had to give away the fifty thousand as soon as he made it. The fifty he already had, as well. He, of course, could not explain, and that deadlocked a situation wherein Funny Pegger and Vix would go on misunderstanding him and opposing his efforts.

The only solution he could see was to leave them and strike out on his own. That would save argument, at least.

"I—goodbye," he said.

He started for the door at a walk, saw Funny Pegger was going to try to head him off, made a jump, got there first, got the key out, bounded through, slammed the door, and locked it on the outside.

"Jones!" Funny Pegger hammered the door. "Jones! You can't do this!"

"I fail to see," Jones called through the panel, "what is to prevent me."

He walked down the apartment-house corridor, passed through the foyer, stepped out under a neat green awning which extended across the sidewalk—and a strange voice addressed him firmly.

"Just a second, buddy," the voice said.

Jones found himself looking at a large blue-coated policeman.

IT FLASHED over Jones that he had two alternatives—he could hit the policeman and run, or he could run without hitting the policeman. This was an impressive cop, large, remarkably lean and athletic for a policeman.

"Does that car"—the cop pointed at a lead-colored coupe at the curb—"belong to you?"

"I— No, indeed," Jones said.

"Okay, then," said the officer. "I figured you was a guy who would know a fire plug when you saw one."

Jones walked on with a dry taste in his mouth and a curiosity as to what the cop would have done if he'd known he was addressing the remark to probably the one man in New York who did *not* know what a fire plug might be.

"Gracious!" Jones exclaimed. "What a narrow escape!"

The splash in his emotional pool which the appearance of the cop had caused, subsided as he strode along, and with the settling of the ripples he realized that he felt better than before it happened. It was a relief to know the police were not going to recognize him with his hair dyed; he had proved that point. Why, he was free to go anywhere he wished! His jaw lifted, his breath came more freely than it had for several hours, and a spring entered his step.

The morning air had a washed freshness, sidewalk and street looked scrubbed, the people stepped out with the vigor that a recent rainstorm seems to impart, and the proprietors of stores were rolling up awnings, while the numerous taxi drivers, for once, were giving each other pleasant looks.

He compared a new feeling of freedom with his previous mental discomfort, and frowned critically. His troubles must be having more of an effect on him than he'd realized.

Jones spoke seriously to himself. "If," he remarked, "dispensing with one problem affords such relief, it might be a good thing to pursue the idea further."

He deliberately made his mind take the matter of quickly making fifty thousand dollars, chuck it in a cubbyhole for later attention, and in its place substitute one of his personal thorns—Lyman Lee. As Jones thought about Lyman Lee, his jaw stuck out, and his fists clenched.

Abruptly, Jones got into a taxicab. He understood taxicabs, having ridden in them with Funny Pegger.

"Take me to Polyphemus Ward's office," he said in a determined tone.

He reasoned that Lyman Lee would work in Polyphemus Ward's office, since he was the financier's confidential secretary.

THE RIDE to the financial district gave Jones time to think—he could draw back, figuratively, brush the sawdust off the new plan he had constructed, and see how it looked. Having done so, he was satisfied, even pleased. What he planned to do was the very thing that needed immediate doing. He settled back comfortably and waited for the end of the ride.

He did not tip the taxi driver because he did not know that you tip for every service in New York, but he did wonder why he got such a dark look from the driver. Standing on the sidewalk, he found himself beside a gigantic building into which ran a river of people. He entered the stream. Elevators were mysteries, but he followed other persons into one, and stood in it listening to the passengers call out for floors by number, and having no number, grew embarrassed, and when they got to the top, realized the operator was looking at him in a surprised way.

"You just come for the ride?"

"Er—not at all," Jones said. "I wish Polyphemus Ward's office."

"This whole building is Polyphemus Ward offices," said the operator shortly. "Who you wanna see?"

"Lyman Lee."

"Mr. Lee is on the fifty-eighth floor."

The fifty-eighth floor was a vast place. Jones discovered, and he began to realize that this whole building must hold a multitude of offices—all dedicated to making dollars for Polyphemus Ward, piling up the fortune which he, Jones, presumably would take over and administer to charity if he succeeded in giving away one hundred thousand dollars before a thirty-day time limit expired. Jones got out his handkerchief and blotted his forehead. He was having an attack of awe-of-a-financial-tycoon vertigo.

Grasping his determination again, he passed through the door which was the busiest and found a vast room full of typewriters, bookkeeping machines, girls and men who looked harried—and Lyman Lee.

Lyman Lee sat in a glass-walled pen, behind a tremendous mahogany desk.

"Who did you wish to see?" It was a trim young woman asking, and Jones became more uncomfortable.

"See? Er—oh, yes." Jones decided to be cautious. "I—ah—am waiting for a man. I—well—I should like to continue to wait, if you please."

He saw other persons sitting in chairs waiting, and he sat in one and waited, too. He was patient. Once more, he turned his plan around and around, and he could see nothing wrong with it. It looked excellent.

After a quarter of an hour, during which he made several telephone calls, Lyman Lee arose from his desk, took his hat and walking stick, and walked out, passing within arm-length of Jones without a sign of recognition.

Jones stood, holding his breath, with Lyman Lee in the descending elevator, but was not recognized, then followed the man out onto the street and into a nearby bar. Lyman Lee ordered something that came in a tall glass with sprigs of green vegetation on top. Jones did not order anything, because he did not know what to order, which he decided must be a breach in etiquette from the way the bartender was frowning. At length, embarrassed, Jones said to the bartender: "An Air Conditioned, if you please."

The sign over the bar said *Air Conditioned,* and Jones presumed it to mean a drink.

Thereafter the bartender, between servings, stared at Jones in a peculiar sort of way.

LYMAN LEE left the bar, took a subway, got off at Grand Central, walked a few blocks up Park Avenue, and entered an exclusive apartment building. Jones managed to trail along by doing exactly what Lyman Lee did. Lyman Lee rode in a black and chrome elevator and got out on a black floor walled around with dark blue mirrors, and Jones, getting out with him, was reminded of a clear Arctic sky in the middle of the six-months-long winter.

Lyman Lee adjusted his monocle and inspected Jones. "There is," he said coolly, "something familiar about you."

"That is conceivable," Jones agreed.

"What do you want, fellow?"

"First," Jones said, "I would like to know if this is your home."

Lyman Lee said, "I have the penthouse here. Does it happen to be any of your business?"

"Why, no, it is not. I merely intend to have a discussion—"

"You'll have to make an appointment—"

"—a discussion with you," Jones interrupted, "or I shall have to—ah—knock your block off."

Lyman Lee began to look nervous, and retreated through a door. Jones followed him. The magnificence of their surroundings increased noticeably. After he had looked around, Jones didn't know what he was reminded of. Splendor, certainly; the walls were either mirrors, or plate glass, or solid yellows and blues, or faced with great photographs of Lyman Lee—always photographs of Lyman Lee: He played golf, shot grouse in Scotland, steered his racing sloop, flew his plane, caught blue marlin off Bimini, danced with beautiful girls, and posed in swimming shorts, all on the walls. It was Lyman Lee's tribute to his own personality.

"Tent," Jones remarked, looking at one of the African photos, "is a portable lodge of canvas, strong cloth or skins, supported and sustained by poles, used for shelter. Also a sweet reddish wine made near Cadiz, Spain, and used for ecclesiastical purposes."

"Jones!" Lyman Lee exploded. "Jones off the iceberg!"

Jones contemplated Lyman Lee. If the other man had been endowed with all the good qualities attributed to preachers, and if in addition he had been as innocent as new-born babes are supposed to be, Jones knew he still wouldn't like the fellow.

"I came here," Jones announced grimly, "to make a short but important speech."

LYMAN LEE decided to change expression. He took the startled glare off his handsome face, replacing it with a wide smile. "Jones, old boy! My friend!" he exclaimed heartily. "I wondered what had happened to you. Where have you been, guy—"

"Guy," stated Jones, "is a rope or chain used to steady an object which is being hoisted. Also a person of grotesque appearance. I am not enthusiastic about either implication."

"Jones, my friend—"

"I," Jones interrupted, "will do the talking. Please."

Lyman Lee looked amazed. "Jones—what—what has happened to you?"

Jones took a deep breath. "You," he said, "are not fooling me. Not a bit."

"Why, I—"

"I now know," Jones continued, "that you are no friend of mine. Your performance in getting me a room in the city was not a gesture of kindness, as I thought. I suspect it was a move to put me within reach of a certain absent-minded fellow who sold me a house full of fake orphans for fifty thousand dollars."

"Why, Jones!" Lyman Lee looked hurt. "This is a terrible injustice you are doing me!"

"I think not!" Involuntarily, Jones' brown hands became formidable fists. "It is with the greatest difficulty that I restrain myself from taking a measure of physical vengeance."

Lyman Lee's manufactured grin slipped. He drew back uneasily.

"I—now Jones! There must have been a mistake—"

"No!"

"But—"

Jones took a step forward, grasped Lyman Lee firmly by both

coat lapels and held the impeccable fellow so that the tips of his toes barely touched the floor.

"All that restrains me," Jones announced, "is the fact that I lack proof."

Lyman Lee wriggled like a barracuda on a gaff hook. "But—"

"I am giving you the benefit of the doubt," Jones said, "which is possibly more than you deserve."

"But, Jones—"

"In the future," Jones said, "you will keep out of my affairs, or various things will happen to you."

He shook Lyman Lee for emphasis.

"You won't," Jones said, "like it!"

And he walked out.

CHAPTER XX

MAKE A PLAN

JONES HAD DONE some freak things, but had done them unwittingly, through lack of experience. Or so, at least, Jones had been assuring himself that was the case. However, he had now done something with forethought. There was no doubt in his mind that Lyman Lee had plotted against him, but whether the emphatic remarks he had just delivered would have a dampening effect on any future activities of Lee's was something else.

He stepped into the gaudy elevator, said, "Lower me, if you please," in a firm voice, and rather enjoyed the strange sensation which the dropping elevator gave him. He stepped out in the lobby, brushed past a doorman in a uniform resplendent enough that it would ordinarily have been a source of awe.

Initiative was the thing! Instead of letting events happen, go out and cause them. That was the idea. Make aggressive war on problems. His enthusiasm called for a quotation.

"Mars," he remarked, "was the Roman deity of war, also regarded as protector of the fields and leader of militant colonists."

All wrapped up in the smoke of his own enthusiasm, he bumped into someone. He pardoned himself, then took a second look.

"Glacia!" he ejaculated.

A vision in cream and gold looked him over blankly.

"Glacia!" Jones exclaimed. Then he remembered. "I am—er—Jones. Jones in disguise. You are—er—my fiancée—Glacia."

Of course it was Glacia. Glacia, if anything, more gem-like than when Jones last saw her on Polyphemus Ward's yacht. Her cream and gold frock was from Paris; her shoulders carried a silver fox; and all about her hung a trace of delicate perfume. She was something to give any man a buzz.

"Why—darling!" Glacia murmured. "How different you look! Why didn't you let me know where you were?"

"I—uh—" Jones said.

"You ran away when the yacht docked," Glacia accused. "Why did you run away, darling?" She looked contrite. "Did I do something that offended you?"

"Oh, my, no!" Jones said hastily. "To tell the truth, I became confused by my first glimpse of New York. I got into an—er—frame of mind. A state. It occurred to me that the only remedy was to be alone. I am accustomed to doing things for myself."

"Why, darling, how quaint!" Glacia squeezed his arm. "But, angel," she murmured, "I wanted to help you."

"But—well—" Jones gave his determination shots in the arm. "I—er—desire to cope with my problems myself. I hope to do so, even in the matter of making fifty thousand dollars."

Glacia stared at Jones. "What's this—fifty thousand—?"

"I must," Jones explained, "earn such a sum quickly."

Glacia swallowed. "What with?"

"I have fifty thousand to use for what I believe is called capital."

"You're using that hun—" Glacia clicked her white teeth together on the rest. She'd remembered she wasn't supposed to know about the hundred thousand dollars which Jones was to give to needy persons.

"What did you start to say?" Jones inquired.

"You're using that honey-lamb head of yours too much," said Glacia. "What you need is some recreation. You need to have fun."

"Fun?"

"Darling, we'll have dinner tonight and see a show," Glacia said enthusiastically. "I'll call for you. Where are you putting up?"

"Putting up?"

"Staying. Where are you living?"

"Oh. With Vix."

A flicker of annoyance crossed Glacia's well-turned-out face. "Vix?"

"Er—"

"Just who," interrupted Glacia, "is this Vix?"

IT MUST have been instinct handed down by generations of male ancestor victims of possessive females that supplied Jones with inspiration. "I am staying," he corrected himself, "with Funny Pegger. Sometimes I call him Vix. It's—it's just a whim."

Glacia frowned at Jones while she took out a cigarette, tapped it on one fingernail and lighted it. "Jonesy, you wouldn't two-time me, by any chance?"

"Two-time?"

"Oh, all right. I don't suppose you're learning that fast." She gave him her smile and another pat on the arm. "What is your address?"

Jones had learned that addresses were important things to remember. He gave her the one of Vix's apartment.

"Goodbye, darling," Glacia said. "I'll call for you this evening at eight o'clock." She tucked a finger under his necktie. "And here's something you don't deserve, you naughty boy." She kissed him.

Jones experienced, definitely, the usual explosion. It began at the ends of his toes with simultaneous heat in his fingertips, but otherwise the concussion followed the pattern of those that had preceded it. It was the third or fourth time Glacia had kissed him, but there was certainly nothing lost in repetition.

"Goodness!" he gasped.

"Eight o'clock, remember," Glacia said.

SHE WATCHED Jones depart. "There," she assured herself, "goes a well-hooked fish."

When Jones was out of sight she continued toward her original destination—Lyman Lee's penthouse.

Glacia had passed a bad minute. Womanlike, she got out a small mirror and gave her face a critical examination. She smiled complacently at the loveliness she saw.

The doorman bowed to Glacia and greeted her by name, as did the elevator operator.

Glacia frowned at the dark chrome interior of the elevator. Jones' remark about making fifty thousand had her puzzled. Her mother had overheard everything on the yacht, so she knew all about Jones' deal with Polyphemus Ward.

"I wonder," she pondered, "if little Tarzan is using that hundred thousand to speculate with!"

She tapped her heels angrily on the black floor of the penthouse foyer. She was concerned. If Jones didn't dispose of that hundred thousand in the manner expected of him, goodbye to his chances of getting a million. He wouldn't fool Polyphemus Ward, because nobody fooled old Polyphemus Ward.

"I'd better," Glacia decided, "take Jones in hand."

The hundred thousand was chicken feed. Jones must get the million, because he was going to be her future husband.

In that frame of mind, she confronted Lyman Lee.

"Good morning, darling," he greeted her.

"Hello."

There was frost in the atmosphere as Lyman Lee steered Glacia onto a canopied terrace which afforded an inspiring view of Rockefeller Center.

Four men occupied chairs on the terrace, drinks at their elbows. Glacia knew only one of them: Paul Shevinsky, the criminal lawyer; and she shook his hand, which was something like taking hold of a live toad. Paul Shevinsky said something clever with his thick lips, then put his cigar back in his mouth and sat down.

Lyman Lee introduced the three other men: A man named Harold Hover, who was a professor of bacteriology at a local university. A second man named T. Clarence Osborn, called "Forgetful," who certainly looked absent-minded enough. A third man with a long face and sleepy lids, who was never without a lighted cigarette between the two forefingers of his left hand. When Lyman Lee said, "This is Tray Marco," she knew instantly who the man was. True, Tray Marco had been more formidable in the days before the Department of Justice gave attention to the quantity of income tax racketeers paid, but he was still a figure in certain circles.

"It looks," Glacia remarked to Lyman Lee, "as if you had turned snake charmer."

The guests frowned, with the exception of Forgetful, who grinned.

"I hardly think," Lyman Lee said in a pained tone, "that crack was called for."

Glacia looked them over coldly. She did not like them; she considered them a menace to her future security; she took no pains to hide the fact. "I'll bet," she said, "that this gathering of maggots is in honor of a man named Jones."

Tray Marco scowled at Lyman Lee. "I thought you said this dame was your girl."

Lyman Lee made soothing gestures with his hands. "Now, now, Glacia," he said, "let's discuss the matter calmly."

Glacia's eyes glittered. "No," she said, "we won't! We won't be calm about anything! You telephoned me to come here, and I know exactly what's up your sleeve. Well, I won't do it."

"But—"

"No! I won't help you trim Jones. I could have told you so over the telephone. But I wanted to tell you to your face." She shook a finger under Lyman Lee's nose. "And I wanted to tell you another thing. It's this—lay off Jones!"

"But—"

"It's too bad, Lyman my boy, but I don't care what does

happen to you. Polyphemus Ward has another fair-haired boy, and it's Jones. And am I sorry? Am I sobbing?" She stopped and threw them a triumphant look. "I'm engaged to marry Jones!"

She waited for that to explode, as if she had thrown a grenade. No one said anything.

"**NOW,**" Glacia snapped, "you know exactly where I stand. You don't want Jones to get that million—but I do. And I'm warning you, Lyman my sweet, that you'd better play on the other side of the tracks. And that goes for the rest of you gentlemen!"

Tray Marco moved the cigarette in his left hand slightly. He said to Lyman Lee: "I do a better job of training my women."

Glacia settled the fox fur angrily on her shoulders. "Now I think I'll say good afternoon," she said. She moved toward the door, and the man called Forgetful said: "Of course you know that we have taken Jones for half of that hundred thousand?"

Glacia stopped. Stopped as if shot.

Forgetful removed a cigarette from a black case, reached for Tray Marco's cigarette, used it to light his own, replaced the borrowed cigarette between Marco's fingers, and blew in the air before he continued.

"I'm rather proud of it," he said, "because I don't believe the victim is the fish—"

"Seal," Tray Marco interrupted, and smiled.

"—not the seal that some of us figure he is." Forgetful glanced at Tray Marco. "It's a free country, Tray. Underestimate the guy if you want to, but I'm gonna give him plenty of room."

Tray Marco said, "I've never seen him."

Glacia swallowed several times; her fingers choked her purse. "What—how—how did you take him?" she asked.

Forgetful looked dreamy. "Eh? Oh, yes—we are discussing a feat of mine. I sold an orphan home. And the price"—he seemed unable to remember—"let's see, I believe it was fifty thousand dollars."

Tray Marco scowled. "I hope this dame is right. If she ain't, you're telling her a lot."

Lyman Lee moistened his lips and watched Glacia.

"I think she'll be right," he said, "now that she knows how things stand."

Glacia felt things crashing down. Half of Jones' money gone! She sank into a chair. "Oh!" she said hollowly.

Forgetful got a glass of ice water. Glacia pushed it away.

She glanced at him pityingly. "There are times," she said hollowly, "when a lady needs a real drink. This is distinctly one of the times."

TRAY MARCO began to laugh, then leaned back in his chair and continued to laugh. He said, "When I was a kid, I used to like to blow soap bubbles and stick pins in them."

Glacia drank some brandy neat, pushed the glass away, then bent over and held her face in her hands.

"Glacia!" Lyman Lee said.

She did not answer.

Forgetful came over and patted her shoulder. "Let me see, Miss de Grandieu, what's that old axiom? If you don't succeed at first, try second base?"

Glacia knocked his hand away. "What do you mean?"

"Your friend and ours," said Forgetful, "hasn't a chance of giving away one hundred thousand dollars. He now has, if I recall rightly, only fifty thousand to give away. That is not enough."

Glacia stared at him dully. "Go on," she said.

Forgetful smiled benevolently. "We are really not bad fellows at heart and we realize you've been unfortunate and it hurts us—it really does. We'd like to do something about it."

"What?" Glacia asked.

Forgetful looked at Lyman Lee. "Maybe you'd better tell her."

Lyman Lee came over and patted Glacia's shoulder. "I'm sorry, Glacia. I really am—"

"What's the proposition?" Glacia asked.

"The remaining fifty thousand dollars," Lyman Lee said flatly. "We help you get it. You take the whole thing."

Glacia's eye evinced a gleam of interest.

"You mean," she said, "you want me to take him for the other fifty thousand?"

"Yes. With our help."

Glacia stood up. "It's a deal," she said. "I've got a date with him at eight o'clock."

Forgetful sighed gloomily. "I wonder," he remarked, "if there's any ships sailing for the South Seas. Because I'm telling you that this Jones may be a bobcat."

The man named Harold Hover sat in pale silence. He was busy thinking.

JONES looked at the stranger in a blank way. "What," he inquired, "has that got to do with it?"

"It's three o'clock," the stranger repeated patiently. "And because it's three o'clock, it's closed, because it closes at three o'clock."

"Er—the stock market, you mean?"

"Wasn't," the man said, "that what you were asking about?"

"I—yes."

"Well, it's *three o'clock!*"

"In that case," Jones said politely, "thank you."

He was disappointed. Another day wasted. He searched in his mind for a quotation suitable for the occasion.

"Delay," he remarked, "means to cook, as to delay a soup; as well as to retard or slow the progress of a project."

The weather had turned sultry again, pedestrians were carrying coats, and clouds had appeared and hung in smoky wads in the sky. Jones stopped under a movie-theater marquee, intrigued by cold air that came from the conditioned interior.

The more he saw of man and the gadgets he had invented, the more complex everything seemed. There was danger of becoming confused, of losing his perspective: he believed that was probably the worst thing that could happen to him. He wished to confine his thinking to the things that vitally concerned him. He wanted to cope with the fundamentals.

Glacia was certainly one of the fundamentals. Undeniably, when she kissed him, something fundamental happened. Frowning, he wondered if the phenomenon was confined exclusively to Glacia. Was there an explosion when you kissed other girls? That point seemed rather important.

"Test," he announced, "is the discrimination of facts by trial. Also, it is the hard or firm shell or covering of invertebrates such as molluscs, crustaceans and echinoderms."

He resolved to act on the idea. He walked rapidly toward Vix's apartment, and thanks to the close attention he had paid to marking his trail, he reached the red-headed young woman's home in fifteen minutes.

Funny Pegger opened the door, and his grin was immensely relieved.

"It's back again!" he yelled.

"Lock it out!" Vix called from the kitchen.

"Not if it's still got fifty thousand dollars." Funny Pegger peered at Jones. "Has it?"

Jones retained the expression of a young man on a mission of serious research on the subject of the effect of the female lips. He headed for the kitchen.

"Criminy!" Funny Pegger exclaimed. "Something is gonna happen!"

CHAPTER XXI

THE PHILISTINE

ON THE ARCTIC island which had been Jones' home for practically all of his life, there had been leisure to burn. In the course of twenty years, almost nothing had happened except blizzards, snowstorms, eighty-below-zero cold snaps, scarcities of seals for food and occasionally an iceberg which broke off the island glacier while one was hunting on it, but these things could be expected, being more or less orderly processes in such an existence. Furthermore, they happened at wide intervals, so there was plenty of time in between to accustom oneself. But lately, event after event had occurred to Jones in slap-bang haste; there was nothing like the leisure he would have liked to let facts sink into his mind and ripen. There was too much that was new, and no time to assimilate, to enjoy the taste of the unique. Above all, Jones would have liked to go on to each new thing slowly, taking his own time, but that was just what he hadn't been able to do. It was impossible. The lightning had struck so fast that he had nearly lost count—everything was kaleidoscopic, and it didn't seem possible at times that it could be real.

Jones was well acquainted with his own mind; the solitude of his previous life had equipped him with that asset. So he knew the danger of being swept up in the speed of new things, of becoming confused, of letting amazement knock him in the head. He had to prevent that, and the best antitoxin seemed to be to make his mind take hold of only the important things, the fundamentals.

And one of the fundamentals was the effect Glacia had on him. Effect wasn't a suitably inclusive term, the upclap being decidedly conglomerate. But it narrowed down to the fact that whenever Glacia had kissed him there had been an explosion....

He ignored Funny Pegger, and stalked into the apartment's toy-size kitchenette.

Vix was trim and pert in a brown street frock and a saucy little hat that tried vainly to confine her red hair. She still had that quality that made Jones go bump-bump inside.

He didn't stop to analyze—he took an astonished auburn-headed young woman in both arms and kissed her, very well, considering that it was semi-amateur effort.

Jones released Vix and stepped back.

"Hmmm," he said thoughtfully.

"I—uh—what—" Vix said, and looked as if she had a great deal more to say, once she got the breath.

"I am," Jones announced, "disappointed."

Vix stared at Jones as though she hadn't heard right.

"Disappointed?" she said. "Did you say—"

"The explosion," said Jones gravely, "didn't happen."

Vix shook her head sharply, as if she had just taken a dive and wanted to get the water out of her ears. "Explosion?"

Jones nodded. "Yes," he said. "I—er—rather hoped there would be one."

Vix took a step backward, and her angry blue eyes flicked around the kitchenette, and selected a sack of groceries.

"I wouldn't," she snapped, "see you disappointed for the world."

SHE drew a tomato out of the grocery sack and hit Jones in the right eye; and it was a juicy tomato.

Then Jones felt himself seized, realizing he was being pro-pelled out of the kitchenette, heard the door slam, and the key turn in the lock. He had been rescued, he perceived, by Funny Pegger. He folded down in a living-room chair to which the gag-man towed him.

"Er—is she still after me?" he asked anxiously.

"I locked the door," Funny Pegger said.

Jones groped in his hip pocket for his handkerchief. He swabbed tomato seeds and pulp out of his eyes. The situation seemed to call for a statement.

"Er—fiasco," he remarked, defining aloud, "is a bottle or flask, usually having a long neck and covered with plaited straw. The word also implies a complete and ridiculous failure, usually of dramatic nature."

"Either one," said Funny Pegger, "covers you."

"Eh?"

"Skip it. What were you doing?"

"I—conducting an experiment."

"Experiment?"

Jones nodded. "I imagined," he explained, "that I could prove a point."

"So," Funny Pegger snorted, "you have an imagination!"

"I—almost everybody has one, I presume."

"Disregard yours," the gag-man ordered. "It plays dirty tricks on you."

By noon, the office of Genius, Inc., was filled with a multitude of the needy.

Jones blinked at Funny Pegger with watery-eyed earnestness.

"I wished," he said feelingly, "to ascertain whether the result of the kiss was a stable quantity, and more specifically, I desired to know whether the same thing would happen when I kissed Vix as when I kissed Glacia."

"It sounds involved," Funny Pegger said.

Jones missed the sarcasm. "Oh, yes, it was important."

"Did you find out?"

"Oh, yes."

"Which girl won?"

"Er—it was not exactly a contest, but when I kiss Glacia, there is a dependable explosive effect."

"And Vix?"

"A sort of sinking sensation."

"You tell Vix that?"

"I—yes."

"It's a wonder," said Funny Pegger, "that you're still as nature made you."

Jones blinked moistly at the gag-man and perceived that the latter thought what had just happened was anything but serious. Jones wondered if possibly it was so important. A moment ago, it had seemed vital, needing immediate attention. Perhaps he was wrong. He felt suspended.

FUNNY PEGGER frowned at Jones. "I presume," he said caustically, "that you've given up the idea of making fifty thousand dollars to replace what you lost."

"Why, no! What gave you that idea?"

"Well, you were going around kissing girls to see what would happen."

"I—"

"Or maybe you've already made fifty grand?"

"I have not," Jones reminded him uncomfortably, "been away from here more than two hours. That interval is hardly sufficient to acquire such a sum."

"I know. But queer things happen when you're around." Funny Pegger screwed up his round, homely face. "Just what did you do that brought you back here with kissing ideas?"

"I visited Lyman Lee," Jones said, anxious to change the subject.

Funny Pegger jumped. "You—what?"

Jones nodded. "I told Lyman Lee to refrain from molesting me. The alternative, I explained, was to—er—get his block knocked off."

"His block—" Funny Pegger swallowed. "Did it take?"

"I—take?"

"Never mind. It didn't, regardless of what you think. You can't bluff that monocle-wearing fashion-plate." The gag-man sighed. "But at that, trying to throw the fear of God into him was a more sensible idea than some you've had."

"Thank you," Jones said.

"But," continued Funny Pegger, "you left here looking for the stock market, a pony, or a crap game. You wanted to make fifty grand in a hurry. Remember?"

"The stock market," Jones explained, "was closed."

"Providence is kind!"

Jones watched Funny Pegger topple into a chair. "I met Glacia."

Funny Pegger sailed out of the chair. "Light!" he yelled. "I see a light!"

"You—do?"

"Glacia."

"Oh, yes. Glacia."

"The sure bet for a guy to raise himself with a queen is to show a little jack."

"Er—"

"Money doesn't grow on trees, but some girls will reach to pick it."

"Why—"

"The point," Funny Pegger said, "is that Glacia threw the hooks into you. She—"

"I do not," Jones interrupted, "care to hear any more in that vein!"

"Now look here—"

"*You* look here!" Jones said grimly. "I do not wish to hear reflections on the character of my—of Glacia."

Jones realized there was a vehemence in his voice which he had never heard there before.

Pegger frowned, spread his hands on his knees and contemplated them. The clock made tiny sound in the apartment, while outdoors automobiles hooted and an elevated train went volleying along. Jones shifted in the chair to get his hip off the hump the roll of fifty one-thousand dollar bills made in his pocket. Then he sat stiffly, as if thinking.

In the kitchen, Vix struck or kicked the locked door.

Funny Pegger, looking defeated, went to the kitchen door and opened it, and Vix said: "Both you clowns can take your hyena manners and get out—"

"Shush!" Funny Pegger said pleadingly. "The headless horseman rides the countryside."

He stepped into the kitchen and closed the door. Vix stared at him.

"Since when did he ever have a head?" she demanded.

"The citizens of the United States are getting a bad habit," Funny Pegger said. "They're underestimating this Jones."

"You must be the man who still thinks the Democrats will lower taxes," Vix suggested.

Funny Pegger ambled around the kitchen, nosing into sacks, and found an orange, which he began to peel, licking his fingers frequently, dropping the orange skins in the sink.

"You gotta remember," he pointed out, "that he really saw the world for the first time only day before yesterday, when the yacht got to New York. Before that, he was on an island—"

"Wouldn't it have been divine," Vix mused, "if he had stayed there?"

"My point," persisted Funny Pegger, "is that he ain't doing so bad."

Vix sniffed. "He's not?"

"Considering everything, no."

"You saw," Vix inquired, "what happened to me a minute ago?"

"So what? You've been kissed before."

"Not," Vix retorted, "as often as you might expect. Which is beside the question. My argument is that you can never tell what that iceberg hermit is going to do next."

"Only makes him interesting."

"To me," Vix said, "it doesn't! To borrow one of those mummies you call jokes—this is the fishhook."

"The what?"

"The end of the line. I get off here."

VIX walked briskly to the bedroom, ignoring Jones, and began to tinker with her hat.

Funny Pegger came into the living room, hissed at Jones, "You've just about done us out of our boarding-place!" and followed Vix into the bedroom. He closed the door so Jones could not hear them. "Look," he said uneasily. "You're gonna let us go on using your apartment, ain't you?"

"Yes," Vix said.

"Gosh, that's swell!"

"Providing," Vix added, "that it is agreeable with the nice big policeman I'm going to send over to look for rodents."

Funny Pegger strangled on the last slice of the orange.

"Vix! You can't send the cops!"

Vix shrugged. "As a taxpayer, I understand I'm entitled to such service."

"But they'll arrest Jones!" the gag-man said wildly.

"You, too," Vix reminded.

"They'll arrest Jones," Funny Pegger groaned. "They'll arrest him for shooting that German liner captain in the leg. Later, the German died unexpectedly. Don't you remember?"

"My memory is good enough. I seem to recollect that the police would also like to arrest *you* for consorting with and aiding this Jones."

"Great grief!"

"Jones," said Vix, "should be in jail for his own good."

"Oh, Lord!"

"And probably jail will make an improvement in *you,* too."

Funny Pegger slumped on the edge of the bed, arms hanging limply, and when he caught Vix's eye, he turned his palms up and looked disconsolate. Vix sniffed. She dragged a trim brown leather weekend case out of a closet and began stuffing it with feminine apparel.

"Poor Jones," repeated Funny Pegger. "He's a swell guy, and he'd have made it all right if he hadn't happened to meet a lot of zany people."

Vix struck an attitude of thought. "I believe," she remarked, "that I shall wear the rust dress instead of this one."

The gag-man shook his head solemnly. "Of course," he said, "it might not have been so bad if Jones hadn't got the idea that the stock market, the horses or a crap game was the best way to make fifty thousand dollars in a hurry."

"Will you shut up?" Vix requested.

"Jones," said Funny Pegger, "is bound and determined to try one of those three ways of making money. He'll doubtless lose the fifty thousand he already has."

Vix stamped a foot hotly. "I don't care!"

"It's too bad."

"Jones," Vix snapped, "is a—a Philistine!"

"I—"

"I can't remember when I've hated anybody so much!"

"But—"

"Jones," Vix gritted, "insulted me like no girl was ever insulted before."

"He only said he didn't explode—"

"I could take an ax to him!"

"Well—"

"But," Vix said, "I'm not going to leave here and have him lose that money on stocks, horses or an African golf game."

Funny Pegger grinned. "You're not?"

"No, I'm not. Because it was me who gave him the crazy idea."

"You?"

Vix nodded grimly. "Yes," she said.

"What did you do that for?" yelled the gag-man.

"I was kidding him." Vix looked disgusted. "How was I to know he would take it seriously?"

Funny Pegger glanced at Vix's trim shape, colorful hair and her pert and rather delectable features.

"You're an item," he said, "that any man is liable to take seriously."

"I don't make them explode, though!" Vix nipped her lower lip angrily. "The big—seal!"

"Sure." Funny Pegger grinned. "I understand. Clearly."

Vix narrowed her left eye at Funny Pegger, apparently unfavorably impressed by an it's-all-right-if-you-want-to-say-it's-that-way quality in the gag-man's voice.

Funny Pegger looked uncomfortable. "Let's go chain the Philistine," he suggested.

Vix nodded. They opened the bedroom door, went into the living room, and looked around, casually at first, then with quick anxiety.

Funny Pegger blurted, "He's gone!"

CHAPTER XXII

CLOTHES FOR GIRLS

JONES HAD A date with Glacia for eight o'clock. Now it was five minutes past, and Jones was disturbed, because Glacia had not appeared. He stood in front of the apartment house, looked around in vain for his lady and worried. He lacked experience with the feminine habit of being late. He began to pace back and forth under the sidewalk awning and ponder. Funny Pegger and Vix, it seemed to him, opposed almost everything he wanted to do, so he had eased out of the apartment without notifying them. Their attitude troubled him; they were the two people whom he really counted as friends, since they had given him assistance. Jones frowned. Every time he opened a door in his mind, there was a fresh difficulty. Whenever he tried to solve a problem, he unchained a new trouble, so that his progress so far, he reflected glumly, could be put in the eye of a rather small Arctic gnat. There must be needy persons in New York. He had noticed, in glancing at the newspaper which carried the story about the police looking for him, that Congress was considering appropriating another four billion dollars or some such astronomical sum to relieve needy people. He wished he had read the item more closely.

In trying to give away his paltry hundred thousand, he was apparently going into competition with the government.

The idea of a government giving away such a sum made him feel rather incompetent by comparison. He only had a hundred thousand. That a government, any government, could find needy persons for billions, whereas he had not been able to find a single genuinely needy person, was discouraging.

Then a musical voice was sounding at his elbow.

"Why, darling," it said. "I do hope I'm not late."

It was Glacia. Glacia, attired in—Jones thought with a gulp—disturbingly little. Whoever had constructed the scintillating thing she wore had skimped scandalously on the upper area. Still, Glacia created an effect. She hit Jones about the way she hit the average observer—the same as a hatful of diamonds.

"I do hope," Glacia repeated, "that I'm not late."

"I—not at all," gasped Jones. "Not at all. You are ahead of time—er—that is. I wouldn't have minded waiting for you. Not a bit."

The motor car into which Jones found himself helping Glacia was impressive. It was Arctic sky blue. Half the machine was hood, but there was enough left over for an outdoor driver's seat where a small, uniformed brown chauffeur sat, and a closed tonneau of plush, subdued lighting, and delicate perfume.

Before he got in, Jones inspected the small brown man behind the wheel. The flamboyance of the latter's uniform urged forth a quotation.

"Regalia," Jones remarked, "is a kind of cigar of large size. Also the emblems, symbols and paraphernalia of persons of royal rank, or the decorations or insignia of an office or order."

The city at night, particularly the number and variety of the electric signs, still intrigued Jones. He resolved not to let them fascinate him, and looked at Glacia instead, which was almost as distracting.

"I wish," he said bluntly, "to engage in a serious discussion."

"You dear boy," Glacia murmured. "You're always so serious, aren't you?" She gave his arm a squeeze. "Frivolous people bore me to distraction. And it's so seldom that I find a man with a mature mind."

"Er—you think I possess a mature mind?" Jones inquired.

"Oh, very mature." Glacia looked up into his face. "You're

not too mature, though. You have the delightful enthusiasm of youth, tempered by a soberly balanced intelligence."

"Indeed?"

"You have," said Glacia, "a comprehensively rounded personality with an objective essence."

"Objective essence?"

"Tempered," Glacia murmured, "by an affinity for intellectual self-communion."

Jones glowed.

"Thank you!" he said feelingly.

It was mighty good to hear someone say that they thought he might have some brains, and use five-dollar words to do so. Vix had insinuated that he did not have enough gray matter to be running around loose. He found himself mentally contrasting the two women. Glacia was ravishing and owned a flattering opinion of Jones. Vix was a saucy redhead with a nice figure, a caustic wit, and more temper than Jones had imagined could be contained in one individual. The comparison absorbed him. He forgot to go ahead with what he had started to discuss.

ALL AFTERNOON it had looked like rain, but the sky had cleared, and the night was cooled by a breeze from the Atlantic. The blue town car rolled without noise, hardly swayed, and the invigorating air poured in through the open window and seemed to lend a zest to the delicate perfume present inside. It took a turn to the right, fording a dense stream of pedestrians, and entered an electric blaze that rivaled the sun.

Jones stuck his head out of the window. He was stunned. He'd thought he had been seeing some bright lights, but they were candles. The Aurora Borealis had never been like this.

"Gracious!" Jones remarked.

"This is Broadway," said Glacia. "Sometimes called the Great White Way."

A few moments later, their driver was holding open the limousine door, then Jones found himself guided across a crowded lobby, into an elevator which arose many floors, then through a throng of women dressed in the same kind of thing Glacia was wearing, and men attired in dress suits or street clothes such as Jones wore. A large oily gentleman who could bow with amazing speed, called *"Garçon"* by Glacia, escorted them to a table.

"You wait here, darling," Glacia directed. "I'm going to the dressing room and pretty up."

Her tone implied she was going to pretty up for Jones....

At a discreet table behind some palms, Glacia dropped into a chair beside a man who had a long face, sleepy lids, a drowsy expression, and who held a lighted cigarette between the two forefingers of his left hand.

"Hello, Tray," Glacia said.

Tray Marco pulled smoke out of his cigarette, held it a while in his lungs, then let it out, and mixed words with the escaping smoke. "How's it go?"

Glacia said to the other two men at the table, "Hello, Forgetful. Hello, Hover," and Forgetful Osborn looked at her blankly as though trying to recall who she might be, then grinned widely. Harold Hover nodded, moistening his lips with a pale tongue. Paul Shevinsky, the fourth man at the table, said, "Don't I rate a nod, darling?"

Glacia looked at him. Paul Shevinsky was examining her, bending forward a little, his thick lips parted.

"Hello, Paul," Glacia said. "Where is Lyman?"

Tray Marco moved his cigarette slightly. He said, "I asked you how it goes."

Glacia's eyes moved to him. He was probably the only man of whom she had ever been afraid. It wasn't just that she knew his reputation. The deadliness that was within him seemed to hang around him in a faint, bitter aura.

Glacia said, "He's at a table."

"He suspect anything?"

"Of course not." Glacia gave Tray Marco a smile about as

firm as she would have bestowed on a stray tiger. "I think he was impressed by your car."

"What kind of a line are you giving him?"

"Intellectual. I talked with him about his objective essence."

"His what?"

Forgetful Osborn came out of an absent-minded stare and said, "My dear girl, you'll have to speak the language of the criminal classes."

Tray Marco's eyelids sank and he put his cigarette between his lips then put his hands hard, palms flat, on the table.

He said, "What?" in a low voice.

Forgetful Osborn lost his grin suddenly.

He said, "Heck, Tray, I was kidding!" earnestly.

LYMAN LEE arrived. He wore immaculate full dress and carried a monocle in his eye. He was by far the handsomest man in the roof-club crowd.

He greeted Glacia, then asked, "Is it going all right?"

"Swell," she said.

Lyman Lee frowned. "We haven't been able to get everything set to take him. Not enough time. Tray is working on it. When we get set, Tray will give you a high sign, and you manage to talk to him privately and he'll tell you where to take Jones and what to do. Is that clear?"

Glacia nodded. "I'll watch for Tray." She frowned. "But after we take Jones, then what?"

"Lyman Lee turned and looked at Harold Hover. "What about that, Hover?" he asked.

Hover licked his lips, and the lower part of his face seemed to want to shake. He opened his mouth, but he did not or could not say anything.

Lyman Lee moved his upper lip a little, contemptuously.

"Hover will probably get back his voice," he said, "when the police arrest and convict Jones for causing the death of the German liner captain."

Glacia grew pale. "What do you mean?"

Lyman Lee looked at her queerly.

"Nothing," he said. "You'd better go back to the boy friend."

Glacia departed.

A moment later, Lyman Lee moved away, and Forgetful Osborn followed him out of earshot of the others and touched his elbow.

"Let's see—what—I had something on my mind," Forgetful said absently. "Oh, yes. Tray Marco. How about us trying to get along without that guy?"

"Without him?"

"Tray Marco," said Forgetful, "gives me a hobgoblin complex."

"We need him," Lyman Lee said shortly.

Forgetful sighed. "Then," he remarked, "I still wish I was taking a boat for the South Seas. Because I'm telling you, this Jones is the kind of a set-up that backfires, and this Tray Marco ain't got no sense of humor a-tall."

JONES was glad to see Glacia come through the crowd toward his table and he arose to welcome her, as he'd seen gentlemen at the other tables around him doing for their ladies.

"With such polished courtesy," Glacia said in a tone of amazement, "I can hardly believe you never saw another human being until a few days ago."

Jones glowed.

Glacia tapped her water glass with a spoon, and another fellow whom she also called *"Garçon"* wrapped a towel around a bottle, extracted the cork with a pop and flourish, then poured out watery-looking liquid that was full of fizz. Jones took a sip, made a face.

"Champagne," Glacia said with a husky little laugh.

Jones eyed his glass and decided the occasion called for a quotation. "The expensive price of champagne," he announced, "is partially due to the breakage of the bottles caused by the pressure of fermentation."

There was a great deal of noise in the room, but it was a cheerful confusion, with a name orchestra doing its best, and the open floor in the center crowded with dancers. Jones leaned back and found that he was enjoying himself. A friendly spirit prevailed. He noticed this particularly because its warmth was directed toward himself. Men glanced at him, often with pleasant smiles, and the women regarded him with interest. He was pleased, and glowed, because the attention was healing balm on his raw apprehensions that his previous life had made him into something fundamentally different from the rest of humanity. It did not occur to him that the reason for the attention might be that he was a pleasant looking young man of remarkable physical build, accompanied by a gem-like girl.

The lights dimmed, dancers went to their tables, and suddenly there was a round patch of brilliant white light in the center of the floor. The orchestra struck up softly, a young man appeared in the spotlight, bent close to a microphone, crooned a song. A long, thin comedian dressed as a pirate took the other's place at the mike and recited jokes which were about the caliber of those Funny Pegger carried on the tip of his tongue.

Jones suddenly craned his neck. A line of girls had appeared, all kicking in unison, all remarkably undraped. He took several close looks before he concluded they did wear something. But he had never before seen so much undraped female—the girls, pretending to be captives of the pirate comedian, wore little ragged panties and not much else.

"Gracious!" Jones remarked.

He studied the dancers, and began to feel concerned about them. They looked like nice girls.

"Don't they," he asked, "have any more clothes than that?"

Glacia shrugged. "Less, if anything."

Jones shook his head pityingly. He placed a hand on the roll of thousand-dollar bills in his hip pocket, frowned, and stood up.

Glacia said, "Wait a minute! Where are you going?"

"I am," Jones replied gravely, "going to distribute some thousand-dollar bills among those poor girls."

Glacia's eyes popped.

"For pity's sake!" she gasped. "This isn't Turkey! You can't buy a harem outright!"

"I—"

"Although"—Glacia looked at the roll of thousand-dollar bills—"you might, at that."

"Oh, my!" Jones gulped. "You misunderstand me! I have thousand-dollar bills to give to needy persons. Those poor girls are obviously in need of clothing, and I intend to supply them."

"Sit down!" Glacia said in a small, cold voice.

Jones peered at her. He could tell something was wrong.

"Sit down!" Glacia said queerly.

Jones sat down.

"Those girls," Glacia said, "make a union wage scale of sixty dollars a week."

"Er—they do? Then why do they dress as they do?"

"That," Glacia said, "is art."

"Art?"

Jones sat down and thought for a moment.

"Art," he remarked, "is dexterity, skill, or the ability to achieve or perform certain actions, usually difficult, or requiring a knack." He considered further, then shook his head. "I fail to see where taking clothes off is art."

CHAPTER XXIII

THOUSAND-DOLLAR BILLS

JONES FELT SOME embarrassment. A dictionary he had once memorized said a *faux pas* was a false step, or an act injurious to your reputation. He'd just accomplished one. He glanced at Glacia to see if she was laughing at him. She wasn't. He thought it very nice of her, and indicative of a character containing a great deal of virtue, kindness, and the common garden variety of horse sense. He suddenly remembered that he had been for some time in need of a person of judgment, experience, skill, and kindly toleration. Someone to whom he could bare his secret longings, and not get spiked with a word, or deflated with a second-hand gag.

"Glacia," he said.

"Yes, dear boy," Glacia responded.

"Er—earlier in the evening, I started to mention a matter, but it was sidetracked by something or other. I should like to broach the subject at this time."

"Do," Glacia invited warmly.

Jones fortified himself with a deep breath.

"I must give one hundred thousand dollars to needy persons," he said, "within the next thirty—er—twenty-seven days."

He waited for Glacia to tell him how many varieties of crazy he was. Glacia put a hand on his arm, and the hand squeezed a little.

"How wonderful!" she murmured. "I should so love to help you."

"I—what?"

"Help you," Glacia repeated.

"Oh," Jones said, "that is impossible. I am trying to prove I have judgment, according to the bargain with old—er—that is—I must do it all myself."

He'd come near telling her that he and old Polyphemus Ward had a deal. He sat for a moment with chin in palm and reviewed the difficulties of giving away thousand-dollar bills.

"The government," announced Jones, "expended for the relief of needy persons during the year 1935 the sum of three billion, sixty-eight million, eight hundred and three thousand, fifty-three dollars and twenty cents. I read that in a newspaper."

"Yes," Glacia said. "There have been rumors."

"They evidently found persons in need of such a sum."

"They claim they did."

"I," said Jones, "have not found even one needy person." He shook his head. "Conceivably the government has got them all."

He sat there and wrestled the question. He went into a dissecting session, took the matter apart, and examined its aspects.

"Hmmm," Jones said at last, thoughtfully.

DURING the course of the floor show, they were served food. Hitherto, Jones had subsisted on bear, seal, white whale, narwhal, fox, Arctic hare, auks, birds, bird-eggs, an occasional musk-ox, or other tidbit varied by clams dug from mud along the edges of glaciers. New York night club food was not quite the improvement he expected.

While a snappy-looking girl was handing Jones his hat and glaring at him because he failed to tip her—he didn't know he was supposed to—Glacia tucked her arm in his.

"Just what," she inquired, "was your thought in bringing up this matter of needy persons?"

"Why, I had no particular object, other than to discuss it. Discussion, you know, causes a plan to stand more clearly in one's mind." He smiled. "In catching a seal, I used to make it a practice to discuss my intended procedure aloud with myself. Seals are very wary animals. There is scientific basis for the belief that they sleep with their eyes open."

"I see," Glacia said.

The château of a town car wafted them around to a theater. They were late, of course, and it was first intermission, a crowd standing in front smoking. The usual collection of panhandlers was around, and the town car drew them to Jones like China attracts the Japanese.

But Jones ignored the outstretched palms.

Glacia looked curiously at Jones as they went inside. "Those people told you they were needy," she remarked.

"I have," Jones said, "formed an opinion on the subject of needy persons."

An usherette showed them their seats, and they saw a play about the vicissitudes of two agile-witted gentlemen who were attempting to produce a play on the money they were trying to get out of a man called the angel. Jones reflected that he had troubles which compared favorably with those the actors were encountering. The play ended, Glacia announced they were headed for a night club, that it was in the next block, and they would walk.

They reached the sidewalk, realized there was rumbling and whooping overhead, and Jones glanced up, forced to conclude the New York weather was as erratic as the human inhabitants of the place. Another rain was coming. The rain arrived before they had gone fifty paces, spattering big drops coming suddenly.

Jones and Glacia dashed for the nearest doorway, which happened to be the lobby entrance of an office building. They stood inside, watching the night sky empty itself of rain.

There was a slight noise in the lobby, and Jones turned around.

An elderly lady with white hair was on her knees wielding a scrub brush on the lobby floor.

Jones looked at her with interest.

THE OLD LADY breaking her back on the floor tiles was well past middle age, with a face that was rather pleasant in spite of the lines of fatigue. She had, in spite of the kind of work she was doing, a neat look.

Glacia turned and looked. She saw only an old scrubwoman, whereas Jones was seeing someone's mother.

He was also seeing the Big Idea. The Big Idea that he had been looking for.

"Inspiration," Jones announced, "is the act of breathing, accomplished by elevating the chest walls and flattening the diaphragm muscle. Also a power which exerts a stimulating effect on the intellect."

Glacia frowned. She took a quarter from her purse.

"Go to the corner and call our car," she ordered shortly. "The large blue town car with the Japanese chauffeur."

The rain came down in moaning sheets that twisted and writhed, boiled on the sidewalks, gorged the gutters. Lightning jumped continuously in the sky, made glare and noise. The wind moaned, banged signs, filled the doorway with a boil of spray.

The old lady reached for the quarter. Evidently twenty-five cents meant something in her life.

"Er—just a moment," Jones said.

The woman smiled at Jones. She had a pleasant little smile. "I'd like to get your car," she said. "I don't get many chances to make extra money."

Jones liked her voice. It was sincere.

"I wonder," he remarked, "if you would mind telling me the amount of your salary."

The small old lady shrugged cheerfully. "It is all the work is worth. I have no kick coming, young man."

"You are satisfied?"

She studied him with birdlike earnestness. "There are two answers to your question, young fellow. If you are asking whether I am satisfied that I am getting paid what my little job is worth, the answer is yes. But if you want to know if I am satisfied with my position in life, the answer is no. Hardly." She chuckled pleasantly. "I'm one of those creatures in whom hope springs eternal."

"On what do you base your hopes, may I ask?"

"That's a funny question." She cocked her head to one side. "Yes, a strange question. But the answer is candy."

"Candy?"

"The best you ever tasted." She nodded emphatically. "Melts in your mouth. I make it. I make a little on my day off, and peddle it around, and put the money in the bank. When I have enough"—she looked enthusiastic—"I'll set up a business."

Glacia was getting impatient. She pecked at Jones' arm.

"You're not interested in her and her candy," Glacia said impatiently. "Let's get going."

"On the contrary," Jones declared, "I am interested to the extent of one thousand dollars."

The little old lady stared at Jones, puzzled.

"Just what are you driving at?" she inquired.

"A few minutes ago, I saw a play in a theater," Jones said thoughtfully. "In the play, there was an individual called the angel, who furnished the money. I presume I might be called the angel,"

"Angel?"

"I propose," said Jones, "to furnish one thousand dollars for the candy business."

The old lady stared at Jones perplexedly. She shook her head and made a *tsk-tsk* noise.

"Young man," she declared, "you're crazy!"

Jones flushed. "I—that seems to be a general opinion not shared by myself." He made his voice as businesslike as he could.

"I propose to supply one thousand dollars. I understand interest is charged. I shall not charge interest. I also understand security is usually demanded for borrowed money. I shall require no security."

He paused to let this sink in.

"But," he added, "I shall expect the money to be repaid as soon as the candy business can repay it."

THIS was a radical departure from previous efforts. He did not know how it would set with old Polyphemus Ward. But he had thought everything over, and come to a conclusion—namely, that giving a person money outright did no lasting good. He realized he did not know much about human nature. Still, if you gave a man money, the fellow would expect to be given more. That was a natural fact. If one polar bear slipped and broke his neck while you were hunting him, you automatically hoped they all would do that.

"What," asked the little old lady, "if I lose your thousand dollars?"

"In that case," said Jones, "you will have lost more than I."

The old lady pursed her lips. She nodded.

"I believe you are right." She smiled at Jones. "Young man, you're strange. But I don't believe you are the wool-head I thought."

A grin spread over Jones' face. It lasted until Glacia grabbed hold of his arm. Glacia's fingers bit him. Glacia was seeing herself robbed of a thousand dollars.

"Have you gone crazy?" she asked angrily.

Jones looked at her. He frowned.

"You do not approve?" he inquired.

Glacia's "No!" was electric.

"That," said Jones, "is unfortunate. I intend to go ahead."

Something about the way he made the statement caused Glacia to swallow a great deal she had to say. It was like getting an unexpected peek at the Rock of Gibraltar through a fog.

"Your name?" Jones asked the little old lady.

Maud Thatcher was her name, and she lived in Brooklyn, and she supported a little grandson. "We've been getting along fine, the boy and I," she insisted.

She put the thousand-dollar bill in her stocking.

The rain had stopped by then. "I wish," Jones said, "to go home."

Glacia glanced at him thoughtfully. Her fingers kneaded the gaudy little bauble of an evening bag which she carried. She parted her lips twice without saying anything. "Of course," she said finally.

Jones opened the door of the blue town car without waiting for the Japanese in the uniform. He was experiencing a glow of competence, a genuine kind of a feeling as though he had been in the cold, and had finally come in where it was warm.

In the car he sighed happily.

After Jones went into Vix's apartment house, the Jap looked around expectantly, but Glacia didn't see him. She wasn't seeing anything in particular at the moment. She felt like the colored boy who was calling imaginary lions out of a hole for fun—and got a real one.

The Jap shrugged, put the car in gear, drove a block, and pulled up alongside a taxicab which had been trailing them. Tray Marco got out of the cab, followed by Lyman Lee, Paul Shevinsky, Harold Hover and Forgetful Osborn. These five birds of feather got into the town car with Glacia.

"Around and around," Tray Marco said to the chauffeur.

The Jap drove into Central Park.

Tray Marco was a man noted for taking a straight line to a given point; he did this so literally, that it would some day probably be the death of him. Neither did he waste words.

"We'll take him tomorrow night," he said. "The spot is my gambling house on Forty-ninth Street. He's hunting a crap game. We'll have it. Steer him there. Forgetful is going to be the house man."

Glacia did not look around and did not indicate by any particular sign that she either heard or was interested.

Forgetful Osborn said, "I—ah—am going to wear a disguise."

Tray Marco reached over and touched Glacia. "What's the matter?"

"I—oh!" Glacia said. "Why, I—nothing. A little trouble inside, is all."

"Maybe," Forgetful said thoughtfully, "you caught it from me."

CHAPTER XXIV

GENIUS, INC.

JONES HAD BEEN sleeping deeply, absolutely untroubled by the fact that last night he had spent a good part of the money he had decided to invest in Genius Jones, on Glacia. His was the kind of slumber that soothes away fevers of care, injects vim in jaded bodies, and puts its victims in danger of burning up if there is a fire. It was wonderful. Jones awakened from it with somebody else's hands around his throat.

"Urk!" he said. *"Wug!"*

He swung at random with both arms, kicked for good measure, rolled over and over wildly, and brought up against the living room wall with force. Then he sat up and looked at Funny Pegger.

"I was beginning to think," said Funny Pegger, "that life was extinct."

Jones felt of his neck. "You—ah—had hold of me?"

"Previously I tried hitting you with furniture."

Jones examined the window and concluded it was morning. He got up, stretched and began dressing. He had slept on the floor.

"What time did you call it a night?" asked Funny Pegger.

"Er—about two o'clock. I took a walk before coming in. I wanted to think. You were asleep and so I did not wake you."

The gag-man stared at Jones anxiously. "How much money have you got left?"

"Forty-nine thousand dollars. A little less, in fact." Night club: thirty dollars. Theater tickets: twenty-two. Investment in Jones.

"Forty-nine—" The gag-man missed strangling by a hair. "You got rid of a thousand dollars! A thousand! It must have been an evening!"

"It was not," Jones said, "entirely unproductive."

Leaving Funny Pegger to cogitate on this, Jones ambled into the bath and showered hot, then cold. Hot water was a luxury which he appreciated. He rubbed himself with a rough towel, and combed his hair, noting that the dye had not faded. Then he dressed and strode to the bedroom door and gave it a tap.

"If it's a telegram," Vix called sleepily, "I don't live here until noon."

"It is time," Jones announced, "that you were getting up."

"That man," Vix said wearily, "is back again!"

When she appeared in the bedroom door, she was sufficiently awakened, and a very bright and colorful article. She surveyed Jones, and puckered her forehead.

"A glass of hot water every morning," she remarked, "will make you feel like a tiger."

"I—"

"Especially," Vix added, "if somebody throws it on you while you're asleep."

Jones frowned earnestly.

"I am starting a campaign," he announced. "I wish to tell you about it."

"Shoot," Vix said. "I'm helpless."

JONES withdrew a few paces and surveyed Vix and Funny Pegger as a general might examine two soldiers before a battle. "I should like your cooperation," he declared.

"None from me!" Vix declared.

"Then," Jones said gravely, "I shall have to think of persuasive measures."

Vix took a step forward and peered at Jones. "Look here!" she said sharply. "What's happened to you?"

"Today," said Jones. "I form Genius, Incorporated."

He paused to approve of himself. He'd hoped that finally there would come a time in his career when he could make an announcement and not feel warmish when Vix examined him with those lively blue eyes and gave him a going over with her wit. The time had come. It was here—it was Genius, Inc. He basked in pleasant self-approval. One of his ideas had finally survived a test, assaying twenty-four carat, and it wouldn't matter whether Vix approved orally or not. The assay was an unconscious process conducted in Jones' mind; it satisfied himself enough that no one else mattered.

Jones turned to Funny Pegger.

"May I ask when your job of writing humor for the radio is to begin?" he inquired.

"Two weeks."

"Would you," asked Jones, "care to associate yourself with a project of mine in the meantime?"

"Say *no* to him!" Vix ordered.

Jones stated earnestly. "I do not think he will refuse."

"Eh?" Funny Pegger squinted. "You mean you'll take measures with me, too?"

"No," Jones said simply. "You are my friend."

The gag-man examined his hands thoughtfully, then inserted them in his pockets. He grinned. "No man could pay me a higher compliment."

"You—ah—are with me?"

"I am," said Funny Pegger.

"You," Vix told the gag-man, "are an impressionable quadruped of the genus *equus*. In other words, a sentimental jackass!"

Jones looked at Vix hopefully.

"I—what about you?" he inquired.

Vix started to show him the end of her chin, but didn't, and shrugged.

"Me, too," she said wearily. "I'm always a weak woman this early in the morning. Now, what about Genius, Inc.?"

Jones withheld the rest of his plan. He thought it a commendable piece of contriving, but at the same time he'd had painful experience with Vix and Funny Pegger—they were enthusiastic pin-stickers. He thought it just as well to give them one piece of the meat at a time.

They had breakfast, and Jones got acquainted with the grapefruit, a victual individual in taste, difficult to consume, unexpected in performance, none of these being qualities which met with his approval. After breakfast, he fired his first gun.

"Advertise," he announced, "comes from the French *avertir,* meaning to warn. Currently, it denotes the giving of public notice."

"As an old newspaperman," said Funny Pegger, "I can say that you hit the nail on the head."

"We are going to advertise."

"Advertise what?"

"Genius, Incorporated."

"Which?"

"That," Jones explained, "is the name I have decided to give my enterprise."

The gag-man put down his coffee cup, wiped his mouth with his napkin, wiped his forehead, put the napkin down, leaned back and grasped firm hold of his chair. "Let's hear it. I've got an awful feeling."

"It can't be as awful as mine," Vix said.

Jones ignored their tone.

"We are," he announced, "going to advertise for people with ideas who wish to start small businesses of their own, but who lack the capital. I am going to supply capital, up to a thousand dollars, without charging interest, the money to be repaid whenever income warrants."

Funny Pegger frowned. "Is this what giving a hundred thousand dollars to needy people has developed into?"

"Exactly," Jones nodded. "I—ah—have decided that giving money to a person outright is undesirable, in fact wrong. It is something for nothing, contrary to the first law of existence. A gift degenerates the moral fiber of the person receiving it. I confess that it does not seem to me that man has yet sufficiently separated himself from the animal status to ignore fundamental laws of nature. I recall from my childhood the sled dogs off my father's expedition ship. I remember particularly the fact that, when we gave them meat, thereafter they sat around the igloo door, howling and whining for more meat. Whereas, if we did not give them meat, they foraged for themselves and grew just as fat, and in some cases fatter, and were always more contented."

Funny Pegger contemplated his coffee cup, picked it up and drank, then fell to looking at the cup again. "Somebody ought to tack up what you just said in the halls of Congress."

Vix pointed a spoon at Jones. "There's just two things wrong with it," she said.

Jones looked puzzled. "Two?"

"First, giving away one hundred thousand is crazy and I don't care what system you use."

"But—"

"Second," Vix said, "how are you going to tell the honest people from the moochers? How are you going to distinguish the dogs that want to hunt from those that want to whine for food? Kindly answer those two."

"Polyphemus Ward."

Vix jumped. She jumped rather more than Jones thought mention of the financier's name called for. Vix also looked somewhat strange.

"What—what do you mean?" she asked.

Jones arose.

"I shall endeavor to demonstrate," he announced.

TO GET in contact with Polyphemus Ward, one could telephone his office and get in touch with one of thirty-seven assistant secretaries, and if an important person, be connected with one of eighteen secretaries, and if the caller was very important, he might get to talk to Lyman Lee, the financier's confidential secretary, but he was unlikely to get any further. The other system was to pick up the telephone, say the first large figure that came to mind, add the word *dollars*, and Polyphemus Ward would be on the line in short order. Old Polyphemus Ward was a beagle for dollars. Jones used the dollar system.

"You—again!" Polyphemus Ward yelled. "Say, I told you not to bother me until you'd made a go of our deal, or had flopped! What are you calling me for? Goodbye!"

"There is," Jones said, "a favor you can do for me."

"What? Favor? *Me?*"

"There is," Jones said patiently, "a matter which I believe you would not care to have publicized."

A Vesuvian sound came over the telephone wire. "If you mean that business of my hundred thousand you're giving away," the financier yelled, "I'll tie knots in your arms! I'll wring your neck if you tell anybody!" He mentioned more that he would do and went into his background of cowpunching and hard-rock mining for words.

Jones interrupted. "If Wall Street heard about the matter, they'd think you had gone crazy. Er—wolves always eat a wounded comrade."

"You blackmailer!"

"I wish," Jones said, "to borrow the private detective agency which you have for some time employed to search for your missing daughter, Janice."

Mention of Janice was always cold water on old Polyphemus Ward. The snarl went out of him, and like a man dazed by a blow, he must have misunderstood, for: "You've found some trace of Janice?" he asked hoarsely.

Jones frowned at the telephone mouthpiece. Men were strange things. Here was a ranting old dollar-magnet with the qualities of a crab, including the shell, and he had a soft spot. He would loot an international banking ring with high glee, trim the budget of a squawling European dictator with gusto, and if someone shot at him, he would reach for the six-shooter he probably kept in his desk drawer. But Polyphemus Ward's daughter had left him because she was afraid his contrariness was contagious. She'd vanished; gone off to get human, like other people. And if she stayed away long enough; it might be that Polyphemus Ward would get human, too.

"I am not," Jones said, "engaged in a hunt for your daughter. I merely wish to use your detectives. I—er—think you will consent to that."

"You scamp!"

"You will send the chief of your detectives to me at once."

"Yes. Yes, of course—I mean—dammit! Who do you think you are giving orders to?"

"To an old dollar-trap with more money than manners," Jones responded. "I trust you will comply with my wishes at once."

"Hell you say! I'm through with you. Goodbye!"

"The address," Jones said, "is Number Twelve, Fiftieth Avenue."

"When I get hold of you," yelled Polyphemus Ward, "I'll stamp on you so hard you'll have to unbutton your shoes to breathe! Goodbye, you idiot! Er—are you in any fresh trouble? If you are, I've got good lawyers."

"Thank you," Jones said. "But I—ah—once read a lawbook."

FUNNY PEGGER got up and made a quick circle around the room, holding his head with both hands, then fell in a chair and threw up his arms. He looked heavenward.

"Don't, don't, *don't* do this to me!" he yelled. "I can't stand it! Anyway, dear Lord, I don't deserve it!"

"Eh—what have I done now?" Jones inquired, puzzled.

"Just," said the gag-man, "tied knots in the lion's tail. Don't you know old Polyphemus Ward eats babies? Don't you know he's the only guy Mussolini is scared of? Don't you know that—oh, bird-cages! I give up!"

Jones shook his head seriously. "All I did was secure the aid of private detectives to investigate applicants of Genius, Incorporated."

"Genius, Incorporated," said Funny Pegger, "is another thing that worries me."

Jones frowned. "It is our new company for loaning out one thousand dollars to a person."

"That," Funny Pegger groaned, "is all this day needs."

CHAPTER XXV

THE MORE THE SCREWIER

DESPITE PREDICTIONS, BY six o'clock in the afternoon, everyone was enthusiastic. The fact that people read afternoon newspapers had already started the firm of Genius, Incorporated, to functioning. There was still somewhat less than forty-nine thousand dollars in Jones' pocket, but only because the private detectives he had extorted from Polyphemus Ward needed time to investigate applicants.

GENIUS, INC.
Will Loan up to $1,000 without Interest or Security to Any
Honest Person Who Wants to Go into Business for Himself.

This was the advertisement which Funny Pegger inserted in the daily papers at Jones' request, and it was evidently good sugar, because applicants arrived like buckshot, including a percentage whose interest subsided when they heard they would be investigated by private detectives. But there was real grist left for the mill. Among the applicants were: An elderly and almost blind chemist who had a clever idea for making self-lighting cigars, a woman who wanted to raise chickens, a lobster fisherman who wanted to buy a boat and traps and go back to his trade, and a soda-jerk who was out of work, but who knew where he could start a soft-drink stand for a thousand dollars. A man wanted to breed cats, a mechanic needed tools, a fellow wanted a small filling station, and five Greeks desired to go into the lunchroom business. Seven Italians wanted fruit stands, three Irishmen thought they could make a living in the trucking business, and two Chinamen yearned for laundries. These people were typical human beings, so some of them would doubtless lose a thousand dollars and others would go ahead and get rich, while some would get jitters and back out, before they got started.

The chief of the private detectives was a middle-aged man, rotund, placid of face, neat of attire, his one noticeable peculiarity being a haircut that would be called a crock job in the farming regions. Watson was his name. Funny Pegger instantly dubbed him, "Doctor."

Watson said: "We'll get after these people. You want to know if they're worth risking one thousand on? Is that it?"

Funny Pegger nodded. "That's Jones' idea, as near as I can make him out." The gag-man frowned. "Look, Doc, Jones wants you to make a duplicate set of your reports and turn them over to Polyphemus Ward."

The detective tamped tobacco in a short pipe, drew in smoke and laughed it out. "Old Polyphemus," he said, "is running true to form."

Funny Pegger agreed, "The old reprobate is always running somebody."

"Men don't fool him." Watson smoked thoughtfully. "He's got the guts to back his judgment. I guess that's the difference between Polyphemus Ward and guys like you and me. Now you take me. Damned if I would take a fellow I found on an iceberg and give him one hundred thousand dollars to give away, just to find out if he had common sense enough to handle a job I had in mind for him."

"Yeah," agreed the gag-man absent-mindedly. "Me neither—what? *What?*"

Watson peered at Funny Pegger. "Is something wrong?"

"I—uh—oh, my!" Funny Pegger beat the left side of his chest with his right fist.

"I used to have them spells myself," Watson said sympathetically. "But when I laid off seventy-five-cent-a-pint whisky, they left me."

"I—whew! Great grief!" Funny Pegger got up shakily. "I— goodbye! See you tomorrow!"

THEY had rented a pair of furnished offices in a more or less ratty Forty-fifth Street building as a cradle for the newborn organization of Genius, Inc., and into the second of these sancta Funny Pegger went staggering in search of Jones. He peered around, squinting as if there wasn't enough light, and saw that Jones and Vix had gone, after which he rushed out of the building. All the way to Vix's apartment, he either made mumbling noises, or pleaded with the taxi driver for more speed. He tore into Vix's living room and gasped. "Where is he?"

"If you mean *it*," Vix said, "it's in the kitchen feeding itself. When it's not getting in trouble, it's usually feeding itself."

"Shhhh!" Funny Pegger hissed dramatically.

The glance Vix gave Funny Pegger changed from casual to blue-eyed intentness. There was heat and dampness on the gag-man's moonish face, obviously much animation inside him.

"I had a hunch," Vix said, "you'd get pixilated before this was all done."

She turned away, shaking her head.

"Shhh!" said Funny Pegger. "I just found out where he got the hundred thousand."

"Who'd he rob?" Vix looked blank, then concern jumped over her face. "Look here! He didn't—didn't—or *did* he?"

"Polyphemus Ward!"

"What do you mean?"

"Old Polyphemus gave it to him. It's a test of whether Jones gets a job. *The* job!"

"And *the* job is what?"

"I forgot to tell you," Funny Pegger explained excitedly. "Polyphemus is gonna hire a man to administer his fortune to philanthropies. He's going to give the man an outright gift of a million to keep him honest. He told me about it one time. He must have told that detective, too, and told him he had Jones in mind, because the sleuth took it for granted that I knew, and he let it slip—"

Vix looked queer. "Why didn't you tell me?"

"I just found out—"

"I mean about Polyphemus Ward giving his money away!" Vix's voice edged. "Why didn't you tell me?"

"I—"

Vix took handfuls of Funny Pegger's coat lapels. "Maybe you thought it didn't concern me at all?" she shrieked.

"Uh—shhh!" Funny Pegger admonished. "He'll hear you!"

Vix inhaled deeply. "Of all the low-grade intellects! You—you monkey!"

Jones appeared in the door. The way Vix and Funny Pegger dropped everything and stared at him made him feel uncomfortable.

"Er—monkey," he remarked. "The most interesting monkey is the howling monkey of Central America, which is equipped with a peculiar enlargement of the hyoid and laryngeal apparatus which permits it to make unearthly howling noises."

"We've just found out," Funny Pegger told him, "where you got that hundred thousand."

Jones broke out in smiles.

"I'm certainly glad of that," he declared. "Keeping my promise not to reveal the matter to anyone was a great nuisance."

There was a knock on the door.

FUNNY PEGGER and Vix looked at Jones, and Jones looked blank, then the knock came again, and all eyes went with one accord to the handiest window.

"Probably police," Funny Pegger hissed.

"They still want to arrest me, I believe," Jones said nervously.

Knuckles gave the door a third banging, and the sound sent

Vix a step toward the window before she tightened her lips and approached the door. "What is it?"

"Telegram."

Vix reached for the door latch, but Funny Pegger, rushing over, blocked her hand and hissed: "An old phony to get doors open!"

The gag-man said loudly: "Shove it under the door!"

A telegram whisked over the threshold, and Funny Pegger, grinning foolishly, opened the door and signed a yellow delivery slip presented by a pint-sized urchin with freckles who stood outside.

"For you," the gag-man told Jones.

Jones took the telegram and scrutinized it curiously. "The telegraph," he stated, "is an invention attributed to Samuel Morse in 1832, but history of its development actually goes back to Musschenbroek in the eighteenth century."

Vix stamped a foot.

"Willies," she said, "are what quotations give people! Open that thing. That's what it's for."

Jones painstakingly extracted contents of the yellow envelope, and ran his eyes over a row of words on a tape stuck to the yellow blank.

"Well, well," he remarked.

Vix picked the sheet from his fingers. It said:

CALLING FOR YOU AT NINE TONIGHT. I HAVE LOCATED A CRAP GAME FOR YOU. LOVE,
GLACIA.

Vix frowned. "Who is Glacia?"

Funny Pegger said, "Daughter of Countess Mark Montignal de Grandrieu. You know her."

Vix puckered her forehead. "Yes, I remember her. But how did she meet our amazing friend?"

"The countess," said Funny Pegger, "mooched a trip on the yacht for herself and her chick."

Vix went to a small modern metal-table, and picked up a cigarette and struck a match, then turned to eye Jones as she drew flame against the tobacco. She seemed to be scrutinizing him in search of mysterious characteristics. She shook her head, and pointed the cigarette at Jones, but looked at Funny Pegger.

"I don't see it," she said. "But it's hanging on to him somewhere. It has to be!"

"What?" asked Funny Pegger.

"I think it must be *Nepeta cataria*," Vix said.

Jones frowned; the zany goings-on of this pair having him baffled again.

"*Nepeta cataria,*" he remarked, "is ordinary catnip, for which cats have a peculiar fondness."

"Yes," Vix said. "I know. I was thinking of Glacia."

"Also a million dollars," Funny Pegger added.

The wrinkles of Jones' frown got deeper. A muscle gathered in a knot on each side of his jaw, and without further words, he turned and stalked into the kitchen, shutting the door behind him with a bang.

Vix stared at the door. Then she looked at Funny Pegger. Her blue eyes were incredulous.

"What got into him? Always before, he stuck around and let us march back and forth across his quivering flesh."

"Glacia," said Funny Pegger.

"Eh?"

"Jones," said Funny Pegger, "is open to education on every subject except the Countess' chick. Anything you say against Glacia tends to bring out the porcupine in him."

WITH an impatient gesture, Vix stubbed the red nose of her cigarette against an ash tray, then obeyed the universal impulse of womankind when confronted by a problem; she went to a mirror to give herself a critical examination. She moulded a tendril of bright hair into place with a fingertip.

"I don't understand it," she said.

"Neither do I." The gag-man grinned. "You've got Glacia trimmed seven ways from the bat."

Vix said quickly, "I didn't mean that!"

"Oh!"

"If you think I care whether that female goblin gets him," Vix snapped, "you're crazy."

Funny Pegger carefully took his grin off. "Oh, well, for the sake of harmony, old man Pegger will let you think you're fooling him. Suppose we discuss that telegram. It worries me."

"I wonder what he's doing?" Vix frowned at the kitchen door. "Maybe he's skipped out the back way!" she exclaimed.

She ran to the door, opened it, then looked relieved. Jones was in the kitchen, and also half inside the electric refrigerator, exploring.

"This," he remarked, "is an interesting mechanical device."

Vix sighed. "I'm glad to see you've got something harmless like a refrigerator on your mind."

Jones smiled. "By the way," he said, "I noticed during my expedition last night that most of the gentlemen wore the kind of garb which I have heard Mr. Pegger designate as toad suits."

"Toad suits?"

"He means," Funny Pegger explained, "evening dress. A tux. Suit of tails. Soup and fish. Monkey plumage."

"If he continues to get his vocabulary from you," Vix stated, "he's going to have a honey."

Jones interposed, "What I was trying to ask is this: May one acquire such raiment at this time of the evening?"

"They rent dress suits, if that's what you mean," Funny Pegger admitted. "You just telephone one of the places you'll find listed in the classified telephone directory."

"Thank you," Jones said. "I shall do so."

Vix said: "Wait a minute! Does this yen for a dress suit mean you're going out with Glacia tonight and visit that crap game?"

"Why, yes," Jones admitted.

Vix's lips tightened. "Listen, if you think we'll let—"

Funny Pegger took hold of her arm and pinched.

"Confucius," he said, "was the Chinese wise man who said it is a wise dog that knows when not to bark at the tiger."

Vix had much on her mind and a choice assortment of words with which to make delivery, but she held back, allowing Funny Pegger to tow her into the living room and close the kitchen door so that Jones would not overhear.

"I'd like to wring his neck!"

"Shhh!" the gag-man admonished soberly. "This is an emergency, and for once I'm not lacking."

Vix frowned. "What do you mean?"

"Listen," Funny Pegger ordered, "to a masterly idea, as follows: First, I volunteer to go out and get friend Jones his toad suit."

"But—"

"And I'll buy," interrupted the gag-man, "something to make the guy sleep. We slip him the Mickey Finn at dinner, and our troubles are over."

Vix peered at him. "Are you sane?"

"It's a swell idea."

"So was Haile Selassie's idea that he could whip the Italians."

"This will work."

"Drug him, you mean?"

"Sure."

Vix sighed. "We've got to do something to him so we can get some sleep."

Funny Pegger picked up his hat. "I'm off on my errand of mercy."

THE GAG-MAN proceeded to a drug store and made the discovery that sedatives were sold only on prescription from a physician, but profiting by that knowledge, he straightway visited a doctor in the neighborhood, and described an imaginary but terrific case of jitters which, he moaned, had kept him awake night after night. Unfortunately the doctor turned out to be an osteopath who was an enthusiastic bone-cracker as well as a high-pressure salesman, so that Funny Pegger, before he could help himself, was stumbling out of the place, minus five dollars, and also possessor of a remarkably disjointed feeling. Having satisfactorily deceived a second doctor with trumped-up symptoms, the gag-man secured a prescription, got it filled, and returned to the apartment, picking up en route a full dress suit somewhat near Jones' dimensions.

Jones scrutinized the black dress attire, his face expressionless.

"Crow," he remarked, "is a large glossy black, oscine bird of *Corvus* and allied genus, having loud vocal equipment and an appetite for young corn. Crow is also a type of door knocker, a croaking sound, a cry of exultation, the southern constellation of Corvus, and a tribe of Indians."

He retired to the bedroom to don his new plumage.

Funny Pegger winked at Vix and exhibited the package of sleeping drug.

"How are you going to give it to him?" Vix asked.

"We'll have hot chocolate for dinner."

"But he may notice the taste."

"We'll tell him," said Funny Pegger, "that it's the way chocolate should taste. He never had any chocolate before." The gag-man considered. "Here, I'll stick the stuff in this vase until we're ready for it. Then I'll help you get dinner...."

THE SINGING sound had been there for some time—it seemed to Funny Pegger that the interval had been several hours. It did not change tone, and was like something made by a bumblebee with half-portion wings, and it had become monotonous to the point where there was an urgent necessity for taking measures. If measures were not taken in a hurry, there might be a disaster, because the singing noise had gotten synchronized with the vibrating point of his skull or something, and was about to pop it wide open, the way they said Caruso could shatter wine glasses with his voice. With a mighty effort, a Herculean summoning of energies, Funny Pegger got awake. At first he could see nothing.

The side of his face felt gummy. It had, he saw, been resting in a plate of soup.

He peered at a hazy something that was located across the table, winking both eyes, and finally with the aid of his fingers, dispelled enough of the haze to recognize the object as Vix.

Suddenly Funny Pegger sprang up and as promptly fell to the floor. He got up, held to chairs and stumbled into the kitchen, then sloped into the bedroom, and finally came rubber-legging back into the living room.

"Vix!" he yelled. "Jones is gone!"

Vix stirred a trifle.

"Vix!" bellowed Pegger. "He switched the stuff and we drank it. He's gone! Oh, damn the luck! Him and his forty-nine thousand dollars are both gone!"

CHAPTER XXVI

TRAIL OF THE LAMB

THE HANDS OF the electric clock on the apartment living room radio said seven minutes until eleven. Funny Pegger glared at the clock, unable to get his foggy mind to think of anything but crap games, and resenting the coincidence of the seven and eleven on the clock. It was dark outside, and in the kitchen the electric refrigerator buzzed as it cooled itself. Funny Pegger let go the chair to which he had been holding, and promptly fell down.

"I do rather well," he remarked. "All things considered."

He lay there for a few minutes, wanting to go back to sleep but knowing he ought to go help Jones. After his better nature had emerged victorious, he got up and lurched to the table.

"Wake up!" he said thickly, to Vix.

Getting no answer, he fumbled around on the table, sprawling among the dishes, until he got three glasses and sloshed what water was in them onto Vix. Vix rolled her head on her arms just enough to show one blue eye. She winked the eye two or three times.

"Where did all this smoke come from?" she inquired drowsily. "There's a good deal of it."

Funny Pegger peered at her. "Wake up!" he said. "There's not any smoke."

"What?"

With as much clearness as he could manage, Funny Pegger said. "The place is on fire! Wake up! Wanna get burned alive?"

Vix moved her head again, a very little, then gave it up and shut her eyes. "That's too bad," she mumbled, and dozed off.

Funny Pegger went into a small futile rage during which he rubbed a thumb and middle finger together soundlessly under the impression he was snapping them in desperation.

"Jones!" he yelled.

"Leave him alone," Vix suggested drowsily. "He's probably sleepy."

"Jones—" screamed Funny Pegger—"is gone!"

Vix squirmed.

"Jones," roared Funny Pegger, "has gone with Glacia to find that crap game!"

"What?" Vix pushed herself up by pressing on the table top with both hands. She pulled her eyebrows together, pushed out her lips and shook her head. "What's wrong with me?" she asked. "Where is Jones?"

"Jones switched that sleeping powder on us!"

Vix rubbed her eyes and kept on shaking her head. "How? Didn't you put it in his chocolate?"

"I put *something* in his chocolate."

"Then what—"

"Oh, shucks! You remember I hid the stuff in a vase while I helped you get dinner. He must have got it out and put sugar or something in the box. And he put the powder in our soup. I remember he came fooling around in the kitchen and offered to put the soup on the table. And the soup tasted funny."

"Why didn't you say so?"

The gag-man groaned. "I thought it was the way you made soup."

"I must be good! You can't tell when my soup has Mickey Finns in it."

Funny Pegger shuffled from one room to another again and came back and said, "He's sure enough gone." Then he thought of something else and ran stumbling to the electric clock and put his round face close to the rounder one of the clock.

"We've been asleep two hours!"

Vix asked: "Where would he go?"

"How do I know?" Pegger planted himself in the middle of the room and looked in different directions. "He's with Glacia. She's taking him to that crap game."

"You said that before!" Vix experimented to see if she could stand. She could. She said: "We're wasting time."

IT SEEMS to be the misfortune of man to have his foibles become his necessities. The uniformed doormen, for instance, in front of all New York apartment-houses.

The doorman of Vix's apartment was taller by a foot than the average, and he had a noteworthy development of forearm and biceps muscles, as well as curly hair, and a grin both engaging and remarkable for the number and dimensions of the white teeth it revealed. He looked rather Irish, except that his skin was as black as that of Haile Selassie.

"Yass'm," he said. "I'se done been noticin' dat young gen'lman what's stayin' with you-all."

"By any chance," asked Vix, "did you notice him about two hours ago?"

"Hot doggie!" The doorman rolled his eyes.

"What do you mean—hot doggie?"

"Dat boy sho' done pick himself a scintillator fo' a mama," declared the doorman.

"Having seen Glacia," remarked Funny Pegger, "we understand you perfectly."

Vix glared, clenched her fists, stamped one foot and otherwise imitated a small auburn bull which had been shown a red flag.

"Where did they go?" she demanded.

The doorman shrugged mighty shoulders, "Dey done go where Boze take 'em, Ah guess."

"Who is Boze?"

"He's a frien' of mine."

"By any chance," Vix inquired patiently, "does Boze drive a taxicab? And was he hired by Jones and the—scintillator?"

"He sho-nuff does."

"Where can we find Boze?"

"Ah wouldn't know. Ah sho' wouldn't. Guess maybe he might come monkeyin' around again tonight. Gen'lly he does."

Vix produced a five dollar bill and held it under the doorman's dark nose long enough for him to become interested.

"Find Boze," she said, "and you'll be rich."

"Mah goodness!" the doorman said.

JONES had not been enthusiastic about eating a second dinner that evening. But Glacia hooked herself onto his arm, gazed up warmingly into his eyes, and asked him if he wanted her to starve, and of course he didn't, so they went to a Japanese place on Forty-seventh Street for *suki yaki*. He paid the check and added another sum to the total mentally designated: invested in Jones, personally.

Glacia looked at him and smiled a siren smile. She had been propped on an elbow, absently studying two chop sticks which she was moving about with her fingers.

Glacia arose. "Excuse me," she said. "I'm going to do things to my face. Back in a little."

She walked to the rear of the place, through a door, up a flight of steps, and into a private dining room where Lyman Lee waved to her from a table.

"Hello, there."

Glacia gave Lyman Lee her hand and looked past him at Tray Marco, who was of steel coolness, and Paul Shevinsky, who gazed at her with a loose-lipped intensity. Harold Hover, the bacteriologist, sat behind a half-emptied pint of scotch; he looking more strained than the last time Glacia saw him. Forgetful Osborn peered at Glacia as if he couldn't remember who she was. The five men greeted her in their various ways.

"All set?" Tray Marco asked suddenly. His voice was so like a knife blade snapping that Glacia winced.

"Yes, I—guess so."

Tray Marco's eyes held her and she could not get away from their coldness even after she looked away. The eyes were not sleepy nor lifeless—just emotionless. The whole man did not seem to have a movable muscle. The cigarette between the fingers of his left hand gave off a curl of bluish smoke that might have arisen from an Indian signal fire.

"I'd hate to see you showing doubts," Tray Marco said.

Glacia wanted to say something cool and hard, but her mind would not supply the words, and her throat was too tight to make them if it had; she was scared of Tray Marco. The man was so obviously deadly. Something was happening inside her. Suddenly she hated the thing they were doing, and hated, most of all, her part in it. And abruptly she wanted to tell them that she was not going through with it. She was surprised that she should feel that way; she could not have explained it. She raised her eyes, intending to refuse to go any farther. But Tray Marco's look froze her.

"We're all rigged," he said. "Steer him to my gambling house on Forty-ninth Street. Better do it right away." He lifted the cigarette in his left hand and drew on it. "Forgetful, here, is going to run the crap table," he added.

Forgetful Osborn said, "I had something to tell you—let me think— Oh, yes. I'm going to wear a disguise."

Lyman Lee chuckled softly. He looked at Glacia. "You can get rid of Jones as soon as we take him. I'll have your money. You get everything we take him for, as we agreed. We'll go somewhere and celebrate."

Glacia's lips felt dry.

Tray Marco looked at his cigarette. "The dame is getting a big cut. Forty-nine grand, the sucker has left, hasn't he?"

"That's all right," Lyman Lee said. "She's steering Jones for us."

Tray Marco frowned. "And me, I'm using one of my houses. What if Jones yaps to the cops? They'll close me up."

Lyman Lee shook his head. "Jones knows that the police want to arrest him for murder. Do you think he would go to them?" He grinned at the gambler. "I'm paying for this. If the price isn't satisfactory, I might sweeten it a little. Say five hundred and fifty for Forgetful."

Forgetful Osborn said, "You can see who is low man around here."

"This is swell!" Tray Marco put his cigarette on his lower lip and got up, paced once around the table, then took the cigarette away. "It's so swell, it stinks! It's too easy. There ain't nothing to it. And I don't like things there ain't nothing to!"

Forgetful Osborn said, "I remember that I've been telling you good gentlemen that this Jones may be an Arctic wildcat—"

"Shut up!" Tray Marco said. Forgetful Osborn subsided and looked as mild as he could. Tray Marco went to Glacia and put his forefinger, rigid, against her chest. "Look, babe," he said. "I don't know about you. I don't know about any woman. But I figure that it won't hurt you to know something you don't—"

"Marco!" Lyman Lee interrupted.

Tray Marco looked at Lyman Lee. "This is my part of the

show and I'm running it. I'm telling the girl off." He pressed the forefinger against Glacia. She could feel its pointed hardness. "Did you know," Tray Marco asked coldly, "that your boy friend Lee hired Hover to knock off that German liner-captain?"

Glacia's lips twitched apart. "I—"

"I just wanted you to know," Marco said, "how deep it is. And you're swimming in it with the rest of us."

Glacia swallowed.

"So I'd play the game if I was you," Marco added. He sat down and lit another cigarette off the one he had been smoking.

GLACIA was pale as Lyman Lee and Forgetful Osborn accompanied her as far as the head of the stairs. They stood and watched her descend, going slowly, as if she was dazed. "I was just thinking," Forgetful Osborn said, "that maybe Tray Marco hadn't ought to have done that."

Lyman Lee shrugged. "It'll scare her into line if she had any ideas about stepping out on us."

"Marco is great at scaring people," Forgetful grumbled. "He scares me all the time."

Lyman Lee said nothing. He was frowning after Glacia. She went through the door at the bottom of the stairs and Lyman Lee removed his monocle and fingered it, still not saying anything.

"Tray Marco," said Forgetful, "reminds me of a trained tiger."

Lyman Lee scowled at the foot of the stairs.

"I once had a friend who owned a trained tiger," Forgetful continued, "but it ate him up one day."

Lyman Lee gestured at the stairs.

"Dammit!" he said. "I believe Glacia *has* got a yen on this Jones." He chuckled. "Now wouldn't that be one for the book?" He glanced at Forgetful. "What was that about lions?"

"It was tigers." Forgetful sighed. "It didn't mean anything— much."

The two men went back to the others.

Glacia had been struck by lightning. She sank into a chair in the ladies' lounge and got out a handkerchief, although her eyes were dry. There was pounding all through her. She felt the way she had the time her car turned over twice.

There wasn't anything she could do about it. She had thought wildly all the way out of the private dining room and down the stairs, and the distance had seemed five miles. She wanted to flee from the Japanese restaurant. Run away. But she couldn't. She had no money. Neither had her mother. There was no one she could borrow from; they had exhausted the gullibility of the people who had been her mother's friends before she married the foreign nobleman who frittered her fortune away.

Even before she had learned of the murder, Glacia knew she had stopped liking the plot. She knew the reason. She was a girl who prided herself on being cool and calculating, and she had tried to fool herself about why she had changed. But she knew. She had fallen in love with Jones. And it irritated her, because he was so absolutely naïve. How could she even like anyone so—so boorish? But Jones had some quality about him that had tripped her.

And now she was scared.

She had supposed the death of the German captain was what the papers said it was—the result of an infection. Infection. An infection was germs, or bacteria, and Harold Hover was a bacteriologist…. She shuddered. Her hands and face felt hot and the rest of her cold. Tray Marco wouldn't play—with murder, she thought first! And second, that one killing breeds another, often.

She got up and went out to the dining room, walking stiffly.

CHAPTER XXVII

CHIPS

JONES WAS PLEASED with everything. He had been fed well, he was in interesting surroundings, had an attractive companion, and what was best of all, he seemed to have a fair number of his troubles crowded into a corner and was all set to knock them in the head. He could not escape the conviction that he was approaching a high point, bringing everything to a head. Little, as they say, did he know.

"Apex," he remarked, "comes from the Latin *apices*, meaning a small rod in the top of a priest's cap, and can refer to a part of a Hebrew letter, a diacritical mark, a section of a copper vein, the tip of a mountain, or the culmination of an activity."

Glacia reached the table, sank into a chair and stared at Jones. "I was referring," Jones said, "to the present array of circumstances."

Glacia smiled rather woodenly. Her lack of enthusiasm moved Jones to offer an excuse for his unusual remarks.

"Dogs," he said, "like to sit in front of igloos and bark at the moon."

His companion looked puzzled.

"I believe that they do so to relieve their canine feelings." Jones smiled apologetically. "My remarks serve the same purpose."

When they were in a taxicab, Glacia made an intent business of putting light to a cigarette. Jones leaned back on the cushions, watching the glitter of Broadway through the windows, feeling warmed by the brilliance.

"An improvement," he stated, "over the Aurora Borealis."

"Over which?" Glacia asked absently.

"The Northern Lights. Aurora Borealis." Jones rolled down the window to get a better view. "This is—er—the first time I have felt a preference for this form of illuminative display."

"Oh," Glacia said. "I wasn't noticing. I'm sorry."

Jones looked at her intently. She was preoccupied. And that, for Glacia, was unusual.

"Is something wrong?" he inquired.

Glacia put her head back so that the line of her neck and chin was a smooth sweep from quadratus muscle to clavicle, with a small and entirely rhythmic pulsing from an artery. "Everything," she said, "is perfect...."

The sign in front said, *Bar.* In the rear was a door, beyond the door a corridor half way down which was another door and a flight of steps leading up to an enormously fat man who sat at a desk. A sign said, *Theater Tickets,* and there were four telephones on the desk. The fat man got up and nodded at Glacia and looked speculatively at Jones as they passed through another door into a long room with a low ceiling, full of refrigerated air, and tables were scattered about. Well-dressed people sat at some of the tables, having good food and excellent service.

Jones said: "I do not believe I could eat another meal immediately."

"The food is free," Glacia explained. "And very good, too."

Jones frowned. "But I thought you were going to show me where I could find the speculative business called craps."

"This way," Glacia said. "I was just telling you that the house gives food to its patrons."

THEY crossed that room and went through a door hung with velvet. The walls were dark, the ceiling low, the lights subdued. A number of tables of assorted variety stood about, surrounded by a fashionable, fast crowd.

"The dice table," Glacia volunteered, "is over this way."

Jones was pleased. "Am I to understand that the—er—performance of craps is only a partial activity of this establishment?"

"That's right."

"What are these other tables?"

"Roulette, faro, poker—"

"Are they all a means of making money quickly?"

"They're all gambling." Glacia looked at Jones. On impulse, she said, "You know that you can lose money here as well as win it."

She knew that she wanted Jones to say that he hadn't dreamed of such a possibility, then she wanted him to get frightened at the idea of losing money, and hurry away to some place where he would be safe from Lyman Lee and Tray Marco and the rest.

"Yes," said Jones. "I know I can lose."

Glacia stared at him. "Then why are you going through with it?"

"I have to make fifty thousand dollars."

There was a quality in his voice that made Glacia look at him and think that it was as though something had cracked open and let her see grim determination to make fifty thousand dollars at any cost.

"I have to acquire the sum to replace funds which were swindled from me," Jones added, with a trace of desperation. "I have learned enough to know that I am not competent to earn such a considerable sum in the time which I have. Ah—I had thirty days after the yacht docked."

Glacia bit her lips. "But you may lose!"

Jones looked determined. "I have made up my mind," he said, "what I am going to do."

"But—"

A sleepy voice at their side said, "Good evening. Is there something I can do to help you?"

Glacia shrank inwardly from Tray Marco's leaden manner.

"We—we're looking for the crap table," she said.

"This way."

In a moment Jones found himself before a table ten feet long, five feet wide, edged by sideboards eight inches high. The whole interior was lined with green felt. A black leather cup stood on the table, and two amber dice with white spots.

Behind the table stood a squarish man with dark curly hair, beetling black brows, and a carefully waxed moustache. He wore full evening attire, had a scarlet ribbon across his shirt bosom. He manipulated a small rake, dragging in the dice and placing them in the black leather cup. The rake was black, with a blade a foot long, an inch and a half high, and three-fourths of an inch thick.

Glacia looked at the rake wielder a second time before she recognized Forgetful Osborn.

"I think," Jones remarked, "that I shall watch, in order that I may see how to do this."

Glacia moistened her lips. Tray Marco was watching her. Forgetful Osborn watched the dice. They rolled, stopped with four spots showing. A man muttered, "Little Joe! Hit me again, boy!" The man was Harold Hover. His hands shook so that he dropped a few chips on the floor. Forgetful Osborn reached out with the rake for the dice, and Hover rolled again. The dice came Little Joe. The house paid.

Forgetful sent the rake after the dice again. This time, he squeezed the rake handle at the right instant, and a cleverly concealed trap in the rake blade opened and two different dice dropped out, and simultaneously another little contrivance whisked the original two dice out of sight in the rake blade. It happened with lightning speed, and only a faint click. No one noticed. The only way they could have noticed was by the slightly altered position of the dice against the rake blade, which was almost impossible with the rake moving. The rake was retailed at ninety dollars by houses which dealt in such equipment.

Hover threw three consecutive sevens. The house paid.

Glacia touched the table edge.

"This," Jones declared, "seems to be what I have been looking for."

Tray Marco asked, "You want to try it?"

Jones examined Tray Marco. "I came here to do so," he explained seriously. "However, I should first like to ask some questions."

"Go ahead," Tray Marco said.

"Er—they may be of delicate nature."

"Go ahead."

Jones took a deep breath. "Is this honest?" he asked.

GLACIA caught her breath involuntarily—she knew Tray Marco's temper. But Tray didn't move a muscle. "It's honest," he said and smiled thinly. "But I run the place and you don't have to take my word. Suppose you circulate around and ask some of these people."

"Why," Jones said uncomfortably, "that will hardly be necessary. Your word will be enough."

Tray Marco nodded. "Want to try a small bet?"

"Er—may I?"

"Of course."

Jones looked enthusiastic. "Then I should like very much to indulge."

He produced his roll of forty-nine thousand-dollar bills. He peeled off one.

"I shall wager this," he said, "to begin with."

Tray Marco smiled at the cigarette in his left hand. "The banker," he explained, "is over this way."

"Banker?"

"You buy chips," Tray Marco explained, "and bet the chips."

Jones considered this. He frowned. "I thought," he said, "that money was wagered."

Tray Marco was patient. "Sure. You bet chips. They're money."

Jones picked up a red chip and examined it, then scrutinized a blue and a yellow chip. His conclusions called for a quotation. "Chip," he announced, "derives from the German *kippen,* meaning to clip. It also means a crack or fissure, to break into a bud, or designates a Cuban Palm, a wrestling trick or a trivial object."

Tray Marco frowned. "Huh?" he said.

"My point," explained Jones, "is that I do not need chips. I need money. Therefore, I wish to play for money."

Tray Marco got rid of his frown and looked patient.

"That's all right."

"I may wager money?"

"Yeah. We'll humor you."

Humoring him meant, it soon appeared, taking him for the tune of two hundred and fifty dollars in four smooth passes. Jones' eyes were brightly interested, and he seemed neither surprised nor upset that he lost. Tray Marco, watching Jones as closely and as impassively as Jones was watching dice and rake and croupier, could not tell whether Jones was spotting the tricky antics of that dishonest, oh-so-clever little rake. Jones' face was impassive. And so was Tray's.

After the fourth pass, he turned to Tray with a pleasant smile.

"You—pardon me is there a washroom anywhere about?"

Tray told him.

As he crossed the gambling room, Jones stared intently at a blank-faced, beefy man in tight-fitting dinner jacket who stood in the doorway, obviously a bouncer or guard of some sort. Although Jones was not familiar with the term, he found it simple enough to place the man.

On his way through the door, he stopped for a few seconds' earnest conversation with the blank-faced husky. A bill changed hands—quite a small one—and Jones had secured the other's cooperation. Jones, it appeared, was expecting a young lady with blue eyes and very black hair. She would be gowned in green lace and wearing a corsage of yellow roses. Her cape would be mink, trimmed, with a red velvet tie at the throat.

The bouncer nodded woodenly.

"It's important that I know the moment she arrives," Jones said. "So if you would just report to me—I shall be at that table over there—every three or four minutes. Be very careful that the young lady with me doesn't hear what you tell me." He smiled in a creditable imitation of the Casanova-about-town manner, and continued on his way to the washroom, where he stood watching a fat man who was washing his hands. When the fat man had gone, Jones unscrewed one of the light bulbs, standing on a toilet seat to reach the bulb.

He took a dime out of his pocket, also his handkerchief. He folded and rolled the handkerchief until he had a tight cylinder of cloth nearly three inches long and not more than half an inch in diameter. He balanced the dime on one end of this, and inserted it in the light socket.

When the dime short-circuited the socket, there was a devil-spit burst of blue sparks and whizzing and popping.

The lights went out. It got very black.

Jones walked out of the men's room, hurrying, and crossed, with skill born of a life spent where the nights were six months long, to the crap table. He felt around. He got hold of the rake. Then he got hold of Forgetful Osborn's arm. He put his lips close to Forgetful Osborn's ear.

"I wish," Jones said, "to converse privately with you."

Forgetful Osborn recognized the voice. "Gleeps!" he said.

CHAPTER XXVIII

THE LAMB'S GOLD FLEECE

FUNNY PEGGER WAS never a patient man. He came rushing out of the apartment kitchen now with a bottle.

Vix frowned at the bottle. "That's swell," she said. "Get drunk!"

"What else do you expect me to do?"

"Nothing. It's exactly what I expected."

Funny Pegger planted the bottle on the table. "Watch me take an oath!" He raised one hand dramatically. "I do hereby pledge me to have nothing more to do with Jones, so help me." He picked the bottle up. "Where's the corkscrew?"

Vix said, "So you're walking out on him?"

"Out on *him?* He walked out on *us!*"

"Maybe," Vix said gloomily, "we shouldn't have tried to give him that Mickey Finn."

"I don't know what we shouldn't have done." Funny Pegger put the bottle down again, and said, "It's time for my regular five-minute visit to that doorman." He left.

He was back in a moment shouting and shoving two flustered-looking colored men ahead of him. One of the darkies was the doorman. The other was a smaller, rounder piece of ebony with a taxi driver's cap.

"They were standing out front talking." Funny Pegger yelled. *"Talking!* And us in here with our wheels about to fly out!"

"Boze only jes get back," said the doorman.

Boze looked injured. "Ah don' do nothin'," he insisted.

"Where'd you take him?" Funny Pegger roared.

"Ah don't know."

"You don't know?"

"Ah don't know what you' all talkin' 'bout."

Funny Pegger explained that he was talking about a tall, well-built young man who was a magnet for trouble and who had, it was rumored, hired Boze's taxicab for himself and a glittering female companion. The explanation was emphasized with arm wavings.

"Oh, dem folks," Boze said. "Dey went—"

"Can you take us there?" the gag-man interrupted.

"Sho', Mike," Boze said.

FUNNY PEGGER sat on the taxicab cushions, and every two minutes, regularly, he poked Boze in the back and asked him why he thought he was driving a hearse. The rest of the time he sat with his fingers fastened on his knees and his mind stabbing itself with thoughts.

The taxicab shaved a parked car, two-wheeled a corner, scared a cop pale, and kept going.

"This ain't a funeral!" Funny Pegger yelled. "Get a move on."

He grabbed his knees again. Maybe Jones would be all right. Jones had a lot of that scarce commodity, horse sense.

The more he thought about it, the nearer Funny Pegger came to concluding that Jones' Genius, Inc., was the best piece of clear thinking he had seen since Roosevelt made the banks insure the depositors' money. The taxi came in to the curb like a badly disturbed rabbit. Boze looked around.

"Dey go to a rest'rant fust," he said. "Den heah."

Vix got out. "Whew!" She stared at the cab. "What a ride! I feel accordion-pleated."

"You may be yet," Funny Pegger muttered, peering at the establishment they were about to enter. "Know what this is?"

Vix examined the place. "It's made of brick."

"And Tray Marco," the gag-man muttered, "is made of trouble. This is one of Tray Marco's joints."

Vix pondered. "I seem to have heard of a Tray Marco."

"Your education," said Funny Pegger, "wouldn't be complete if you hadn't." He squared his shoulders. "Well, here goes."

They went past the bar through the door and up the stairs to the sign that said *Theater Tickets,* and Funny Pegger said, "Hello, Atom," to the enormously fat man behind the sign, then, after that they went on.

Inside the door, a slick man with dark skin and large teeth looked them over, then looked away, and Pegger breathed, "Joe Kirx, who got stuck in the vice racket trials." Of a man who might have been a banker, Funny Pegger said, "Collector for policy."

"Nice people," Vix suggested.

"Uh-huh."

"You know them so well, I'm getting suspicious."

They had paused near the door.

Suddenly Funny Pegger stopped. His jaw dropped. He grabbed Vix's arm.

"There he is!"

Vix stared at a knot of people, all well-dressed, who were doing everything but climb over each other to get close to something that was happening. A moment later, she saw Jones' head appear above the other heads, remain for a moment, then sink from sight.

"They've already taken him!" Funny Pegger croaked. "A mob like that would only gather to watch a killing!"

"Come on!" Vix raced forward.

"But what can we do?" the gag-man wailed.

Vix didn't answer. She sank an elbow in a fat man's ribs, twisted and pushed.

Funny Pegger struggled in her wake. They reached the craps table.

"Jones!" Vix gasped.

Jones, who was holding the black leather dice box aloft, looked at her. His face lighted.

"Eight," he announced, "is one more than seven. In Iceland, the word eight is called *atta*, in Gaelic it is *ochd*, in Danish *otte*, in Gothic *ahtau*. Rowing crews have eight members. Er—these amber cubes have five combinations totaling eight."

He rattled the dice in the box. "Eightur from Decatur!" he announced seriously. He threw the dice.

They came eight.

Vix clutched Jones' arm. "How much have you lost?" she asked wildly.

Jones gravely accepted the leather cup after Forgetful Osborn had raked the dice back into them.

"It is my wish," Jones said with dignity, "to permit accumulations to remain astride whatever it is they remain astride of."

A voice gulped, "He's letting it ride!"

The dice sailed against the bump wall, staggered back, end over end and stopped six and ace.

"Oh, criminy—he's doing *that* again!" an onlooker groaned.

Jones picked up a stack of greenbacks and gravely counted them. He looked at Vix.

"I have won," he announced, "one hundred seventy-two thousand and ninety-eight dollars, six wrist watches, eleven rings reputed to contain diamonds, other jewelry, and a deed to an item called a Rolls Royce."

"Don't forget," a man croaked, "my sixty-foot yacht!"

BOZE, the blackamoor taxicab driver, was waiting at the curb downstairs, and he did not seem surprised when Funny Pegger and Vix come flying out on the street dragging a reluctant but elated Jones. With wild haste, Boze opened the door, helped hurl Jones into the cab, slammed the door, jumped behind the wheel, and took the cab away from there with the speed and noise which will probably characterize interplanetary rockets.

"From de way you-all look," he said, "Ah done figger somethin' happen."

Vix leaned back, took two or three deep breaths and patted her chest with her left hand.

"Ah done figger it's jes' beginnin' to happen," she said.

"Ah-men," muttered Funny Pegger. "And ah-me!"

"I earned," Jones said proudly, "much more than fifty thousand."

Jones devoted some of his attention to remaining upright on the swaying taxicab cushions and the rest of it to stowing currency, jewelry, deeds and I.O.U. slips more securely in his pockets.

Vix looked at Funny Pegger. "They let us walk out of there with Jones."

"You're not as surprised as I am," Pegger said. "We ran, not walked, however."

Having completed stevedoring his winnings, Jones gazed amiably at his two companions. "My financial condition has improved."

"That's all that has improved, I'm afraid," Funny Pegger muttered.

"I only needed fifty thousand dollars," Jones pointed out. "But I made—"

"One hundred and seventy-two thousand and ninety eight dollars, six watches, eleven rings, and the Rolls Royce item," said the gag-man. "We remember."

Jones was elated. He had to hand himself a bouquet.

"Er—I did rather well, don't you think?" he inquired.

Funny Pegger wiped his forehead. "Ask me again in a few days, after I see what Tray Marco is gonna do about this."

Vix echoed this sentiment with a grim kind of nod.

Jones felt deflated. Having just completed a major coup, he had reasonable expectations of being approved—if not dancing in the streets in celebration, at least some dignified elation. Instead of assuring him he had done well, they were acting as though he had stepped on the baby's kitten. Maybe it was after-effects of the sleeping powder. He held to the seat as the cab skidded around a corner.

"You—ah—seem in excellent health," he remarked.

Vix grimaced. "Just give us time."

"I refer," Jones explained, "to your recovery from the sleeping potion which you—er—consumed unwittingly."

"Unwittingly is right." Vix eyed Jones. "We wish to confess that we had ideas of feeding you a Mickey Finn to keep you out of that crap game. We admit we were in error. And we state that henceforth we believe in miracles. Lastly, we wish to know how *we* got the Mickey Finn instead of you?"

Jones smiled.

"I am endeavoring to become a student of human nature," he said.

"Eh?"

"I noticed a strange note in your behavior. Er—I formerly noticed a kindred note in the deportment of my pet seal after it had consumed a fish to which it had no right. I—well—I eavesdropped, saw where you hid the sleeping potion, and the rest was—ah—rather simple."

"I like the seal part," Vix said.

"The *simple* is descriptive, too," agreed Funny Pegger.

Jones beamed on them.

An unavoidable encounter with a cop who had a loud whistle and an extensive vocabulary chastened the progress of the taxicab, and also equipped Boze with a slip of paper informing him he would be expected in court the following day to consult a judge about speeding, reckless driving, running past traffic lights, and the oversight of not having his meter registering. They arrived at Vix's apartment house in a spell of silence.

"Ah sho' is havin' bad luck," Boze complained.

"You're around where it's contagious," Funny Pegger informed him.

Jones examined Boze with concern. "Do you," he asked Boze, "own this vehicle?"

"Nope. After what done happen', ah jus' same as don' own no job, neither."

Jones explored pockets until he located a thousand-dollar bill.

"Here," he said. "Buy a taxicab for yourself, and pay the money back out of your profits."

Boze made sounds.

"The money is loaned to you by Genius, Inc.," Jones advised, "for the purpose of setting up a small business for yourself. There is no interest or security required."

"De Lawd," Boze said, "mus' love black men."

JONES was not unaware that Vix and Funny Pegger were regarding him as if he was something weird, as they entered the red-headed young woman's apartment. Vix flung off her hat, turned on an electric fan, fell into a chair, lighted a cigarette and began to smoke it industriously. She did not say anything. Funny Pegger did not say anything either. But both he and Vix looked at Jones. They seemed expectant. They were waiting for something. Jones didn't know what.

Jones began to feel uncomfortable. He ambled around the apartment, then emptied his pockets of wads of bills, and jewelry, making a stack on the table. He hoped that would break the conversational ice. It didn't. Vix and Funny Pegger just stared at him.

Jones feigned indifference, ambled over to the electric fan and contemplated it. In a moment, he did what every person does at one time or another in his life. He put a finger in the fan blades just to see what was happening in there.

"Ouch!" he said.

Funny Pegger got up out of his chair, came over and took Jones by the arm. He led Jones politely to a chair, carefully forced him to be seated in the chair, then patted Jones' arm.

"Please," he said pleadingly. "Please, all we ask of you is to be patient with us. We are trying to understand you. We really and truly are."

Jones was puzzled. "I do not comprehend. Both of you seem to be acting queerly."

"It's reaction," Funny Pegger said. "After-effects."

"I—"

"It's the lobwollies," Vix said. "We've got them."

"It is amazement," said Funny Pegger. "Simple and pure wonder. We feel like Darius."

"Er—the Darius named Green, with the flying machine?" Jones queried.

"No," said Funny Pegger. "The one who saw Daniel come out of the lions' den."

"Oh."

"Would you like to keep us from going entirely mad?"

"Why, I—"

"Then tell us how you *won*."

Jones frowned. "It was—ah—simple. I merely placed my money on the table, shook the little box and let the small cubes roll out."

"Oh!"

Jones smiled self-consciously. "I—er—also talked to the little cubes. Such things as, 'Baby needs new shoes!' and 'Come a natural!' Various persons were kind enough to coach me as to the accepted remarks."

Funny Pegger looked at Vix. They both shook their heads.

"Jones," said Funny Pegger, "there must be an explanation. There's got to be." He frowned. "What happened before you started playing?"

Jones considered. "Well, I asked if the establishment was conducted on an honest basis."

"You—ahem!"

"They said it was," Jones explained.

Funny Pegger swallowed and waited.

"Hire," Jones remarked, "is a word derived from the Greek *heuer,* which is similar to the Latin *hircus,* meaning the he-goat, or buck."

Funny Pegger wiped his forehead with the backs of both hands.

"So," said Jones, "I hired the gentleman who operated the craps table to work for me."

"You what?"

"It seemed quite a logical thing to do," Jones explained seriously. "They assured me the place was honest. Therefore I saw no harm in employing the operator of the table. I—ah—asked him what he considered a fair night's income for himself. He replied, naming a sum called 'five grand.' I was surprised to learn this designated five thousand dollars, so I inquired if he thought my chances of winning were good enough to warrant such an outlay. He replied in the affirmative. In fact, he said: 'Brother leave it to me!' So I hired him." Jones gazed about.

"Ah—my employee is to call here sometime tomorrow evening for his salary," he finished.

Funny Pegger shook his head.

"Wait!" He held tightly to his chair. "Wait, wait! I think my head will stop swimming in a minute."

"When it does," Vix said, "paddle over and rescue me."

Then Vix got up slowly, came over and peered at Jones. "Where was Tray Marco when you were doing this *hiring?*"

"I—he didn't notice."

"Why not?"

"Ah—I had extinguished the lights for the interim."

"You—"

"Yes," Jones said. "To tell the truth, I did not like the looks of this Tray Marco, who was the proprietor."

Vix seemed to have difficulty with her breathing.

"You hired the house man to throw the game to you!" she croaked.

"I—what?"

"You mean you didn't know what you'd done?"

Jones swallowed uncomfortably.

"Craps," he explained, "means a gallows from which people are hung, as well as the dice game in which the odds are 251 to 244 against the caster of the dice."

Jones grinned, almost boyishly. That was the only thing he could have done that would have prevented Vix from heaving the electric fan at his head.

"There was more to it than that," she said darkly. "A lot more."

"Well, yes," Genius admitted. "There was. You see it seemed to me that the croupier bore a strange resemblance to the gentleman who got me to back that spurious orphanage. In fact, I am positive it was the same man. And I am equally positive that he knew I knew who he was…."

"It certainly," Vix said, "was dandy for you to get it all straightened out so nicely."

"I think also that the little man was afraid I might—ah—retaliate," Genius went on. "I decided to play upon his fears. In addition to *hiring* him to be on my side, I made dark hints. A sinister-looking individual made regular trips to the table to whisper in my ear. I told the croupier that this fellow was watching him and that if he did not live up to his bargain, there would be—well, violence."

Funny gasped. "I wish I understood about logarithms. Or relativity. Or something. On account of I certainly do not understand what you are talking about. Who was the sinister-looking gentleman and what made him come up and whisper menacingly in your ear at three-minute periods?"

"I made him. I hired him to do so, in fact. He was, I believe, one of Mr. Marco's employees."

Vix made a strangling noise. "You hired one of Marco's men to come up and frighten Marco's croupier? I mean, that *is* what you said, isn't it?"

"Well," Jones said. "He didn't know he was scaring the croupier. He merely came up to tell me that the black-haired girl in the green dress hadn't arrived yet."

"I," Funny announced firmly, "give up."

Vix's reaction was more feminine. "What girl?" she demanded.

"Oh, there wasn't any girl. I invented one as an excuse to make the bouncer come up and whisper to me every three or four minutes. It was really very simple. I pointed out to the croupier that since money had already won over one of Marco's men, he might just as well join the parade—rather than become seriously damaged. The bouncer really was quite a ferocious-looking gentleman. He was very convincing. So what with this croupier fellow's being apprehensive about me in the first place, and scared of the bouncer in the second, he apparently figured that he might just well come and work for me. Elementary, really."

Vix extinguished her cigarette-end with tender care. "Anything that happens from now on will be an anticlimax," she said. "With arsenic."

The telephone rang and Vix went to the instrument. She held it out toward Jones. "For you."

"Me?" Jones was surprised. "Who is it?"

"Fate, I'm afraid," Vix said.

Jones put the receiver to his ear and said a polite, "Good evening," into the mouthpiece.

He would have had no trouble recognizing the voice, although the voice lost no time in explaining who it belonged to.

"Tray Marco. Cough up, Jones. The whole take. Otherwise, flowers and slow music," the voice said.

"But—"

The owner of the ugly tones at the other end hung up. Jones put the telephone down and frowned.

"What event," he inquired, "is associated with flowers and slow music?"

"Weddings," Vix said. "But not if you were talking to Tray Marco."

CHAPTER XXIX

THE WILD MEN

THEY DID NOT go to bed as early as Jones had hoped. Funny Pegger's pre-bedtime talk was nothing to induce sleep, either. The gag-man remembered a number of things, one of them being that Tray Marco might not be the best man from whom to win a hundred and seventy-two thousand and some odd dollars.

Jones was glad when the sun came up, even if it was raining again.

During the ride to the little suite of offices they had rented for Genius, Incorporated, Funny Pegger spent most of his time on his knees on the seat cushions, peering through the rear window of their taxicab. When they got out, he was a little pale.

"Whew!" he muttered.

"Has something happened?" Jones asked curiously.

"It's getting ready to happen." Funny Pegger pointed to a large dark car which cruised past. Two rather grim-faced young men occupied the rear seat, and they made no pretense of not looking Jones over intently. "You see that?" the gag-man demanded.

"Why—"

"Tray Marco's boys. They followed us from the apartment."

"They looked somewhat young," Jones decided.

"Uh-huh. That's because they don't live to get very old in their racket."

"I do not quite understand."

"They're gunmen."

Jones pondered this, and immediately had an uncomfortable sensation. "Goodness!" he muttered.

"They're waiting around to see when you pay Tray Marco back the money you earned—as you quaintly put it—in his gambling house."

Jones did not need to be reminded of that. He had surmised as much.

Funny Pegger added, "No telling when they'll get tired of waiting. They aren't famous for patience."

Jones was glad to get upstairs and plunge into the business of giving away money with his new firm of Genius, Incorporated. Fortunately, there was plenty to take his mind off other things. First, they had to wedge their way to the door, aided by Polyphemus Ward's borrowed private detectives, who were there in force to conduct the investigations of applicants to Genius, Inc. By the time he had squirmed through the mob of applicants, Jones had a hearty respect for the power of advertising, the notice he had inserted in the newspapers having been approximately the size of his thumb. He also began to feel that giving away a hundred thousand might finally be accomplished. He would have glowed over that, under other circumstances.

The first applicant for a thousand dollars without interest or security was an Italian who wanted a fruit stand. The next was a lady who wished to lease a rooming house, and the third was another Italian who wanted a fruit stand. Fourth came an aviator who needed a thousand to finish financing a flight across the Atlantic, a project about which Jones was enthusiastic until he discovered there was already a regular trans-Atlantic passenger air service via Bermuda. Then there was an Italian for a fruit stand, a baker who wished to go into business, a tailor, a truck farmer, and another Italian, but this one wanted to make spaghetti.

ABOUT eleven o'clock, Tray Marco telephoned. "Cough. Last chance. A hundred and seventy-two grand. Or it's curtains."

"Your statements," Jones said, "are cryptic and not quite clear."

"You savvy, don't you?"

"Er—I presume you think you can coerce me into returning the funds which I earned in your establishment last evening."

"Coerce?"

"I—to constrain by threat or force."

Tray Marco said: "My boys'll go to town if you don't kitty up." He banged down the receiver at his end of the wire.

Funny Pegger peered at Jones anxiously. "Tray Marco again, eh?"

"Well—yes."

Funny swallowed.

"How'd he sound?"

"Rather violent," Jones confessed. "He said something about going to town."

Funny Pegger groaned and sank into a chair. He grasped the back of his neck, as was his habit when he was trying to get something out of his fertile mind. "This is bad," he moaned.

"I," said Jones, "am not going to fret. I have one hundred—ah—two hundred and eleven thousand dollars, that is, to give away."

"Great grief! You're gonna give all your earnings?"

Jones nodded. "Exactly."

"But why?"

"In order, as you would put it, to do the job up in a well-baked complexion." Jones smiled. "There is a million at stake, you know," he added, not unreasonably. "The million is to be my reward if I win, along with a job of disposing of the Ward millions to philanthropies."

"Somebody's got to look out for you!" Funny Pegger said desperately.

He wandered outside to sit in another chair and hold the back of his neck.

During the afternoon, Jones found himself losing trace of

Funny Pegger. The Tray Marco possibilities were also pushed into the background temporarily. Genius, Incorporated, was doing a rushing business, and by four o'clock, the private detectives had okayed nearly a score of applicants, and Jones had reduced the firm capital by as many one-thousand dollar loans. He was pleased. Three or four boom days like this, and he would have fulfilled his bargain with old Polyphemus Ward.

At five o'clock, Jones optimistically told the other customers to come back tomorrow, and put on his hat. He found Funny Pegger outside, and noted that the gag-man was in earnest consultation with several of the customers of Genius, Incorporated. When Funny Pegger saw Jones, he said, "It's all up to you, boys," and came over to Jones. The gag-man seemed resigned to the future.

They got into a taxicab. Remembering what had happened that morning, Jones turned to look through the rear window. His apprehensions sprang up.

"We are being followed!" he gasped.

"How many cars?" Funny Pegger demanded.

"Oh, four or five at least."

"It ought to be quite a war," the gag-man said grimly.

In a chastened mood, Jones reached Vix's apartment. He was inclined to examine the dusky doorman with an eye to the latter's potential abilities at gangster-repelling. And for the first time, the door of Vix's apartment seemed a fragile piece of equipment. Vix made them fried chicken and waffles.

JONES was examining a wishbone somewhat wistfully when there was a knock on the door. Jones had a peculiar sensation up and down the back of his neck, and the feeling must have been telepathic, because Vix and Funny Pegger put down their implements.

"Er—who could that be?"

Funny Pegger took a deep breath. "The police," he said.

Jones winced and his stomach lost its desire for food as he

conjured up an unpleasant assortment of perhapses…. Perhaps the police had stopped seeking a largish young man with red hair and a remarkable red beard. Perhaps they were now looking for a largish young man who had dyed his red hair black. The biggest perhaps was the perhaps that they had traced him here. The knuckles tattooed the door again.

"That," Vix said, "*couldn't* be a cop."

Jones looked at her hopefully. "No?"

"It lacks," Vix explained, "the coppy quality."

Jones hunted around in his memory, trying to find someone else who might be visiting him. He sprang up—he had remembered something. He hurried toward the door with long strides.

"Glacia!" he exclaimed. "I lost Glacia somewhere last night!"

"If this is her, let her in," she ordered. "I'll go hunt the hatchet."

It wasn't Glacia. It was Forgetful Osborn, who still wore his disguise—curly dark wig, fake waxed mustache and full dress, although it was early in the evening for the latter. He looked as though the hounds were after him. Forgetful flew inside, slammed the door, locked it, then propped himself against the panel.

"I'm damned"—pant—"glad I"—pant—"found you!"

"Won't you sit down?" Jones suggested politely.

"I want—my—five grand," Forgetful puffed.

Jones looked solicitous. "Er—won't you have a cup of coffee? You seem to need one."

"I'll have five grand! Quick!" Forgetful peered around the apartment. "Got a telephone? Maybe there's a plane leaving tonight."

"The telephone is that doll," Vix said, pointing at a corner.

Forgetful Osborn rushed to the corner, grabbed the doll, extricated the phone, and tried to hold it with one hand while he riffled through the directory with the other.

Jones walked to the agitated con-man.

"I am," Jones stated, "crediting you with the five thousand, or grands, as you call them."

Forgetful Osborn looked up blankly. "Crediting?"

"Exactly. It follows, therefore, that you owe me only forty-five thousand dollars, or as I understand it, forty-five grands."

Forgetful went pale. His words stumbled. "What—what—"

"Of course, technically, there would be some interest due," Jones continued, "but we will charge that up to—ah—experience."

Forgetful Osborn peered at the door, then at Jones, and evidently concluded Jones was too much obstacle in the way of flight. He crabbed sidewise to a chair and sank into it.

"I told 'em so," he mumbled.

"Told them what?" Jones asked curiously.

"That you was something to look out for." Forgetful squinted at Jones. "You spotted me, huh? I knew it! I thought so last night."

Jones nodded. "Naturally. You have a false mustache and a wig, but you are still the absent-minded person who sold me a bogus orphan home for fifty thousand dollars."

There was a pause.

"We started to discuss forty-five thousand dollars you still owe me," Jones said firmly.

Forgetful Osborn swallowed large pieces of nothing. "I—I haven't got it."

"No?"

"Lyman Lee took it. He and Paul Shevinsky, Harold Hover and Tray Marco, hired me to pull the job on you. They gave me five hundred." The con-man looked disgusted. "I never took on more trouble for five hundred."

Jones frowned. "Lyman Lee has my money, you say?"

Forgetful Osborn stared at Jones. "You'd better skip town."

"Eh?"

"Tray Marco!"

Jones swallowed uncomfortably. "What do you mean?"

"Tray Marco," said Forgetful Osborn, "has blowed his top."

"He—what?"

"Came unconnected. He's a wild boy. He thinks Lyman Lee and Paul Shevinsky and Harold Hover and me and you and Glacia and this girl here and this newspaper guy—he thinks *everybody* doublecrossed him."

"Er—did what?"

"He thinks this whole thing was a rig to take him for the hundred and seventy grand."

"Goodness!" Jones said.

"Tray Marco," said Forgetful, "has his boys together."

He moved uneasily.

"His boys?"

"His gorillas. They're looking for everybody. I went out the back door of my rooming house when they came in the front."

Jones frowned. "You mean that they contemplate violence?"

"The darned fools want to kill everybody."

THEN there was another knock on the door, which did not exactly soothe any of them. Forgetful Osborn flew out of his chair and turned white on his way through the handiest door, which happened to lead into a closet where he would be satisfactorily enclosed for the time. Funny Pegger sauntered to a window with a fire escape. Vix said, "Don't go to the door!" and Jones went to the door.

"Ah—who is it?" he called nervously.

"Lyman Lee."

On the theory that the devil never introduced himself by his true name if he was bent on any mischief, Jones opened the door.

Simultaneously, Vix said, "Count me out of this for reasons of my own!" and vanished into the kitchen.

Lyman Lee came in, looking worried, followed by two other

worried people. The first was Paul Shevinsky; the second was Harold Hover.

"Er—how do you do," Jones said.

Lyman Lee spoke in low tones. "Jones," he said, "I do not want you to misunderstand this visit."

"I shall try not to," Jones announced.

"I thought it over seriously before I came," Lyman Lee explained. "I did not want to offend you. I did not want to aggravate the position."

"What position?" Jones asked, recalling that there were several.

"My position," replied Lyman Lee gravely, "wherein I find that you no longer consider me your friend."

"Oh."

"I am your friend, you know."

"Are you?" Jones looked thoughtful.

"Yes, indeed. Very much your friend. But I am sorry to say that you have been poisoned against me." Lyman Lee looked accusingly at Funny Pegger. "Poisoned," he added, "by certain persons who have an unreasonable dislike for me."

"Is that so?" Jones remarked. Funny opened his mouth, then closed it.

Lyman Lee nodded. He took out a white silk handkerchief almost large enough to be a sheet and dabbed at his forehead. Obviously, he was a young man trying to sell a bill of goods under difficulties. "Would you consider putting aside everything that has happened?" he asked.

"Gladly!" Jones said enthusiastically. "I would put Tray Marco aside with the most willingness of all."

Lyman Lee winced. "I hoped you would let me give you some advice," Lyman Lee said earnestly.

"Advice," Jones agreed, "is certainly what I need."

"Jones," Lee said, "you've got to give Tray Marco back his money."

"Yes?"

Lyman Lee looked relieved. "That's the smart thing," he said. "I figured you would know what was good for all of us."

"The 'yes,'" said Jones, "was purely a conversational stimulant."

"It was—what?"

"It didn't mean anything," Jones explained. "I have not the slightest intention of giving Tray Marco any money. On the contrary, I expect to collect fifty thousand dollars from you."

Lyman Lee straightened the front of his coat and looked stunned. "Are you crazy?"

"Chestnut," Jones remarked, "is a name variously designating a nut, an elderly joke, or a callous on the leg of an ass."

Lyman Lee began to get sunset coloration.

"You are trying," Jones continued, "to pull your chestnuts out of the fire." He took a step forward. "You swindled me out of fifty thousand dollars. I now have a witness to prove this fact. The only reason I do not have you arrested at once is because I am giving you a chance to return the money. The fifty thousand will do humanity more good than seeing you behind bars, where, I will add, you belong."

"Tray Marco," said Lyman Lee wildly, "is going to shoot somebody if he don't get his money back."

Jones grabbed Lyman Lee and gave that gentleman's well-tailored behind a kick.

"If you wish," Jones shouted at Funny Pegger, "you can help me throw them out!"

Jones opened the door with one hand while he held Lyman Lee with the other.

Tray Marco said, "Thanks. I was wondering how we would get into the nest."

MARCO did not have a gun. Jones looked, first thing. Marco walked into the apartment with stiff-legged wariness, then took a quick step to one side to get out of the way of his boys who were behind him and came in after him. They had the guns.

Forgetful Osborn sidled toward a window. Tray Marco said, "You lose something over there?" Forgetful stopped.

Jones said, "This intrusion is unwelcome—" and shut up when he found the black gullet of an automatic pistol looking at him.

Tray Marco said: "Case the lay."

Two men searched the apartment and hauled Vix out of the kitchen, after which one of them gave the *coup de grâce* to that part of proceedings by announcing, "The joint cases clean."

"Any do-ray?" asked Tray Marco.

"Not a red."

"Frisk the gulls."

Jones judged from the adeptness displayed that the friskers had previous experience.

"No rods or shivs," one stated.

"Any flash?"

"Just cackle."

"No folding jack, eh?"

"Nix."

With firmness, Jones put away an impulse to ask for a translation. The impulse, he realized, was out of place. "Er—what can we do for you gentlemen?" he asked nervously.

Tray Marco said: "We'll do for ourselves."

A tightness came into Jones' throat as he got his first close look at Tray Marco's eyes. They reminded him of chips off a glacier.

"Relax," Tray Marco advised. "We got some more company coming."

He glanced at Lyman Lee.

Jones was surprised. "Company—"

Tray Marco showed his teeth unpleasantly. "I'm putting on a little get-together. I thought everybody would like to know that I expect somebody to hand me two hundred thousand dollars."

"Two hundred?" Jones frowned. "But I won—er—earned one hundred and seventy-two thousand and ninety-eight dollars. Ah—how do you account for the difference?"

Tray Marco said: "Costs of collection."

Someone rapped on the door, and Tray Marco took out a gun, held it behind his back, opened the door, presented the gun quickly and said, "Don't run away, chick. Come on in."

Glacia entered. Glacia, with fingertips pressing tightly to her cheeks and her eyes staring, and both her face and her hands slowly losing color. "But I received—a telegram—from Jones," Glacia said, with halts.

Tray Marco looked interested. "You did?"

"Yes. It—asked me to—come here."

"Did it say Jones loved you and nothing you had done mattered?"

"I—yes."

"Then it was the one I sent," Tray Marco said.

"But why—"

"You're part of my collection," Tray Marco said. "Sit down."

Glacia sat down and her lovely face proceeded to lose all of its color. Jones now expected Tray Marco to proceed with whatever he had in mind, but he was disappointed. Marco perched on the edge of a table, put a fresh cigarette between the fingers of his left hand, and waited patiently.

When the delay got on Jones' nerves, he tried to temper it with a quotation.

"Wait," he said tentatively, "means an ambush, a snare, a horn of the oboe type, a piece of music sung by serenaders, as well as to rest in expectation."

"I can't stand much of that," Tray Marco said grimly.

"Er—what are we waiting on?" Jones persisted.

"The other guest."

"Who—"

Tray Marco said: "Shut up!"

For lack of anything else to do, Jones began to notice that Lyman Lee was staring at Vix most strangely.

A CURL of smoke rose lazily from Tray Marco's cigarette. One of his men began to eat peanuts, extracting the salted goobers from a paper sack and popping them into his mouth, crunching them with his teeth, licking and popping his lips, occasionally sucking in.

Twenty minutes later a fist practically caved in a panel of the door.

Those in the room exchanged looks, understanding looks. Instinct told every one of them who had crashed knuckles against that door. Such hard-fisted violence meant—old Polyphemus Ward.

Vix said, "Oh!" in a loud strange tone.

Jones stared at Vix. He had never seen her expression so queer.

Tray Marco went to the door, opened it, and stood so that old Polyphemus Ward could see only Tray Marco.

"Who are you?" roared Polyphemus Ward. "Where is Jones? What do you want?"

Tray Marco said: "I wanted to let you inspect a piece of my personal property."

"Personal property? What personal property?"

Tray Marco said: "This." He let one of the world's richest men look into the destructive end of his large blue automatic pistol.

Polyphemus Ward had seen gun snouts before. He cocked his head to one side and peered to see if the safety catch was off.

Tray Marco said: "I'm Tray Marco. If you haven't heard of me, you should have. Sit down!"

Polyphemus Ward yelled, "Say what kind of locoed—"

"Sit down!" Tray Marco interrupted.

The financier began to get a lobster color. "Who do you think you're talking to?" he bellowed. "I've heard of you, all right! And you've heard of me. I've roped and hogtied plenty of your kind. You tinhorn, if you think you can run a whizzer on me, you're riding the wrong range." He took a step forward. "I'm gonna take that hardware off you and make you eat it!" he roared.

He took another step. Tray Marco took a step backward. Most of his teeth were showing.

Jones began to have a rather low opinion of the self-control of his possible future employer. Old Polyphemus Ward wasn't bluffing Tray Marco.... Tray Marco was going to kill him if something didn't happen.

Something did happen, and something quite astounding. It occurred when Polyphemus Ward, angling sidewise to get closer to Tray Marco and death, chanced to turn enough to see Vix. The auburn-haired young woman's gaze met Polyphemus Ward's.

The two of them stared at each other with hypnotic intentness. Their lips parted, parted at almost identical instant; their lips moved a little; neither of them made any sound.

Old Polyphemus Ward took in a deep breath, shut his eyes and fell on his face on the floor. Vix ran to the financier, dropped at his side, and her throat ached with apprehension.

Tray Marco sprang back.

"Watch it!" he flung. "Something screwy here!"

Jones felt confused. Events had turned into rabbits that were coming too fast out of the magician's silk hat. There was obviously a connection between Polyphemus Ward and Vix. Jones realized he had suspected this before. On an occasion or two, Vix had reacted strangely when Polyphemus Ward was mentioned. Vix had also known Glacia, and Glacia was distinctly not of the circle to which Vix belonged at the present time. Vix had known a great deal about Polyphemus Ward, so much so that Jones had been led to suspect some kind of an association, a nice one, of course. The discrepancy was that Vix claimed to be a radio singer. Jones perceived that Tray Marco was staring at Vix with intense interest. The man began to grin thinly.

"Get the dame!" he commanded. "That one."

His men looked blank. Tray Marco said: "Kayo her. Take her out to the cars. If anybody says anything, tell 'em she got tight and passed out."

One of Tray Marco's boys said, "You—we—you—"

Tray Marco said: "We're gonna snatch her."

"Snatch?"

"Sure. Get going."

"But the Feds! The G-men—"

"It's worth the chance," Tray Marco said grimly. "It's a chance at the biggest snatch in the world. It's worth a million, if it's worth a dime."

"A million?"

"She's the old buzzard's girl."

"His sweetie?"

Tray Marco said: "Not his sweetie, you fool. She's old Polyphemus Ward's missing daughter."

CHAPTER XXX

EVERYTHING HAPPENS
AT ONCE

JONES FELT RATHER proud of himself, because he had reached an identical conclusion a few moments earlier. It was all perfectly logical. Polyphemus Ward's daughter had left home because she was afraid she'd get to be like her male parent. But it was natural that the girl would want to keep tabs on her father and see how he was taking her absence. It was logical for her to use Funny Pegger, the moneybags' public relations counsel, to do the checking up. That explained how Vix happened to know Funny Pegger in the first place. Jones saw that it was all clear enough.

Tray Marco ordered: "Get her out of here!"

Three men grabbed Vix. She struggled, struck at them. One of them struck back and hit her mouth. A red string of blood came off her lip and wriggled over her chin.

Something hot and wild blew up inside Jones, and he jumped, swung a fist at Tray Marco and connected. Tray Marco very nearly turned end for end. After he hit the floor, he kicked, his hands twitched, and his gun let out noise, lead and cordite smell.

The door opened. A man came in. A dark, short, wide man, whom Jones thought looked familiar. The man ran and grabbed one of the boys struggling with Vix. Jones then recognized the dark, short, wide man as one of the beneficiaries of a thousand-dollar loan. More men came in the door. Some of them had clubs, others had bottles. In from the window fire-escape came another man. He was an Oriental gentleman who wished to start a laundry. Jones became confused. More guns were going off. The Chinamen shouted in Mandarin. The others shouted in English.

Harold Hover, who had been stumbling around wildly, holding his hands above his head, ran suddenly and jumped out of the window. Another man instantly jumped out after him. And a third man climbed half out of the window but came back in when he saw three floors down to a hard concrete courtyard.

Jones upended the table at Paul Shevinsky, made a chest-hit, and the rush of air blew a set of false teeth out of the shyster lawyer's mouth. The man rolled on the floor and coughed. Jones headed for Lyman Lee; he had a large juicy bone to pick with Lyman Lee. But Funny Pegger got there first with a chair, and turned Lyman Lee's profile into a difficult job for a plastic surgeon.

"I hated him before you did," the gag-man explained to Jones.

The fighting was down on the floor for a while, before it slowly subsided. A final fist smack or two, one splintering report of a chair, and comparative quiet came inside the apartment.

However, an uproar arose outside as excited tenants dashed around inquiring what had happened, and spreading rumor that the G-men had cornered another public enemy and were fighting it out.

Jones grinned widely at the wreckage, at Funny Pegger, at Tray Marco, at everyone. The fireworks were decidedly over. But he was wondering who had lighted the fuse.

The Italian of the fruit stand, the Chinaman of the laundry, the baker, two Irishmen who had received funds for trucks, and assorted other clients of Genius, Inc., stood around and grinned back at Jones. They seemed pleased with themselves.

"I am surprised to see you gentlemen," Jones remarked when he had recovered his breath.

"Sure, and we figured yez wouldn't be mindin'," said one Irishman.

"Oh, no," Jones said. "Not at all."

"Hope velly much you all lightee," volunteered the Celestial.

Personally, Jones was feeling fine, but he glanced around to see about the others. With two exceptions, everyone was present, and after more or less patching up, would be able to get into a taxicab or a police wagon. The exceptions were Harold Hover and the other man who had jumped out of the window.

Several, however, were not moving.

"I cannot understand how you gentlemen"—Jones surveyed his benefactors—"how you gentlemen came to arrive so conveniently."

Boze, the taxi driver, said, "Boss, yo' sure ain't think us is gwine let nobody make an angel out'n you, does you?"

"But how did you know about the angel proclivities of the— ah—boys?"

"Oh, dat was what de vice president done tell us all about."

"De—I mean, the vice president of what?"

Funny Pegger said: "He means me."

"You?"

"Sure." The gag-man grinned. "I'm the vice president of Genius, Inc."

"Why," Jones said, "I didn't know that."

"Well, I intended to get around to telling you. This other thing was sort of on my mind. I knew you couldn't call in police protection. The cops want to arrest you. So I thought of tipping these people off. They're your friends. I told them the whole story. They volunteered to see nothing happened to you."

JONES was touched. He had tried for several days to throw bread on the waters, had finally cast part of it without it bouncing back, and now some of it had already returned. The occasion seemed to call for a quotation.

"The word grin," he announced, "means, variously, a noose for hanging persons, a trap, or an instrument of torture, as well as to draw back the lips from the teeth to show merriment or good humor. Er—the latter is my present impulse."

An additional client of Genius, Incorporated, came in through the door. He was a fat man who stuttered and who had been financed for a lunchroom, and he seemed perturbed.

He said: "The gug-guy who fell outa the window kik-kik-kik-kik—"

"It has been my experience," offered Funny Pegger, "that a drink of water helps."

"—kik-killed the German captain," finished the future proprietor of a lunchroom.

Jones took a step forward. *"What?"*

The fat man said, "He was huh-hired by Luh-Lyman Lee. His name is Hover. He used germs to do the job. He thinks he's duh-dyin', but he ain't."

"What," Jones inquired, "is wrong with him?"

"He luh-lit sitting down."

There was some doubt in Jones' mind about the court value of a confession from a man who had descended freely for three stories and landed seated. The question revolved around the number of witnesses present at the confessing.

"How many persons overheard this statement?" he asked anxiously.

"A dozen, anyway."

Jones relaxed. A dozen witnesses should convince a jury by sheer majority.

"Goodness!" he said wildly.

Funny Pegger peered at him. "Now what's wrong?"

"I do believe," Jones said, "that I haven't a trouble left, comparatively speaking."

At this point old Polyphemus Ward grumbled, turned over on his back and sat up, then peered around at the battlefield.

"Who hit me from behind?" he roared.

ON A typical early September day in New York City—it was drizzling rain steadily—Jones tipped back in a swivel chair, glanced at the clock on his desk, and noted that it was now thirty days to the hour since he had stepped ashore from the Polyphemus Ward yacht. The occasion called for a pronouncement.

"Months," he declared, "are of several types, namely: The calendar month, the lunar month, and the synodic, anomalistic, nodical, dracontic, tropical, sidereal, solar and consecution months, not including the colloquial month of Sundays."

The Jones desk was an impressive affair of mahogany, ornamented with six telephones, and an article resembling a midget radio for communicating with Vice President Funny Pegger in the office next door. There was a dictaphone and a conference chair and the walls were mahogany, paneled with white, the windows offered an excellent view of Radio City, if anyone cared to look.

On the desk, anchored with a paperweight so that it would not blow away if there had been a draft, lay a greenish-colored slip of paper. This was a check, duly signed by Polyphemus Ward.

For the tenth or twelfth time, Jones scrutinized the figures on the check. As on the previous ten or twelve occasions, he looked rather pleased. "One million dollars," he said aloud, just to hear how the sum reacted on the ear.

One of his new secretaries appeared in the door.

"A lady," she announced, "to see Mr. Jones."

"Er—which lady?"

"Glacia Montignal de Grandrieu."

It struck Jones as appropriately synonymous for Glacia to appear so hot on the heels of mention of a million dollars.

"Show her in," he ordered.

He watched the door expectantly, and he was not disappointed. A moment after Glacia appeared, there was a bump-bump inside his chest. He relaxed. If by chance he had not bumped, he would have been worried, convinced that his reflexes were off. If you were normal, you at once bumped when you saw Glacia at her best.

And today Glacia was definitely her best. She gave him her most electric smile. "Darling," she murmured, "you've been neglecting me."

"Ah—have I?"

"Of course," Glacia admitted, "you have been terribly busy, what with the trial of Lyman Lee, Tray Marco, Paul Shevinsky and Hover for murdering that poor German liner-captain. Do you think they will be electrocuted?"

Jones frowned. "I am afraid so. A foreign gentleman by the name of Adolph Hitler keeps cabling that there will be another war if they aren't."

Glacia sighed.

"You naughty boy!" she exclaimed.

"Er—"

"You haven't called me once! You might have. Just one tiny time."

"I telephoned you half an hour ago," Jones reminded.

"Your secretaries," continued Glacia dramatically, "always said you were out. I was heartbroken."

"I—you were?"

"I was distraught."

"Distraught?"

"Actually ill!"

"Goodness!" Jones said.

He took a moment to put his more impressionable emotions back in the box, then arose. Of late, he had become an addict of the motion pictures, and as a result, in taking Glacia in his arms, his technique showed great improvement over the last occasion nearly a month previous.

"Pardon me."

INVARIABLY, when he had kissed Glacia before, there had been explosions. Not just a bang. Explosions! Something distinctly worth remembering, usually starting at his toes, and getting more cataclysmic as it climbed. This time, it started off all right—but got about to his ankles and fizzled.

"That," said Jones cheerfully, "is all I wanted to know."

"Darling, I don't understand!" Glacia was astounded.

"Er—it didn't happen."

"What didn't happen?"

"The explosion."

"Explosion?"

"For the first time," Jones explained, "there wasn't any."

"But, darling—"

"I am rather pleased." Jones' smile widened. "The event proves conclusively that it would be a mistake for our engagement to continue."

"Mistake—"

"I do not," said Jones, "wish to be engaged to anyone who does not cause me to explode."

Glacia's glamour slipped a trifle. "I do not understand!"

"It's off. Starting now, it is off. Our engagement."

Glacia took a step forward, put a forefinger against Jones' large chest and tapped.

"Listen, my pet!" she said. "You're engaged to me! If you think you're not, you're crazy. I'll sue you for every penny you ever hoped to have. I'll—"

"Would you mind leaving?" Jones asked.

"Listen, you iceberg hitch-hiker—"

"Either get out," Jones said gravely, "or I shall take you by the nape of the neck and the equivalent of the seat of the pants, and throw you out!"

Glacia glared. However, when Jones took a purposeful forward step, she wheeled and fled through the door.

Hardly had Glacia made her departure when Vix appeared in the same doorway and gazed quizzically at Jones. He gazed back, thinking she was rather remarkable this morning. Vix was rather remarkable any morning for that matter. She lacked several things that Glacia had, but he heartily approved of the shortcomings. Today Vix wore a trim rust outfit and a saucy little hat which sat on her wealth of auburn hair and went very well with her pert little face.

"There," Vix remarked, "went a woman who looked as if she'd been fighting for her honor."

"I—honor had very little to do with it," Jones stated uncomfortably.

He swallowed several times, and realized they were in the middle of a silence, the overly still kind of a silence that frequently precedes a stroke of lightning.

"I—ah," Jones said. "That is—well—"

Vix tilted her bright little face to one side. "Word trouble, eh?"

"No, no, not at all," Jones said. "It—er—ah—well—that is—I guess so."

"That's too bad."

"I—yes."

"It's really something."

"Well—"

"Well?"

"I—well?"

"We're certainly making progress."

"I—oh, my!" Jones said miserably.

Vix had been waiting patiently and rather expectantly, but it began to appear that this might go on and on far into the day, and she showed traces of exasperation. She threw the victim a rope.

"Love does it," she declared. "Also a bump on the head."

"I—is that so?" Jones mumbled.

The silence returned and if anything, it was more silent. Even the clock on the desk seemed to bog down with its ticking. Jones heard his own loud breathing.

"With that opening," Vix said disgustedly, "you fall down!"

Jones gulped. "Ah—" he said. "Well—"

"Darling," Vix said desperately, "what are you waiting for?"

"Great Scott!" Jones burst out. "What am I?"

There was a kind of paralyzed moment or two when it seemed there was not going to be any explosion on this occasion, either, but that was misleading. The blast was just winding up, crouching, digging in its spikes, and getting set.

Old Polyphemus Ward was a man who liked to come through doors yelling at people, and when he stamped onto the scene, he bellowed, "What is keeping you? My lawyers are here to draw up those papers about your job. D'you think they've got all day?"

He stopped and took a second look. "What is this?" he yelled.

Jones came up for air, but it was necessary to get his breath. "Explosions," he said.

"What?"

"Explosions," Jones said, "that assuredly are explosions."

UNTITLED OUTLINE

Villain's name—Angelo Moroni

Girl's name—Flit

Locale—Tulsa

Situation—Old Polyphemus Ward has interests in Tulsa. They include a newspaper, a bank and oil interests.

Moroni is a crook who is trying to take over the town. Moroni is a political boss.

Polyphemus Ward has noticed his Tulsa properties are not returning the income they should. He sends Jones down to do trouble shooting.

CHAPTER I

Begin story with a delineation of Jones' character. Explain about his life on the iceberg and fact that Polyphemus Ward gave him huge fortune to distribute to charity. Bridge to Jones being called into Polyphemus Ward's presence and assigned job of going to Tulsa to see why the Ward interests there were not making more money.

CHAPTER II

Jones runs off and leaves Funny Pegger and Vix because he wants to cope with his problems alone. Jones goes to Tulsa. Carl Block, Polyphemus Ward's manager in Tulsa, meets Jones, gives him a rousing welcome intending to befuddle Jones and to cloud the main issue. Jones meets Flit. It is intended for Flit to vamp Jones.

CHAPTER III

Carl Block and Moroni have a consultation. Moroni has something on Carl Block. Moroni orders Block to "give that dog Jones a bone to gnaw." In other words, they are going to concentrate Jones' attention on a small and unimportant company which is failing, and hope that Jones will concentrate on this mouse and let the rats run loose.

CHAPTER IV

Jones is visited by Herman Bunderson, a local manager of Polyphemus Ward working under Carl Block. Bunderson's idea is to learn if there is anything to this man Jones. In other words, is Jones worth cooperating with? Bunderson is honest. Bunderson leaves with a bad impression of Jones.

CHAPTER V

Jones does not react to the invitation to take over the small company as Moroni had hoped he would. Moroni visits Bunderson and makes a threat ordering Bunderson to keep in his place. Then Moroni visits Jones and tells him the same thing. He is thrown out on his ear.

CHAPTER VI

Jones seeks out Bunderson and cooperates with him. Learns the city is organized by Moroni. Polyphemus Ward's companies are being systematically looted by Moroni.

CHAPTER VII

Funny Pegger and Vix arrive in Tulsa, and Moroni learns that Jones is engaged to Vix. Since it is necessary to get Jones' attention away from ferreting out what is wrong with the Polyphemus ward interests in Tulsa, Moroni decides to stir up trouble between Jones and Vix.

Moroni's scheme results in Jones being compromised with Flit. Vix breaks her engagement as a consequence.

CHAPTER VIII

Jones takes hold of small company and Moroni, to further harass him, causes the company to go broke.

ABOUT THE AUTHOR

A ONE-TO-THREE-HUNDRED-MILE JAUNT from his northeast Missouri hill-country home in La Plata to the public library in Chicago, St. Louis or Kansas City is no problem for Lester Dent, author of mystery novels. When he is stumped for a new murder method, he simply hops in his lightplane and visits a metropolitan library.

For example, in a novel titled *Dead at the Take-off,* Dent wished to murder a character and wind up the yarn at a metropolitan airport. He simply hopped to the city, studied control tower and airport terminal routine for a few hours, got data on the new airliner he wished to use, flew back home and finished the book that night.

On the same trip, he saw the millions of dollars worth of surplus bomber plant machinery for sale, and got the idea for another novel, *Lady to Kill,* which was published by the Crime Club.

Dent is a member of the Chicago chapter of the Mystery Writers of America, a trade group of whodunit authors, and drops into their monthly meetings by plane. A prolific fiction producer, he believes he has had more novels published about one character that any contemporary—a hundred and sixty-eight booklengths about Doc Savage, a character he created. He formerly resided in a New York City suburb, but now says he can fly to a metropolitan library about as quickly as he could once commute from his suburban apartment to the New York Public Library.

SERIES 1 INCLUDES:

* DENT * KETCHUM * KLINE *
* MacISAAC * ROSCOE *
* ROUSSEAU *
* SELTZER *
* TUTTLE *
* WIRT *
WORTS

THE BEST FICTION
FROM THE FRANK
A. MUNSEY LINE

GENIUS JONES
BY THE CO-CREATOR OF DOC SAVAGE
LESTER DENT

WHEN TIGERS ARE HUNTING
THE COMPLETE ADVENTURES OF CORDIE, SOLDIER OF FORTUNE, VOLUME 1
W. WIRT

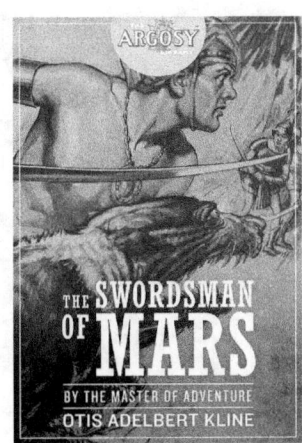

THE SWORDSMAN OF MARS
BY THE MASTER OF ADVENTURE
OTIS ADELBERT KLINE

THE SHERLOCK OF SAGELAND
THE COMPLETE TALES OF SHERIFF HENRY, VOLUME 1
W.C. TUTTLE

GONE NORTH
BY ARGOSY READERS' FAVORITE
CHARLES ALDEN SELTZER

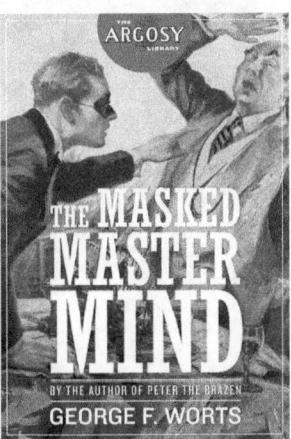

THE MASKED MASTER MIND
BY THE AUTHOR OF PETER THE BRAZEN
GEORGE F. WORTS

BALATA
BY THE AUTHOR OF THE RAMBLER
FRED MacISAAC

BRET-WALDA
BY ARGOSY READERS' FAVORITE
PHILIP KETCHUM

DRAFT OF ETERNITY
BY THE CREATOR OF JIM ANTHONY
VICTOR ROUSSEAU

FOUR CORNERS
VOLUME 1 BY ARGOSY LEGEND
THEODORE ROSCOE

SERIES 1 • AVAILABLE SPRING 2015